FOUNDRY
—MAN'S—
APPRENTICE

EDWARD EVANS

Best Wishes

Edward Evans

Author

16/4/19

WORTHSIDE

About Edward Evans

Edward Evans lives in the Yorkshire village of Haworth with Lilian, his wife of forty eight years. They have three children; all have flown the nest and have families of their own. Haworth was the home of the famous Bronte sisters, and this connection together with their frequent visits to France is what provides his inspiration to write. All his books have a distinct Anglo-French flavour and it is from the sale of these that he raises money for various charities.

He has a wealth of experience which has been gained not only from his work in the nationalised industries and through his private companies, but also as a juvenile magistrate where he became involved in Youth Justice. It was during this time that he witnessed the injustice meted out to those from poorer social and economic backgrounds. He has written about this in *Babes in Gaol* (manuscript form only) where his passion to improve the system is apparent as is his vehement support for the underdog.

About his books

11 PY

When wealthy businessman Robert Conway flies to New York to fulfil the dream of a lifetime – to buy a beautiful vintage Rolls-Royce – he little knows that he is bidding for more than he bargained for. Dream turns to nightmare as he discovers that the Rolls-Royce – the II PY of the title – is the confiscated property of a convicted drugs dealer, John Maitland, who will stop at nothing to get it back. As Conway and his family fall victim to a series of increasingly terrifying crimes, they gradually realize that there might be more to II PY than meets the eye.

'I have never read a book from cover to cover in my life but I started reading this at 5 p.m. on the Thursday and finished it at 11 p.m. on the Friday. I couldn't put it down. It had my imagination running wild and has sparked an interest in books I never knew I had. I can't wait to read another of his books.' **James Reed**

LIKE *a* FISH OUT *of* WATER

When newspaper reporter Clive White is asked to interview a well-heeled eighty-something lady about her life history, he is expecting the usual run-of-the-mill tale of marriage and children with perhaps a bit of charity work on the side. The indomitable and spirited Alexandra Fraser, however, turns out to be a completely different kettle of fish, and she slowly reveals a dramatic and diverse life, encompassing sporting achievement on the cricket field and courageous service in the WAAF as well as a passionate wartime romance. But there's something even more remarkable about her story – for Alexandra was brought up as Alexander ... as a boy.

The PIANO

The indefatigable newsman Clive White – who will already be familiar to readers of the II PY and A Fish out of Water – has gone to cover an unusual protest at a large London hospital. Unusual because for once it's not about waiting times or mixed-sex wards but a beautiful old piano that stands in the entrance hall. Originally, the gift of no less than 30s idol Noël Coward, the piano is now to go to auction to raise funds for the cash-strapped hospital.

One by the one the protesters reveal what the piano means to them, and heartfelt tales fall from their lips like old-time melodies from its ebony and ivory keys.

COME on GRANDDAD hold my hand

COME on GRANDDAD provides a vivid and informative portrait of someone with Alzheimer's. It is a disease much feared, yet, as we see here, with the understanding and love of those surrounding the sufferer, much can be done to ease their condition.

'I couldn't put this book down. It's a definitely eye opening and will make you look at people who suffer with Alzheimer's in a whole new light. It has clearly been written with love and care, capturing emotions and feelings in such a beautiful way. At some points I had tears rolling down my face, at others I was laughing out loud! Each character is well thought out and expressed in a way that brings them to life. I can see myself reading this book again and again and will be recommending it to friends.' **Miss C. L. Fothergill**

For the RIGHT REASONS

Like Edward Evans' previous book, II PY, For the Right Reasons is fast-paced and action-packed. Set mainly in East Berlin just a couple of years before the fall of the Berlin Wall, the novel tells the story of down-to-earth Yorkshire businessman Robert Conway who accidentally becomes involved in an assassination attempt on the East German President's life. His heroic efforts to rescue the President win him special freedoms in the East and during his travels he stumbles across secret plans for a terrifying act of sabotage against the West.

'A really good read. The author obviously knows his subject well. Exciting and extremely interesting. I am looking forward to reading Mr. Evans' next book.' **Margaret Waterhouse**

MOONCAR

The deadliest and most feared weapon in the British arsenal – the Rolls-Royce Armoured Car spreads fear into the hearts and minds of the Irish people. This symbol of British might was deemed invincible but now it was in the hands of the Republicans who would use it to devastating effect!

This is a tale of victory, tragedy and pathos, not least the expression of a man's undying love for one woman.

Also by Edward Evans

I enjoy writing and to use an Agatha Christie expression, it keeps the little grey cells alive. By meeting and chatting to people from all walks of life, I am able to glean a wealth of ideas for my novels. However, the greatest pleasure I get from my writing is to donate £1 from each book sold.

So far, we have raised over £20,000 for a number of charities from the following books:

II PY
– The Bradford Day Shelter

LIKE *a* **FISH OUT** *of* **WATER**
– RAF Benevolent Fund

The **PIANO**
– Specialist Autism Services (formally known as Sacar)

Le **PIANO**
(French translation) – Specialist Autism Services

COME *on* **GRANDDAD** *hold my hand*
– Alzheimer's Charity, 'Friends Together'

For the **RIGHT REASONS**
– Help for Heroes

MOONCAR
– Alzheimer's charity, 'Friends Together'

TWO OLD DEARS
– Disadvantaged children with Down's Syndrome

The **FOUNDRY MAN'S APPRENTICE**
– Mind Charity

***

Books yet to be published will also be
supporting charities. These include:

The **BENT COPPER**

***

MURDER *on the*
WORTH VALLEY RAILWAY
(Sorry Agatha)

***

DOCTOR JOHN

Ode to Ted

Your Magistrates' duties have ended.
The gavel is silent at last,
And hundreds of sentences rendered
Will soon be a thing of the past.
Perhaps much more time for your writing
Is something you're thinking about.
Perhaps something just as exciting,
There are plenty of choices, no doubt.
You've made quite a mark with the locals.
There's some who've been pleased and some not.
Some just want to hear their own vocals
But that bothers you not a jot.

Acquaintances you have so many
But would they help you in distress?
These folk are for sale ten a penny.
Your true friends don't need to impress.

The JPs will miss you, that's certain,
And most call you 'Edward', it's said.
There's no need to bow for your curtain.
To us you will always be 'TED'.

John Conquest

First published in Great Britain in 2015 by
Worthside Holdings Ltd
Worthside House
2 Belle Isle Road
Haworth
West Yorkshire BD22 8QQ

Printed in Britain by Short Run Press
Typesetting and page layout by McColm Design

A catalogue record for this book is available
From the British Library

ISBN 978-0-9928642-2-4

Contents

Dedication

I suppose the older you get the more funerals you seem to attend and 2016 started badly with the loss of three of our friends – Mavis Utley, Betty Taylor and Patsy Holmes, the wife of David a long-time friend and fellow Francophile, albeit in a different part of that lovely country. Patsy, an accomplished artist, was lucky and lived life to the full; she will be sadly missed.

David is one of the most amazing craftsmen one could ever know; his ability to restore furniture to almost the original has made him well known all over the world. His skill in copying the original is such that it has given me the idea for a new book which will be written in the near future.

Betty's health suffered greatly in later years. However, she had five children, and I have often said that in life we are lucky if we can count on one hand the numbers of real friends we have. Well, one of her children, Mark and his partner Sandra are amongst such.

Mavis was another of those ladies who lived life to the full. Her life was so full of incidents that it would be a series and not just one book. She was very kind and generous, but I thank God I didn't get on the wrong side of her.

Acknowledgements

First, I would like to thank Irvine Rawson, whom I have known for many years, and who gave me the idea for the book. His stories about his early days and the hardship he and his family suffered in his childhood could have come straight out of Dickens. But it was the recollections of his uncle Frank who became a foundry man's apprentice which really took my breath away and is the main feature of my book. I have, of course, given my input to the story which I hope you will enjoy.

Special Thanks

To my editor, Christina Harkness, who works tirelessly on my novels, especially this one, for which I have been really grateful. Her ability to find the smallest of errors, not only in the grammatical sense, but also in the factual presentation, her knowledge and the sixth sense she appears to have when perceiving something is wrong is second to none and very difficult to contradict. I really don't know what I would do without her. She has been poorly of late but thankfully making a good recovery and is busy again.

To Jill Buchanan, my reader, my critic, good friend and neighbour of nearly forty years. Without her, I would not have the courage to submit the book to Christina's mighty pen.

Of course I cannot go on without dedicating yet another book to Lilian, my lovely wife, whose help and influence is so important to me. Her tireless reading and re-reading of this and all my books, just to make the story flow better is amazing and I am sure it will be appreciated by the reader.

Introduction

Allow me to introduce myself: I'm Clive White. I work for the *Mail* and have done so for many years as an investigative reporter. George Stevenson is my editor with whom I have a good working relationship and thankfully, this has led to some excellent stories coming to the fore.

We are currently in the midst of celebrating our victory eighty years ago and remembering those who fell during the First World War. My editor, George Stevenson has received a letter from an Irvine Gough which included a copy of a document about an unusual incident which happened during one of the battles on the Somme.

Usually, editors are far too busy to read letters from the public; all are filtered out and dealt with by others in his or her name. Somehow, possibly by divine providence, one letter in particular appeared on his desk and he read it. It fascinated him, especially when he read the enclosed document, which told how all the members of a forward platoon believed that a First Lieutenant Smith had not only murdered a soldier in his command but also taken the credit for the capture of two German heavy machine guns, which were causing major problems for the British.

What was more surprising was a statement witnessed by a Captain William Harmsworth of the South Staffordshire Regiment and I am sure you will realise it was unheard of for an officer to be involved in a complaint along with his men. It was however signed and dated after the war had ended.

George subsequently received a phone call from Irvine Gough, who spoke about the correspondence which whetted George's appetite even more, especially when he referred to a man who had disappeared during that time.

'I've got something right up your street,' George said, as he called me in to his office. 'At least it sounds intriguing,' he continued, gesturing to me to sit down to discuss the matter.

'He sounded genuine enough,' George said, referring to his conversation with Irvine Gough, 'and he must be in his seventies. He told me about the Army cover-up of the murder of a soldier in the First World War, which had never been discovered and of corruption at the highest levels. He also mentioned an article which appeared in the *Daily Mirror* from the early 1950s about untold bravery of a man during the First World War.

'Anyway, go and have a word with him. You know the form. Stop if you think it's not going anywhere and keep me informed. Oh, you'll need these,' he said, pointing to a pile of papers on his desk.

His phone rang and we all knew what a great talker he was and none of us could ever tell how long he would be on, but whatever; he was always a long time, so I took the opportunity to get up and go. I picked up papers from his desk and whispered, 'It must be another interesting one, with this lot.'

He smiled and mouthed, 'OK?' I slipped out, raising my arm as I went.

You may remember some of the 'interesting' ones under the following titles: *Like a Fish out of Water*, about Alexandra Fraser who was awarded the George Cross during the Second World War. This was followed by the fascinating story – *The PIANO*, an actual piano given to St

Thomas' Hospital in London by Noël Coward in 1933, where we uncovered Russian spies, drug dealing, illegal abortion clinics, the six-day war, wartime bravery and the secret affairs of the stars. *Mooncar* followed, a story about Michael Finn who stole a Rolls-Royce armoured car from the British in 1917 and used it to devastating effect. Finally, that wonderful and funny story about the Trenchard sisters, who were arrested in their nineties for alleged armed robbery. I found out they were career criminals with a fantastic story to tell under the guise of *Two Old Dears*.

There were several other stories which all involved members of the older generation and as it seems I am headed in that direction, I am always the one who gets the job. I like to think it's because I have the ability to rake out the story from them and get the best out of it, but you will be the judge of that.

Anyway, back to the investigation. I quickly looked at Irvine's letter then took a cursory look at various news stories around the time he mentioned and found it tied in with a *Daily Sketch* headline: War Hero Disappears. This really whetted my appetite and I spent the next few days looking through Georges' notes and doing my own research into the disappearance of the war hero. It began to make for another fascinating investigation.

I came up with a few ideas and starting points, looking through newspapers around the time and sure enough, a war hero by the name of Graham Smith had mysteriously disappeared. There were even comments that he should have been awarded the VC for his bravery.

Prologue
The First Meeting

I made an appointment to meet Irvine Gough at his home, 14 Tremont Street in Wolverhampton. The following week I booked into a hotel and found myself walking down Wednesfield Road, turning right into Tremont Street, which I found to be a small cul-de-sac of identical blue, brick terraced houses. Several were now boarded up, awaiting demolition.

It was the same on both sides of the street, typical of the early Victorian industrial era and built to house the thousands of people leaving the countryside for the industrial areas in the towns and cities. The occupants were looking for an easier life but all they achieved was the opposite.

Each of the houses had three windows at the front, two upstairs, one down. The front door was only ever opened for christenings, weddings and funerals and for the doctor, but only if he insisted on it. Next to every fourth house was an archway through to the rear, where it joined a path along to the back doors of all the houses.

Again they were the same, all with three windows and a rear door which almost everyone used. They all had a single-storey scullery and an outside toilet, built in the same blue brick as was the outside yard.

The path separated the backs of the houses from a 40-yard garden which although only 16/17 feet wide, was adequate for their needs. You could see many had kept chickens but most seemed to have used the land for growing vegetables; it was either that or go hungry.

I walked round the back until I came to the last but one, number 14. I opened the little gate, now obviously made from old pallets and walked into a double yard; again the entire floor area was blue brick, simply laid directly onto the soil, only this time they were patterned to break up the monotony. I was greeted by several hens that were feeding in the yard on the worms that deigned to show their heads above the bricks and the bits of grass that dared to appear.

I walked to the back door, which was slightly ajar and knocked. There was no reply so I knocked harder, causing the door to open a little wider and began to walk in.

'Mr Gough, it's Clive White from the *Mail*.' I waited a moment before shouting: 'Irvine...it's Clive White.'

'Go on in, Mr White,' a voice from behind said. 'I'm right behind you.'

I stopped in my tracks, but was ushered in. You may imagine the sort of room it would be. There was a huge, black leaded range, with a fire in the middle and an oven either side. A griddle folded over the fire to either accommodate the pots and pans, or grill the meat. Then of course, there was the inevitable roasting spit which could be manually turned, and underneath was the copper kettle which was permanently on the fire.

The room itself was very old fashioned but spotlessly clean with its Lancashire clothes dryer hoisted to the ceiling, and bearing a full load of Irvine's washing. The solid wood table dominated the middle of the room with just one chair tucked into it. Finally, on opposite sides of the fireplace sat two old leather armchairs which seem to have been there since the house was built.

'Hello Irvine, nice to meet you. No need to introduce

myself. I've come to have a chat about the murder of a war hero.'

'He wasn't a hero,' Irvine snapped sharply. 'He was a murderer, a rapist and responsible for many other crimes. And he got the justice he deserved,' he continued, almost spitting the words out in his outburst of anger.

I realised I had touched a nerve and concluded that there was much hidden in this story. What was the justice he deserved? We looked at each other for a few seconds, which allowed him to cool down.

'Would you like a cup of tea?' he asked.

'I would love one,' I replied, breaking the ice and sitting down in one of the old leather chairs, which was so soft and comfortable I could have fallen asleep.

'That's why I keep them,' he said, noticing my apparent comfort. He took his yellow enamel teapot off the table and placed two measures of loose tea into it and then took the kettle from the range, pouring the boiling hot water onto the tea. I could smell that delicious aroma of an old-fashioned real cup of tea and this was a real cup of Sergeant Major's tea – hot, strong and sweet; the second one was just as good.

'Are you interested in the story, Mr White?'

'Yes of course, that's why I am here.'

'How much are you going to pay me for the story then?' he asked.

'Well, it's a bit early yet. We need to see where it leads. A couple of hundred, I suppose.'

'I would want more than that, but I'll wait,' Irvine replied, but I could detect from his tone and hesitation that the story and its publication was the end goal and more important to him than the money.

'This story really is about a murder and it's not a confession, Mr White. I do want to make that absolutely clear. What is most important, we want this story to be published, to let the world know what really happened.'

'Who are "we"?' I asked.

'The families of all those who were involved,' he replied.

'That's fine. Let's see where it takes us then, shall we?'

Chapter 1
Early Days

'Mr White, Irvine continued: 'I have lived this story all my life from being a young boy until today and I hope you will bring an end to it for all our sakes. Time and time again, over the years I've gone over almost all of the facts, re-read the papers and studied all the other evidence we have. I can remember virtually all the conversations I've had. I feel I know all those concerned, and I almost feel as though I was there, taking part in every move, feeling every emotion. I cannot continue what is left of my life in peace until we receive justice for our friend and I can put this to the back of my mind.'

'I can see and feel you are determined to make someone listen. Well, I'm listening.'

'Mr White, I think it's important that I start by giving you the background to the story because it goes back to the 1890s, and you will get a better feel of how and why things happened as they did.'

'That's fair enough. Carry on.'

Irvine recounts the story...

My father was born in 1892, the last of seven brothers and one sister, Alice, all born very close to one another as they were in those days, There was Evan, the eldest with the same name as his father, who was my grandfather, then Charlie, David, Graham, Frank, Alice, Jess and Noel, my father. My grandmother, who was always known as Mrs Gough was also named Alice.

They all lived in this house, which you can imagine was very crowded, but no one knew any better and just accepted their lot.

All the houses were rented and if you believe the modern-day landlords are rough, tough and unscrupulous. I can assure you they are amateurs compared with the owners of these properties. There was no protection for the tenant. The first complaint meant you were out on the street. If you missed one week's rent, you were out on the street and if you fell out with any of the landlord's friends or relatives, you were out on the street, no matter what the size or ages of your family.

They were all poor as church mice, suffering the same ups and downs in life. Children came along at roughly the same time and they too became firm friends. Many children died at an early age because conditions were cruel. If they survived, most of them grew up tough. They all went to the same school as our family did, the Great Bricklin Street Board School. The locals never used the word 'Great'. It was always known as the Board School.

It was worse if your house was owned by your employer. They would deduct the rent from your wages. If you became ill and couldn't work, you were out on the street and what was worse, if you fell out with the charge hand, foreman, works superintendent, or the owner, you lost your job and again you were out on the street. This was the worst of the scenarios, as there appeared to be a sort of cartel between the employers. If you were sacked by an employer, it always signified you were a troublemaker, whether it was true or not and, of course, as the word got round no one else would employ you. So you were not only out of a job and inevitably out on the street, you now had to leave the area because no one locally would give you any sort of employment.

This led to terrible bullying and corruption; men were

cheated out of their wages by the lower end of the management structure and were too afraid of losing their jobs to fight or even argue. Money would be stopped from their pay for the simplest of reasons, which were often made up by the charge hand.

Uncle Evan was a cobbler by trade and one of those who fell foul of his charge hand. He was sacked simply because he stood up for fellow workers and because he was involved with a union. He was so annoyed that he used all his cash to buy a tray of cherries and sold them in front of his works at Queen Square in the centre of Wolverhampton. He was that successful he bought another tray the following day. By the end of the week, he had begun to sell other fruit and vegetables. From then on he never looked back. He bought a horse and cart and hawked the fruit and vegetables around the streets of the town. Within three years, he still had his round but also operated three shops. His business empire grew and grew, but he never forgot his socialist principles, not only helping his family but all those who needed help. He became an excellent employer. The rest of the family were not so lucky or courageous.

Many of the resident families arrived at the same time and in consequence they too became firm friends. There was an esprit de corps and like the musketeers, they were all for one and one for all. They worked at the same place, which was either the Compass Iron & Steel Company, or Compass Castings Limited, which were both owned by Lord Winston Heath, and sited in the same complex.

Lord Winston Heath had a vast empire from the north to the south of England with works in almost every big town. His family was one of the nouveau riche of the time, but he was very much part of the establishment and a man with a considerable amount of influence in all aspects of life, including the church, the judiciary and business. He exercised enormous powers over church affairs, often influencing the content of sermons as well as ordering the pastors to castigate the wrongdoers in his factories, particularly those who were members of the union. On one occasion he fell out with a local pastor over some workers' rights and from that moment banned all his employees from attending the church, or risk losing their jobs. To rub salt into the wound, he had the water cut off to the vicarage as he owned the water rights. That was until the vicar apologised for the mistakes he had made and that was only achieved with the help of the bishop. When it was finally over, his Lordship featured in all but the socialist press glorying in his victory over the church. The cartoons of the day boasted he had a victory over God Himself!

Lord Winston Heath's employees were always in fear of losing their employment as there were ten people for every one job. Men and a few women would work for whatever they could get but wages were extremely low.

The families in Tremont Street were almost joined at the hip. Next door at number 16 were the Guests, Ida and Wilf; they had two children, Bobby and Janet, my mother. The Wearings, Bert and Lilly lived at number 11 opposite and had two boys, Fred and Jack and a girl, Charlotte, the latter becoming inseparable from Janet. At number 9 were Jack and Lottie Ambrose. They had two children, Anne and Seth. Finally, there was Bill Wilson and his wife Victoria at number 8. They had four girls, Anne, Elizabeth, Mary and Lily plus one boy Henry the youngest, the same age as my father.

Bill always joked that when Henry was born that was it. He didn't want to risk another girl. It was bad enough with one wife but more women in the household would have been sheer hell.

The Smith family lived at number 2; they were Graham

Senior as he preferred to be called, and his downtrodden, desperately treated wife, Grace, who was often seen with a black eye, together with their obnoxious son Graham Junior, again as his father insisted he was called. The Smith family arrived a few years after my family and the others had moved in. The neighbours considered them to be posh because they used a removal firm and had a few decent pieces of furniture. Graham Jnr was born a few months after their arrival, about the same time as my father.

They all felt something was not quite right when Graham Smith Snr was made a charge hand at the works after only a few weeks working there. No one respected him as he was not able to do the job he was already doing, and he certainly threw his weight about. A year later, he was made the senior charge hand and things got worse.

The children grew up together and played together, all ending up here at number 14. This yard was much bigger and not divided into two like many others in the street. Grandfather made a gate, closing it to the rear alley which made it safe and prevented the children wandering off.

They were a happy lot and although they had no toys as such, they made wooden swords and became Roman soldiers or made guns when they were playing at being British soldiers. The boys would fight the battles and the girls would become the nurses. Fred Wearing always became the leader simply because he was the most daring. He would be the first over the wall into the sports field and the first to climb the trees or get on the roof of the football stands. He was inevitably the daredevil, but he was always there to help the others, no matter what.

Large cardboard boxes would become boats or even houses like those in Penn or Tettenhall, the upper class areas of Wolverhampton. The only thing which spoiled their pleasure was the constant presence of Graham Smith

Jnr. He always wanted his way and if he didn't get it he would become aggressive and would think nothing of hitting the girls like some enraged boxer. If that didn't work he would run to his parents which caused further trouble. If the children's parents dared to complain, then it was: "Oh, he's only playing, aren't you, Graham?"

"Yes Mummy," was the retort, followed by a supercilious look on his face to denote he had won.

The Smiths were more financially fortunate than the others. The extra money they had meant they could afford better and more food on the table. In fact, young Graham was becoming bigger by the day, not with muscle, but with fat, so much so he was able to throw his weight around and get away with it. The young ones in the area were terrified of him simply because of his size.

He wasn't welcome simply because he was becoming as bossy as his father and just as unpleasant, but every time the children sent him home, his mother would come storming down the street complaining to all their mothers that her son was being ostracized because he was the boss's son. Invariably, they would all give in for a quiet life. On regular occasions, Smith Snr would arrive and lay the ground rules down, treating the dads as though they were still at work and should do as they were told. The sad thing was he had the power to hire and fire and the consequences for any family were dire and not worth the risk.

Smith Snr was becoming more and more corrupt and with it came more and more bullying of the employees. He began to stop money from their wages on the slightest pretext, but the worst of the man showed every time a colleague died, which unfortunately was a fairly regular occurrence because working and living conditions were that dreadful. He would organise a collection for the family of the deceased. It wouldn't be much, but whatever the amount, he would keep half for himself. Everyone knew what was going on but was too frightened to do anything. However, every time his wife Grace Smith was seen with something new, people would shout, "Who's died then, Grace?" She would simply scurry off.

All the children went to the Board School, which Grandmother thought was the most important thing of all. She was determined that all her children learned to read and write, especially my father, Noel. She wanted him to go to one of those new universities that were opening up to help the poorest in society to further their education. She spent hours with all of them after school, going through their homework. When it was just Noel left at home she spent much of the morning teaching him to read and write and to do maths. When he eventually started school, he was well ahead of his peer group.

The problem at the time was the family could not afford to buy Noel a pair of shoes and his father hadn't finished making his rope sandals. He used to tell me every time he saw a posh man or woman walking down the street he would hide in case it was the truant inspector from the Board School. Eventually, he was caught out and his absence from school had to be explained. My grandmother was completely honest and told them they couldn't afford some shoes and that Jess hadn't grown out of his yet. She also explained that he was being educated and not wasting his time. The inspector was very impressed at the standard he had reached and how well his mother had done, advising her to resolve the problem as quickly as possible.

They did make the effort. Grandfather finished the sandals a few days later and my father was off to school, accompanied by his older brother and his sister Alice who held his hand all the way. However, the shock of having to be separated from her when they arrived was almost too much. The boys and girls were separated on arrival and were not allowed to meet or even talk to their brothers or sisters until school was finished for the day. Frank took over the responsibility until he thought my dad and Jess could cope, which had to be the following day.

The others would not wear rope sandals at any price simply because it was only the children from poor families who wore them; they preferred to put cardboard in their shoes if the soles had holes in, but it was all right for a five-year-old. He did get some teasing, but when you had elder brothers still at school, it wasn't too bad. When my dad was older, so were the members of the little gang and then there was always strength in numbers.

Grandmother was right to educate him at home because he was streets ahead of the others and from then on, he was encouraged enormously by the teachers and became somewhat of a favourite, as they too kept up his enthusiasm for education.

After school, every child had to help in the home and was given various tasks to perform before they could play out. This also applied to the other families. My dad had to feed the chickens, Jess had to look after the garden, Alice had to iron some clothes and so on. They also had to take it in turns for at least half an hour, to make the rag mats once Grandfather had shown them what to do. This was a real chore which none of them liked, but after the half hour was up, it was like the bell at school – they came out from everywhere to play. Team games like 'Kick the Can or Cannon' were the favourites. These were games which gave them the chance to get little Smith Jnr out first of all, if only to get him sidelined for a few minutes. Even so, he would go home and complain to his mother. If his father was around this would cause even more problems for the other children.

As they grew older my uncle Graham used his self-taught engineering talent to build racing cars from anything that had wheels. An old set from a pram would be the pinnacle; they were big and went very fast. The rider or driver, call him what you may, sat on the frame and was pushed until he was going fast enough to leave the rest to him. The front wheels were on a swivel and steered by means of string pulled in the direction he wished to go. It was sheer excitement as the car whizzed round the sloping narrow paths in the park, creating mayhem as the rider screamed for everyone to get out of the way.

This was one activity where they could exclude Smith Jnr as no one would push him or allow him to use their car. Then the inevitable happened – he turned up in a well-used pedal car, which they knew was very expensive, even when bought second hand. Everyone knew that a senior charge hand at the factory wouldn't earn money like that. It made people begin to think more about where Smith Snr was getting the extra funds.

The group were growing up and becoming sportier, often playing a little rougher, but the girls continued to be involved. Smith Jnr could see and hear the pleasure they were having and wanted to be included, but he was becoming more and more jealous of my father's relationship with Janet, especially as she was becoming a prettier girl by the day; this was beginning to cause some serious friction.

However, his weight was no longer the advantage it had previously been; in fact, almost all the boys could run faster, hit harder and generally were leaner and fitter even though he still tried to dominate. I remember being told about the sports day. The teachers used to allocate which teams each pupil was in and which races they had to run and which other activities they were to take part in. Well, poor Graham had three races – the 100 yards, the 220 yards and the 440 yards. It was cruel and I am sure that the teachers deliberately chose these races just to bring him down a peg or two. It certainly did. He was last in both the 100 and 220 yards and was lapped by every other runner in the 440, with Frank winning the latter.

He went home embarrassed and in tears which resulted in a visit from Graham Smith Snr, who went to the school to ensure nothing like that ever happened again. He went home with a flea in his ear as Miss Grisdale, the Head Mistress, would have none of it. She was not going to be told by him how to run her school. That was until she was hauled in front of the Town Council and had to apologise to Smith or lose her job. She was a determined lady and resigned, only to leave the area entirely.

It was at this time that we began to realise that the Smiths had someone pulling strings for them.

It was evident to all that Fred was becoming the leader of the group. All the children loved to follow him; he always seemed to look after them particularly if they did anything a little daring. This too became difficult for Smith Jnr. He was already jealous of Noel because he and Janet were great friends and now became very jealous of Fred who had the respect of all of them.

On one particular day Smith Jnr followed the children to the park. It was just after they had been warned he must be allowed to play with them, so he was being King Dick, bossing everyone around and showing off. Suddenly, he grabbed Janet's scarf, wrapped it round the ball they had been playing with and kicked it with enormous force.

The ball landed high into a tree and became stuck. Well, of course Janet began crying and my father, Noel went up to console her, which made Graham seethe with envy. Then of course, my father went over to retrieve it.

This was the first of Graham's big mistakes. My father was about to begin his climb up the tree when Smith pushed him away.

'I did it! I'll get it for Janet,' he announced in his usual brash way and began to climb up the tree. It wasn't the most difficult of trees to climb but Graham, now quite plump would not take advice from Fred as to the best way up and at about 15 feet he became stuck and was nowhere near the ball. Of course, everyone began laughing and as more and more people arrived to see what the commotion was all about, the more they laughed the more agitated Smith became.

Everybody began shouting advice on how to get down. Another would shout how to get the ball and scarf and I'm sure he would not have heard any of it. The more he struggled, the more stuck he became. Someone even suggested calling the Fire Brigade.

'No!' Smith shouted. He didn't want that embarrassment.

'Well, they'll come out for cats,' an old lady called out.

I suppose the audience had grown to about thirty people when the park keeper arrived with his ladder. It was the right height but because of Smith's position in the branches he could not get it near enough.

'I'll do it for you,' Fred shouted.

'What do you mean?' the keeper asked.

'I'll show you,' Fred replied as he too set off up the tree.

'Come back. I don't want two of you stuck up there,' the keeper yelled.

'I won't,' replied Fred as he clamoured up like a squirrel taking food to its young. Within seconds, Fred was level with Smith and gave him a huge cheeky smile. They all saw the look of hate that emanated from Smith in return. Fred passed Smith and retrieved the scarf and ball. He threw them to my father and shouted to the keeper to shift the ladder over to him.

Fred was very mischievous, pushing the ladder near to Smith but making sure it was on a branch he knew would not take Smith's weight.

'It's not very strong here,' Fred shouted down. 'The branch is a bit floppy,' he added, rubbing Smith's nose in it. 'Try moving it round here,' Fred shouted again. He knew that wouldn't work either as Smith would not be able to climb over to it.

The park keeper moved the ladder to where Fred had suggested and Fred pushed it into a safe position. He then held his hand out for Smith to take hold of, again with that cheeky smile all over his face. The offer was refused.

I think Smith would have killed him there and then from what my father told me.

'I can't make it over there,' he whispered to Fred through gritted teeth.

Fred shouted down to the park keeper, making sure everyone heard, 'He says he can't make it over there. Can we move it somewhere else?'

By now Smith was absolutely seething: 'I didn't want you to tell everyone.'

'Oops sorry, I just thought you wanted me to shout and tell the parky.'

'I think we shall have to call the Fire Brigade, the keeper shouted up.

'Oh no,' Smith said despairingly to Fred.

'Wait there, son,' the keeper called up. 'They will be about half an hour.'

Due to a previous emergency it was well over an hour and a half before the Fire Service arrived at the park, at which point they couldn't get the engine to where Smith was. They had to take the huge ladder off the vehicle and wheel it to the tree. By this time, the crowd had grown enormously, all wanting to advise the best course of action. In all his boyishness Fred pandered to the crowd, climbing up and down at will, whilst everyone congratulated him for helping his friend and keeping his spirits up.

Seth had run up to the offices of the *Express & Star* and told them about the incident in the park. Within minutes, a reporter arrived for a story where Fred was the little hero. The park keeper told them how stupid the kid was for thinking he could climb the tree and how brave Fred had been trying to help his friend out of trouble. Within minutes, the Fire Brigade had him down. But didn't he get a telling off in front of the entire crowd.

'You shouldn't do such things. You've wasted all this time. Come on, what's yer name and address.' Smith was reluctant to answer, knowing what would happen to him when he got home.

Fred answered for him. 'He's Graham Smith and his dad is the boss at Compass, isn't he, Graham?'

The good thing about the incident was that they got rid of him as he had ripped his trousers and had to go home. It gave them much to laugh about but they all knew Fred had made a lasting enemy.

Graham was told to stay away from them for a short while which was marvellous as they were sick of his interference and now they tried another method, using a code to get away from him. They always met about 5 o'clock so if Fred's front bedroom curtain was closed they would be playing in the sports field over the wall and if it was open, they would be in the park. It was mostly the football pitch, over the wall because Frank was becoming quite talented at football and wanted to practise all the time.

However, Smith Jnr soon sussed out their scheme and again complained to his father.

Smith Snr, who had now been made under foreman,

called all the men into his office and wanted an explanation as to why his son was being ostracized by their children. By 'men' I mean the heads of families, also known endearingly as the Tremont Street Mob: Evan Gough, Wilf Guest, Bert Wearing, Jack Ambrose and Bill Wilson.

Bert Wearing just had a touch of genius. 'Look boss, we didn't feel you would want your son playing with our children now that you are the under foreman.'

The mere fact that Bert called him boss simply made Smith's chest stick out and his head swell. It worked and they couldn't believe his next remark. 'Come on men, you know I'm not like that. We all live on the same street.' They were all trying desperately not to laugh.

It was another touch of Bert's genius that made the day. 'Not for long, boss,' he said. 'You'll be moving to a place which suits your position. We'll never reach those dizzy heights.' He paused to let his words sink in before adding another line:

'Boss, we'll keep our children away from him to save you the embarrassment.'

Smith Snr nodded, realising he now had a position to maintain.

It worked; they left his office, with him shaking their hands and thanking them. He then had the gall to give them one shilling and three pence to treat each of them to a pint of beer in the Fighting Cocks.

'Thank you boss,' Bert said, touching his forelock.

They got well away from Smith's domain before they allowed themselves to burst out laughing.

'Well done, Bert. Good one my old mate.' They were full of praise for Bert's quick thinking as they made their way to the Fighting Cocks for the pint.

It was the first time for a long time that they had been out together for a pint and it gave them the chance to have a chat. Bert was given the money so he bought the drinks:

'Five pints of Butlers, please.'

'Come into money, Bert?' the publican asked.

'Naah! The boss decided to treat us.' They exploded with laughter again only to stop to watch the pints being pulled. Their eyes followed the froth gently sliding over the sides of the glass and falling into the tray, which some poor sod would drink in his glass of mild. Theirs was a pure pint and with five mouths watering, they were ready.

Bert raised his glass. 'Cheers boss!' The five erupted once more.

'Make it last,' Wilf said after the excitement had waned.

'Oh, don't worry. I've got seven pence so we can have another half at least.'

Between them they managed another pint, but the important thing about this get-together was they were all of one mind.

'Some things I just can't understand,' Bert suddenly remarked. 'How did Smith Snr get the job in the first place? Why is he being promoted continuously? What hold has Smith over the works superintendent if any?'

'It could be Lord Winston Heath. There have been a few rumours about him over the years,' one of the others added.

They knew he was the owner of the business, which had branches all over the country and couldn't believe that he would be mixed up with Smith, so that was dismissed and they continued concentrating on the works superintendent. They chatted for a couple of hours before tramping back home, determined to find out what was behind the rising power of Smith Snr.

Chapter 2
Coming of Age

Life continued as normal; the children were fast growing up. Noel, my father had fallen in love with Janet who would often tease him just to keep him on his toes. She would tell me how he watched her every move. He was simply mesmerised by her and didn't care who knew it. He just wanted to be with her.

It seemed to be a liaison made in heaven and they both knew it, but he was only sixteen years old at the time and the family thought it would pass as they grew up but it never did. Grandmother thought it was lovely.

Grandfather was still very protective of his brood and did not want any of them to follow him into Compass. He wanted something different for them; he wanted all of them to have a trade, do something different and not to be so dependant that they were terrified to criticise or answer back if things were wrong. He managed to get Alice, his only daughter, onto a training scheme at Beatties, where she later became a buyer of soft furnishings for the new departmental store in Wolverhampton town centre. However, three of the boys did follow in his footsteps: Charlie, David and Frank but the latter made sure it was for the shortest time possible. Eventually, David obtained a job in the Post Office, but that was after the war.

Evan, of course, had his business and was doing well without Grandfather's help. Graham joined the apprentice scheme at Guy Motors, founded by Sidney Guy where he became one of the country's experts on gearing. His claim to fame was that he worked with Aircraftsman Shaw (T. E. Lawrence) on his motor bicycle.

The children grew up; games were no longer played and each of them went into their chosen career and consequently their separate ways. My father, Noel studied at school until he was eighteen when he was old enough to take the examinations which would get him into university. He never forgot the day he received his letter of acceptance to Birmingham. Grandmother opened it because my father was too scared to open it in case he had failed.

She pulled the letter out of the envelope and burst into tears, hugging the letter as though it was she who was receiving the accolade. My father told me it was one of the most magical moments of his life. Of course, he was growing up and wanted to spend as much time with Janet as possible before leaving for Birmingham.

Frank was recognised at an early age. He was not academic, and spent all his time on the sports field, over the wall, playing football, or dribbling the ball round the field on his own. His father could see he was developing a rare talent and took him down to Heath Town where they had a junior side. It seemed he was streets ahead of the others and in no time at all went straight into their second team. He was picked for Wolverhampton Juniors and after one year was made Captain.

In the summer, he played cricket but after each match he would practise his keep fit regime. His father knew various teams were looking for talent and managed to get one of the scouts to take a look at him. This worked and he was introduced to the boss of the LMS Railway Repair Yard. He was now sixteen and fortunate, having developed into big strong lad and an excellent sportsman. However, his singular passion was football where he now held his own with the adults. He was brilliant for anyone of his generation, bearing in mind his background and fitted ideally into the mould that every large business wanted.

The big industrialists needed to appear philanthropic so they provided recreation facilities and in many cases each large factory had its own sports ground for football, cricket and often athletics. The trouble was they became very competitive because to the winners went all the spoils and masses of free publicity. The owners of course, would bask in the reflective glory of their winning side. Furthermore, to have any really good player in the team also created much free publicity plus a spirit of esprit de corps within the workplace. This was the main reason the LMS Railway offered Frank a job.

There were no real wages for sportsmen or women in those days so they had to have a job as well. Frank was offered a position in the foundry area at their repair yard, He was to become the foundry man's apprentice, a job he would do admirably because of his physique and where he earned the princely sum of 14 shillings and 11 pence per week, but he was also paid 5 shillings every time he played football and an extra shilling if they won. This was paid into his back pocket; he did not want to lose his amateur status, which was very important in those days. In the 1930s he even played for Portsmouth First Division. Frank became quite well off until, with war looming, he went into the Army where they expected him to play for nothing.

Anyway, I remember him telling me about his first day at work. He was given his boots, his big leather shoulder cover which was slipped over the head and his helmet which was fitted with dark glass to protect the eyes from the white hot glare and finally, a big leather apron, which went down to the floor. All this, according to Frank, weighed a ton before you even started to work and was like being in an oven. That was before you entered the furnace area.

Frank didn't drink alcohol and I don't ever remember him imbibing, but in this hothouse, where the heat was almost unbearable, on the hour and almost every hour they would take a break and drink a pint of Ansell's mild beer. This was to restore the bodily fluids and put the nutrients back in the system which was very important as they could lose a lot of body weight.

Not only was the area like being in an oven, the work was extremely hard. The molten white hot iron was poured into long moulds and after a few minutes, the moulds were cracked open to reveal a red hot bar of iron, often weighing several tons which then had to be hauled to the rolling mill by hand. All the time the men were showered with minute particles of red hot iron. It was hell on earth.

On one particular Saturday, Frank was playing his first match for the LMS. Everyone was looking forward to seeing him play. From the start the manager could tell he was not fit; he seemed exhausted, which of course he was, but there was no way he could drop out. I remember him telling me it was as though he still had his furnace kit on as everything felt so heavy. Even when the ball was kicked to him he didn't seem to have the energy to kick it back to anyone. He collapsed just before half time and the team doctor was called. He immediately diagnosed total exhaustion and complete rest. There were no substitutes in those days and the team lost 3 nil.

This work was hard for a fully developed man let alone a sixteen-year-old boy, but as the charge hand told the boss, he had tried to keep up with the men. He was told to keep Frank out of the furnace area Thursdays and Fridays. That did it, he was back to normal in no time and the LMS won the league, losing only one more match the entire season, which amazingly as it may seem was very much down to Frank's ability.

Frank did his bit for the family, giving his mother the 14 shillings and 11 pence a week for the family and living off the 6 shillings a match he earned from football.

It was a different matter for Jess who was a young thirteen when he started work. Grandfather managed to get him an apprenticeship in the bed factory, where they not only made beds, but bedroom furniture, tables and chairs.

He was very lucky as everyone wanted to work for Benchmans. Mr Benchman was one of those wonderful philanthropic and enlightened employers, who had two main objectives: one to keep the business going and two, to ensure that all his employees were treated properly and fairly and that their working conditions were good.

Jess came home the first day and said how he was introduced to Mr Benchman by Mr Williams, the works superintendent and Mr Daniels the foreman and what nice people they were and then said excitedly: 'They've got a flush toilet which you can sit on and places to wash your hands and faces. As Mr Benchman says they must be kept clean enough to eat you dinner off,' and then added, 'I wouldn't want to do that, Mother.' She hugged him.

He had a proper apprenticeship and was learning to be a carpenter.

With his first week's wage, which was 7 shillings and 6 pence, he had to start buying his tools and that took several weeks. His boss told him only to buy the best; they would last longer and do a better job, which he did. Uncle Edward on my grandmother's side was also a carpenter; he and Aunt Betty were the well-offs of the family. They had no children and always plenty of money to spare in comparison to my father, that is. Anyway when he retired, she gave Jess his tools and he gave them to me when he retired and I still use them.

Irvine took me down to the cellar via the steepest of wooden steps I've ever trodden and there they were – the most amazing set of carpentry tools you could ever imagine. The cleanest tools I had ever seen. Chisels sharpened as new, as were saws of every description. Everything was in its proper place and quite frankly, simply from the historical point of view, it was a diary of carpentry from early Victorian to the present day and was fascinating. They have since been offered to and accepted by a Midland Industrial Museum.

We returned to the big leather chairs where Irvine continued his story:

Believe it or not, they had a canteen at Benchmans where everyone could buy a well subsidised sit-down meal. Even the manager ate in the same room although he did have a special table.

Every morning the canteen staff would give everyone a cup of tea with a biscuit and the same in the afternoon but minus the biscuit. On Fridays, they would be given a large bun with their tea.

Jess had been working there for a few weeks when on the Friday he decided to take the bun home for his mother and placed it in paper and put it under his pullover. On the way out he was seen by the foreman and Mr Benchman.

'Jess Gough,' the foreman shouted. 'What have you got under your pullover?' he asked, thinking he had stolen something.

Jess walked over to the two men, his head bowed sheepishly. He took the bun, wrapped in paper from under his pullover and handed it to Mr Daniels. 'It's the bun I was given this morning with the tea, sir,' he replied, addressing Mr Benchman. 'I'm taking it home for my mother.'

Benchman was visibly taken aback. 'Come with me

young man. I'll deal with this now, Mr Daniels, thank you. Come on, follow me.' Jess followed him up the stairs and into the canteen, where Mr Benchman went straight into the store room and brought out a tray of buns.

'Do you have any brothers or sisters?'

'Yes sir,' Jess replied.

There was a long pregnant pause. 'Well, young Jess, how many?'

'Six brothers and one sister, Alice, sir.'

'Are they all at home?'

'Yes sir.'

'Is Alice your favourite?'

'No, Frank is; he's a footballer and gets 6 shillings a match. He's very good.'

'Who does he play for?'

'The LMS Railway,' Jess replied, sticking his chest out in reflective glory.

Mr Benchmark continued the conversation in a convivial tone, when he finally asked: 'Well, young Jess, you better have one for each of the family, hadn't you?'

Jess didn't answer, but the smile on his face said it all.

Mr Benchman took one of the empty cardboard boxes off the shelf and placed the ten freshly made buns into it, Jess watching every move with a wide grin on his face. His boss then tied the box with a piece of string and handed it to Jess. 'Go on, enjoy them.'

'Thank you, sir. Thank you very much.'

'Eat them today whilst they are fresh,' he added as Jess almost skipped out of the canteen down the stairs and off to the main gate. He sensed that Mr Benchman was watching and turned, looking up at the canteen window. Sure enough, his boss was there. In his excitement Jess waved frantically; Mr Benchman smiled and returned the wave.

He arrived home and immediately gave the parcel to

his mother who opened the box. She was astonished. 'Where did you get these from? Did you pinch them?' she asked worriedly, the colour draining from her cheeks.

'No Mother, I didn't. Mr Benchman gave them to me.' It was only after his lengthy explanation of what had happened that he received a huge hug and the thanks of the entire family.

'Next time you see Mr Benchman, you thank him from me. Will you do that?' his mother asked.

'Of course I will,' he replied.

Mr Benchman's generosity didn't end there. I suppose Jess had been working there for about six months, when Mr Benchman thought that if his employees had one of his beds, it would encourage them to talk about them and encourage others to buy them. To achieve this he decided to offer them the opportunity to buy one of the beds and repay the cost at five pence per week over a period of time. He also thought that it would reduce labour turnover and increase the loyalty factor.

This was too much for Jess. He knew his mother and father had never slept on a proper mattress and decided to take up Mr Benchman's offer. On Friday, pay day, he went to the office, paid his five pence, walked down to the stores and collected his mattress. They tied the one end for him, with tape and string so he could hold it and then helped it onto his back. To the astonishment of all concerned, including Mr Benchman, he carried it out of the gate all the way home. It took him over two hours to get back and by that time his father was home and worried about his lateness.

'I've bought you a present,' he said proudly before collapsing on the floor, almost exhausted.

You cannot imagine what his parents thought of the gesture. They talked about it for years to come. However, on the following Monday, Jess was summoned to Mr

Benchman's office. He knocked on the door and was greeted by Miss Plaidy, his secretary. 'Come on in Jess, Mr Benchman won't keep you a minute. I hear you have bought your mother and father a new bed?'

'Yes Ma'am, they love it.'

'They are very lucky to have such a generous son.'

'Ma'am,' he acknowledged.

'Ah, Mr Benchman is here. Jess Gough, sir.'

'Good morning, Jess and how are you after your marathon walk with that mattress? Did you carry it all the way home?'

'Yes sir.'

'I only expected adults to buy the beds at 5 pence a week. Are you going to be able to afford it?'

'Yes sir. I promise I'll pay for it. It was a present for my mother and father. They have never had a mattress before except for one night on their honeymoon. That's when Evan was conceived, my father said yesterday. Both Miss Plaidy and Mr Benchman looked at each other and smiled.

'Well, young Jess, I think you will do very well in this firm, don't you, Miss Plaidy?'

'Yes I do, sir. A smart and an intelligent young man like him will undoubtedly do well, sir.'

'Run along then Jess and make sure you keep up the payments.'

'I will, sir.'

Jess kept up the payments, but after six months he went to pay another 5 pence when the accountant told him he had finished paying.

'But that's not possible.'

'Oh yes it is, Jess. Look.' Sure enough the payments had been made and the account was closed.

Jess knew who had paid the balance off and at the first opportunity he and Mr Benchman were on their own, he said quietly, 'Thank you sir for the wonderful bed.'

Mr Benchman simply smiled.

Jess had made a strong impression with Mr Benchman especially as he listened, worked hard, never grumbled and when his apprenticeship finished, he was a very competent carpenter. He soon rose up the ranks at Benchmans and thanks to his mother's attention to his education, he was eventually made works superintendent and often went back on the bench with the young ones to show them how to do things. Unfortunately, Mr Benchman died in the 1930s and due to family squabbles, the works was sold and all lost their jobs. That said, Jess was now highly skilled; he started on his own and was never short of work again.

Jess married and had two sons, my cousins and both joined the Army as career soldiers. They became recruiting officers before the Second World War. At the time, problems with Germany seemed to be rising again. When war broke out they rejoined their Regiment. Sadly, William, the eldest was killed at Dunkirk and Daniel, who rose to the rank of Captain was killed at the Battle of the Bulge later on in the war, but not before he had sired two children, a boy and a girl. His wife, Dorothy never married again but we were in constant touch.

Chapter 3
The Worst of Life

Grandmother had achieved her dream when almost the entire family were at the railway station to wish Noel, my father well as he was leaving for his first day at Birmingham University. Janet and he were madly in love, and she was there, sobbing her heart out. Grandmother couldn't have been more proud of her son on that day as she waved him goodbye. Yet Birmingham was only fifteen miles away; it wasn't the ends of the earth. He could have come home every day, but it was simply a question of cost; the family could not afford the daily return fare and because he had won a scholarship and had free residential accommodation, it was eminently sensible that he stayed at the university.

Grandmother had given him the opportunity to achieve something special and he had grasped it with both hands. He was the first in the family to go to university and the first in our area. It had even been in the papers and was on the front page of the *Express & Star*.

Irvine went over to the sideboard, pulled open a drawer and took out a dilapidated old scrapbook, opened the first page and there was a picture of his father winning the prize for Mathematics. On the following page, some six years later, was the photograph of him receiving his Honours Degree in Mathematics and of course, the accompanying story. His initial studies had been halted by the advent of war.

The publicity over my father's success meant that the

entire town knew he was now at Birmingham University and away from the area. It was therefore a good time for Smith Jnr to throw his hat in the ring; in other words, to pursue Janet. She had different ideas and would avoid him at all costs, constantly rejecting his attentions. He would not leave it at that. He wanted something he knew he couldn't have.

Graham Smith Jnr's career was mapped out for him. He would join his father and was now working at Compass; it was obvious to everyone there that he was destined for better things. Any sensible father would have placed his son on a training programme, spending several months in each department and learning things from the bottom up. But Smith Jnr went in with all guns blazing, simply telling the workers he was checking on whether they were doing the job properly – certainly not the right way to engender good working relationships with staff.

He continued as he did as a child, trying to be in control and throw his weight around in more ways than one. By now all the Wearing family were working at the Compass and Smith Jnr was now Fred's boss and didn't he love to lord it over him. 'Not so big now are you, Wearing?' he made the mistake of saying to Fred.

'No, that's right Smith, but I will always be that inch taller than you,' he replied, demonstrating the point with his finger and thumb.

Fred's philosophy was always that you can work anything to your advantage as long as you stop and think about it, which is exactly what he did.

However, from that moment on, Smith Jnr began laying the poison down for our family. He even tried setting them up, putting things in Charlie's pockets and then reporting him for stealing. The threat of a seriously broken arm made by his big brothers soon put a stop to those allegations, but it failed to stop other attempts to discredit the family, especially as he was spending a little time in each department, supposedly learning about the business. All in all, Smith Jnr was a layabout and wasting everyone's time, simply looking for personal opportunities. He became jealous of the closeness of the Wearing family, something he had never experienced. He had a dysfunctional relationship with his father although he spent much of his time trying to emulate him.

There was no doubt that Smith Jnr wanted followers of his own; he wanted to be a leader that everyone looked up to, which became very easy for a lad in his position. He had more money than his friends and would splash it around, so it was only natural for others to sniff him out and therefore not hard for him to find a few that would do his bidding. One in particular, a Johnny Blakemore was from a very poor family and never had anything in his life. Suddenly, he had a friend who would give him a few coppers for doing the odd job and suddenly, he no longer had to pick up nub ends from the pavement, as he could now buy a packet of cigarettes of his own. He felt he had self respect and wanted to keep this friend at all costs. Smith Jnr knew it and used him.

A new family, the Blacks, arrived in the area, also as poor as church mice. They had two sons, Tim and Jack. Being new to the area meant they knew no one, so it was wonderful for them when their sons became friends with the boss's son. Yes, John Black, their father also began working in the factory.

Within days, Smith Jnr had Tim and Jack wrapped round his little finger for the same reasons as Johnny Blakemore. Smith Jnr now had a small gang that began to terrify and bully other youngsters in the area and worse still, they began to shoplift; at first nothing of any consequence – sweets, cigarettes and liquorish. But of course when this became boring and too easy, they moved onto bigger things, eventually to rob anyone including the old and vulnerable.

If they weren't allowed to associate with my father's friends they would simply break up the group, just to spoil things for everybody. There were many times when they wanted to give Smith Jnr and his cronies a hiding but the bigger threat of dismissal was always there in the background.

The troublemakers had drawn police attention on several occasions, but somehow they were always told to leave Smith Jnr alone, especially as Smith Snr had just been invited to sit on the bench of magistrates. People in general were up in arms against his appointment because everyone knew he was a villain and not a fair man, but nothing could be done.

Shortly after his father's appointment to the bench, Smith Jnr was positively identified by the proprietor of the bread shop in Heath Town as the young man who had robbed his shop and got away with over £5. The shopkeeper knew Smith Jnr well because he had experienced difficulties with him some months before.

This became another example of the law being twisted and money used to pervert the course of justice. They all felt the shopkeeper would not be bought off; however, he may have been leaned on because, a few days after a positive identification, he rescinded his statement, stating he could no longer be absolutely sure it was Smith.

It was a while later that the shopkeeper told Frank he had received a visit from a senior police officer who told him that they now had a suspect called Johnny Blakemore in custody who had walked into the Police Station and confessed to the robbery. They had set up an identification parade and dressed Blakemore in the clothes and hat Smith had worn at the time and, of course, the shopkeeper picked him, especially as he had been told which one to pick even though the clothes he was dressed in didn't fit him; they were far too big.

The police felt they had a cut and dried case and were satisfied they now had their perpetrator.

Blakemore took the fall and was sentenced to three years in the juvenile prison at Borstal, which was more than he was expecting. It made him somewhat bitter and created another problem not only for himself, but also for the Smiths, as he continuously talked about taking the fall and that he would get £1,000 when he was released.

That was a small fortune for any young man at the time and, of course, he was talking to other criminals who were perhaps a bit more ruthless than he, so poor old Smith Jnr began to receive visitors who wanted a slice of the £1,000 and it took some major threats and action to warn them off.

Blakemore was released after two years for good behaviour and immediately made contact with Smith Jnr. He had done his time and wanted his money, but of course people, especially young people, move on and now Smith Jnr had the Blacks on his side and they suited his purpose more. Despite promises about his money, it was always 'tomorrow'. Blakemore was furious and started mouthing off, but unfortunately for him, with the exception of my family, no one would listen.

About a fortnight later, Blakemore's body was found in the River Severn at Bridgnorth. At the inquest the coroner stated it was misadventure as he had been seen drinking heavily in Bridgnorth and had obviously fallen into the river. No one questioned the fact that he was found with his pockets turned out or considered the possibility that he was pushed in the river upstream. One reporter investigating the death could not find any pub where he had been, especially as it would have been doubtful if any publican would have served him; he was of mixed race and scruffy attire. Of course, the story hit the local *Express & Star* newspaper as he was a local boy and there were many rumours circulating about his relationship with Smith Jnr and many unanswered questions. The whole affair was soon brushed under the carpet and the matter was dropped by the press. I've often wondered if it was anything to do with the fact that several press barons were friends of Lord Winston Heath.

Everyone knew it was another example of the Smiths getting away with 'blue murder'. It seemed they now considered themselves to be above the law.

Smith and the Blacks continued in their abhorrent ways, but with my father away at university, Smith Jnr decided to ignore Janet's continued rejection of him and began to bother her at every opportunity – wherever she was or whoever she was with. She would complain to the management of the particular establishment she was in and on several of those occasions, Smith would be ejected.

However, on one of those occasions Smith was uncontrollably angry and extremely embarrassed at being told to leave, especially as the place was full. You could see it in his demeanour as he left; he was talking to the Blacks through gritted teeth and snarling as he looked at Janet.

She left the place with her friends and decided to take the short cut home by walking through the park. It was coming up to 9 p.m. just before the park keeper locked the gates when she was stopped by the Black brothers.

'Where are you going to, my pretty maid?' one of the brothers asked in a sneering tone.

'Get out of my way,' Janet shouted, hoping to attract attention; but no one heard. She moved sideward to go round them, but they too moved to cut her off.

She turned round to run back when Smith Jnr stopped her from behind. She was again terrified and screamed at the top of her voice, but it was late. Everyone knew the park closed at 9 p.m. and wouldn't want to be locked in. She was alone with one of the worst kind of filthy animal and his two rats and no one was there to help. They dragged her into the open men's toilet. The Blacks held her arms and legs and the poisonous Graham ripped her clothes off and raped her.

She was crying her heart out when Graham yelled, 'Ooh, she's a virgin!' and then added in a sneering tone: 'Well, my little one, I had you before your Noel. You'll be able to tell him that, won't you?'

The Blacks wanted a turn, but Graham wouldn't let them. He wanted to be the only one for his own vicious reasons.

The whole incident had lasted just fifteen minutes when they left, screeching like wild animals. She lay in the toilet almost naked, bleeding profusely from her injuries until the cold began to get to her. She was hoping that someone would come to her assistance, but the park gates were locked and no one came.

She struggled to put on what was left of her clothes and then almost crawled to the wrought iron gates. She pulled herself up, clinging to the gates for support, in the hope of seeing someone who would help.

It seemed ages before she was seen by an elderly couple walking their dog around the park's exterior. There was no way they could get to help her and both felt useless in their efforts. The man decided to go and get the police whilst the lady remained with Janet who was shivering from the cold. The lady passed her coat through the railings. 'Put it round you dear. It will keep you warm.'

It didn't take long for the police to arrive, followed by the park keeper who lived on the edge of the park.

'Who did this to you, miss?' the constable asked, but

Janet was too shocked to speak.

A new Wolverhampton ambulance arrived and took her straight to hospital.

It was a memory Janet would never forget. She never got to know who the old couple were and always wished she could have thanked them properly.

A policeman went with her in the ambulance and spoke to Janet about the incident.

'Janet, do you know who did this to you?'

'Yes, it was Smith, Graham Smith Junior. He lives at No 2 Tremont Street. He was with two brothers called Black. I can't think where they live but they helped Smith. They held me down while Smith raped me.'

Janet could see the paramedic shudder at her description, but then it all became too much for her.

'I think you should stop the questions now, she's not very well,' the medic interrupted.

The officer nodded and the rest of the journey was made in total silence, save for the ambulance's siren. After all, it was a new toy for the driver. They arrived at the New Cross Hospital not far from the park, where she was rushed on a stretcher into the building. She was in a terrible state and immediately taken to the emergency department where she was treated. There was no opportunity for any further questioning, which left the police no alternative but to call at the Smith's house.

Ironically, Janet was unaware that the Smiths had moved home and were now living in a house and area that suited their new position in life. Fortunately, the police knew where they had moved to, as Smith Jnr had already crossed their paths on several occasions.

They arrived in force at his home and rang the bell. Grace Smith answered the door; she was bruised and battered and this startled the police officers.

'Good evening, Mrs Smith. I'm Sergeant Wilberforce

from the Central Police Station. Is young Graham in?'

'No, he's not. Can I help you?'

'No. I'm afraid we need to speak to young Graham.'

'I'll ask him to call at the station first thing in the morning.'

'Thank you but we need to speak to him tonight. It's very urgent. Have you any idea where he might be?'

'What on earth has he done to warrant this urgency?' Mrs Smith asked.

'It's alleged he has raped Janet Guest who is currently in hospital.' He hadn't finished his sentence when she fainted. Wilberforce was at a loss, but ordered one of the constables to help him carry her inside. The maid arrived just in the nick of time to help take her into the lounge and lay her on a sofa.

'What on earth has happened?' the maid asked.

'She fainted when the sergeant told her we had come to arrest young Graham for alleged rape,' said one of the constables.

Mrs Smith slowly came to and took the glass of water the maid had fetched.

'Have you any idea of where he might be?' the sergeant asked the maid.

'No, I haven't.'

The sergeant addressed Mrs Smith again. 'It seems we have another matter to discuss.' He paused to look at the injuries on her face. 'How did you get injuries like that? Was this also young Graham?'

'No sergeant, I fell down the stairs and bumped into a chair when I fell.'

The maid who was standing behind the sofa was shaking her head at the officer to indicate that this was not the case.

Wilberforce just stared at Mrs Smith. Not a word was spoken. After a few seconds, she added: 'It's true, sergeant.'

'Of course it is,' the sergeant said, turning to leave.

'Show them out, Isobel,' Mrs Smith said, addressing the maid.

The maid opened the door and let them out, immediately following them over to their bicycles. 'It's not true what she said. She didn't fall down the stairs. She was given a hiding by that swine of a husband of hers. That's where their son gets it from.'

At that point Mrs Smith appeared at the door and shouted: 'Come on, Isobel. Come on. Don't let's have any idle gossip. You know what the master will say if he hears about it.'

Isobel went running in to find Mrs Smith almost hysterical at the thought that she had spoken to the police. She begged Isobel not to say anything in case her husband found out. This time though, she realised the secret was out. There was no way a young girl would keep a secret like that, especially when Mrs Smith had added: 'Just like his father.'

Shortly afterwards, the police called at number 16 to tell the Guests their daughter was in hospital. Unfortunately, as Mr Guest was still at work, the police called on Grandmother to go round and comfort Mrs Guest, which of course she did willingly.

Janet was battered and bruised and when the doctors told Mrs Guest what had happened to her daughter, she broke down and wept uncontrollably. They told her she was going to be all right but couldn't allow her to stay with her until the following morning as she was having treatment.

You can imagine the state of mind Mrs Guest was in; she was unable to take anything in and didn't want to leave until she was absolutely sure that Janet would be all right and only left because she wanted to be with Wilf, her husband when he heard the news.

They were met by Wilf on their way back from the hospital. He'd learned from a neighbour that something was wrong, particularly as his dinner had not been put in the oven to warm up.

'What's up, love?' he asked.

Ida burst into tears, blurting out what had happened with all the gory details that she had gleaned. Wilf was dumbfounded.

'Alice dear, thanks for helping her. Can you leave her to me now and we'll see you tomorrow?' he said.

'Of course Wilf, but you will let us know if you need anything or even want company. All right?'

'Yes, of course.'

Grandmother left, realising the importance of that special moment when families come together in times of crisis and they need to be left alone.

Janet was in hospital for over two weeks recovering from the injuries that bastard had bestowed on her. However, things had begun to change; some of the workforce knew what had happened. Graham Smith Jnr could not walk anywhere in the works without someone shouting: 'Rapist' or something equally telling. In fact, it was becoming so difficult at times that Graham Smith Snr had to take back control of the situation.

He made it clear that the next person who shouted any abuse would be sacked. He even put one of his own mistresses in the factory to report back. Graham Smith Jnr was duly sent in to inspect the place, slowly walking down the factory floor. Several people shouted abuse but poor Phyllis Mayfield was the one who could be identified and was sacked on the spot. What was worse, she lost her home and was on the poverty line until others stepped in to help her to find another job.

This action was very effective as the abuse stopped but the looks never ceased.

Smith's wife, Grace suffered so much of the torment. The employees vented their feelings on her to the point that she became acutely aware that the entire neighbourhood knew her son had raped Janet.

I'm sure it was this pressure that made her want to speak with the Guests and this happened one evening when my grandmother was just arriving home with Mrs Guest. There was a car waiting outside the house and they couldn't believe their eyes when Mrs Grace Smith stepped out.

'May I come in?' she asked, walking towards them.

'Of course, Grace, Come in,' Grandmother replied.

They walked through the archway along the alley and into the yard. 'Does it bring back memories?' Grandmother asked.

'Yes, it does. I hated every minute of it.' The two women were shocked at her outburst and stood open-mouthed.

'Why's that?' Grandmother asked as she ushered Grace in.

Grace didn't reply. She was too wrapped up in her worries of the moment but even then they could not help but notice the angst on her face as she looked round, uncomfortable with the scene before her.

'Not like the new house!' Grandmother asked rhetorically.

'No and I hate that too.'

'Why on earth is that?'

'It's my prison and my punishment for my past sins and I'm there for life.' She paused for a moment and then added: 'Mrs Guest, I know the pain you are suffering–'

She was stopped in mid-sentence. 'How dare you say that!' Ida Guest replied, pausing as her anger boiled over. 'My daughter has been raped by your son. What would you know about anything like that... with all your so-called finery?'

'I do know what it's like and I'm really sorry. I too was raped by that boy's father and I had to leave my family in Newcastle and come here to live with that beast of a man because I had no means of support and... everyone wanted me out of the way.' The anger and bitterness in her voice was evident.

'How would you like to live with a man who treats you like a dog, whips you when you do something that's not to his liking and only stays with you because of an allowance he receives?'

She took her coat off and undid her blouse to reveal several wheal marks on her back.

'That insect son of mine also treats me like some leper. I have had no friends. No one will speak to me, even associate with me because both the men in my miserable life are vile creatures. And you say I don't know what it's like. How would you have liked to live here with all the nasty comments made about you, when all the time they were hoping to get at your husband? It doesn't hurt him because he seldom speaks to me and never allows me to speak to him without permission. So he never knows what people think.

'Oh yes, he keeps me in clothes in order to keep up appearances as he is now a JP and the new senior foreman. And he has the ear of Lord bloody Winston Heath, but that's all.

'I'm Graham's mother and I know he has done many evil things and got away with them. I know your daughter was raped by him, but I also know that somehow he will get away with it. I don't know how but I know he will and for this I am truly sorry.

'I have a little money saved up and I want you to have it, but please don't let it be known where it came from.'

With that she handed an envelope to Mrs Guest and left quickly.

Neither Grandmother nor Mrs Guest could believe their eyes when they opened the envelope and found there was £210 in large white five pound notes – an absolute fortune in those days.

The police couldn't find Smith Jnr until the following week when he was arrested and charged. But in those few days, once again he had beaten the law. He had managed to obtain a couple of witnesses who confirmed they were with him at the Rose and Crown at the time of the incident – a pub where he and his father were very frequent patrons. Even the landlord of the pub confirmed he was there at that time with none other than the Blacks.

'He drew attention to himself by throwing his money about,' the landlord was heard to say.

'Can anyone else confirm this?' the police officer asked.

The landlord turned to the barmaid who had been listening and with a slight inflection of the eye let her know he wanted agreement.

'Yes, I can,' she replied. 'He was here all evening.'

'Who was?' the officer asked.

For a split second she seemed confused and then replied: 'That loud mouth. He's always in here. I can't remember his name.'

The landlord, much to the officer's annoyance, helped her by saying 'Smith'.

'Yes, that's it. Smith. Graham Smith,' she added. 'I see so many people here, I can never remember their names.'

The officer thanked them and turning to the barmaid said: 'I think we will need to talk to you again.' He then left, knowing from her last reaction she wasn't telling the truth.

The police were fed up with Smith Jnr and so was everyone in the area; they believed it would only be a matter of time before he was behind bars where he belonged.

My grandmother visited the hospital with Mrs Guest on several occasions and on one occasion the investigating officer arrived to discuss the case with Janet.

'Will you be able to answer a few questions for us, miss?' the officer asked.

'Had we better go?' Mrs Guest asked.

'No, I want my mother here,' Janet said, still sounding distressed.

The officer talked to her about how she was feeling. In those days, officers did not have the training or experience to be able to question a victim in such circumstances, particularly where a charge of rape was invariably considered to be the woman's fault.

Then came the real questioning...

'Are you sure it was Graham Smith? There are four people who have stated he was in the Rose and Crown at the time.'

'Well, they're lying.'

'Four of them?' he asked.

'Yes. I know it was him. He made no pretence of making it clear who he was and I've known him for years. He is a hateful person.'

'You don't like him then?'

'No, I despise him and I have done so ever since he came to live near us,' Janet said, almost in tears, the stress of the situation now getting to her.

'Is this a way of getting back at him, you thinking it must be him?'

'Get out!' she screamed. 'Get out now.'

Hearing the raised voices, several nurses came running in, ordering everybody out. One nurse turned to the policeman. 'Can't you see the state Janet is in? It's a wonder she didn't lose her life. She has experienced an appalling attack. We know and she certainly knows who did it. Now leave her be. She is still too poorly to be questioned. I will fetch the doctor if you wish and he will tell you.'

Mrs Guest returned to comfort her daughter whilst Grandmother left with the officer, who aside from having his tail between his legs was also in receipt of some apt and well-chosen words from her.

Chapter 4
Out of Site

The police decided not to prosecute Smith Jnr because of the weight of evidence in his favour. They knew she had been raped but they couldn't prove without doubt that it was Smith who had committed the crime. Everybody knew the truth and the Rose and Crown began to suffer. They began to lose clientèle. The barmaid was the weakest link, but it was too late and pressure was put on the police to drop the case as they had no conclusive evidence.

Once again my grandmother and Mrs Guest were by Janet's bedside when the police came to give her the bad news. The last thing she wanted to hear. Janet was told what Grace Smith had said, including the fact that she knew her son would get away with it. So at least Janet was fully prepared for the worst. It did take a lot of persuading for her to accept the money, but eventually she did.

However, the most important thing in Janet's life was Noel, my father and she made all concerned swear he would not be told anything. Eight weeks later came worse news; it was confirmed Janet was pregnant. She was not going to stay around for obvious reasons.

She tried in vain to get accommodation in other areas, but the moment they knew she was expecting, it was always an emphatic rejection. I think the worst thing for her was people perceived she was a loose woman and even when the truth was told, she was frequently perceived to be guilty of blame.

Eventually, Mr Guest contacted his brother who, after knowing the full facts, agreed to look after Janet for the princely sum of nineteen shillings and six pence per week. They lived in Haworth, a prosperous little woollen town in the West Riding of Yorkshire. It was also becoming well known as the home of the now three famous Brontë sisters – daughters of the Reverend Patrick Brontë, a former vicar of the Parish Church. A few years earlier, they had written several books, which had sold well and received considerable acclaim.

The sisters had died very young many years earlier and people were now visiting the area to look at where they lived and what had inspired them. Their association with the area was beginning to add to its prosperity.

Approximately two and a half months later, Janet was on her way to Haworth where she was met at the station by Stanley Guest, the local coal man who lived at the back of the railway yard.

Stanley and Ada, his wife, together with their two daughters were kindness itself and when the baby was born, even more so. She had a little boy Henry, born in the April at the start of a terrible summer, which was wet, cold and damp. Dozens of woollen mills polluted the environment and in the railway yard next to house, engines belched out thick black smoke. It was certainly no place for a newborn baby.

It would be fair to say there is a natural bond of love between mother and baby. This was certainly the case with Janet, despite the circumstances of Henry's birth. He hadn't asked to be born, so now it was her job to ensure the child had the best she could give.

She had made herself very useful not only helping with the housework but also doing the books for her uncle's business, something he hated doing. She dealt with the coal mines and the customers who delivered direct in those days; in fact she was so efficient that Stanley was able to concentrate on the deliveries. In nine months, he almost doubled the size of his business.

Her uncle had told her she could stay as long as she liked and was so pleased with her that he began to pay her twelve shillings and six pence a week.

Using her first month's wages Janet paid for her mother and father to come and visit her, staying at the Temperance Hotel on Bridgehouse Lane, just round the corner from their house. I remember my mother saying it was one of the loveliest moments of her life to see her parents again and introducing Henry to them. It was also one of the saddest because she had to make them keep the promise that they would not tell my father where she was or what had happened to her.

Janet's parents could clearly see that things had worked out well with Stanley and Ada. Janet's health was showing a marked improvement. She began to smile again and had built up a wonderful relationship with her uncle's family.

***

I mentioned earlier that the families in Tremont Street were a very close-knit group, parents as well as younger family members, always ready to help each other out. They all knew what had happened to Janet despite the mask of secrecy, but they respected the family's wishes not to tell my father, Noel. That said, there was no way any of them were going to allow the Blacks to get away with their part in the rape.

The Black brothers were seldom separated from Smith Jnr and when they were, they were seldom separated from each other, which only complicated the situation because they felt it was better to get them one at a time.

Not that this would be a problem because the Blacks would be outnumbered; it was felt their family's pain would be extended further because they would be able to warn the other brother he was next and possibly Graham Smith after that. None of them would know when something was likely to happen and none of them knew what would happen; it was psychological warfare, so to speak.

When the Blacks were on their own few people would mix with them, both tarnished by Smith Jnr's reputation. They would hang round the park, trying their luck with the young girls, which wasn't very sensible as the girls knew they were involved with the rape and would have been warned to stay away from them.

Janet's brother, Bobby Guest, Charlie Gough and Jack Wearing were walking by the park perimeter one evening when they saw Tim Black standing idle outside the park gates. It was closing time and the gates were about to be locked.

Bobby gave Charlie a knowing look and walked towards Black.

'Fancy nickin' a boat and having some fun?' Bobby asked.

'Yeah, come on,' Tim Black replied, pleased that Bobby was speaking to him. By this time, Charlie had sent Jack to Tremont Street for a few reinforcements.

Within seconds, the three of them were over the park wall and walking towards the boating lake. They released the ties to three boats, whilst Charlie managed to open the locked boathouse door and went in.

'Come and chose your oars,' Charlie quietly called out.

Black walked in, selected a pair of oars and marched to the boats. He was immediately followed by Bobby and Charlie.

'I'll hold the boat while you get in,' Bobby suggested.

Black was facing the other way, and with one leg in the boat and the other on dry land, Bobby began gently pushing the boat away from the jetty; Black's legs started to stretch apart.

'Hang on, Tim!' Bobby shouted. 'I haven't got hold of the boat yet.'

The boat was quickly leaving its mooring as Tim Black's legs were now fully stretched. It would only be a matter of seconds before disaster struck and he fell in. This was the case and whilst the water was only two feet six inches deep, he fell in head first and was soaked from top to bottom.

'I told you to hold on,' Bobby shouted, tongue in cheek.

'I didn't hear you.'

'Come on, let's have you out.' They helped him out of the water, with Bobby admonishing him again for not waiting.

'Let's go over to the bog and get these clothes off. I'll lend you my pullover and some pants. These can dry off a bit,' Bobby said, pointing to his clothes.

They ran to the toilets where there were five other lads already waiting and the moment they entered, Tim Black was grabbed. He hadn't the chance to yell as an oily rag was shoved into his mouth and wrapped round his neck.

They now had him in the park at ten past nine in the evening, the same time and place where Janet was raped. The park keeper had locked up and gone home. Everywhere was now quiet as the grave, apart from Black's muffled screams.

They stripped him of all his clothes and tied his hands and feet. Bobby explained that Janet was his sister and that they now had an independent witness to the rape but they were too scared to come forward.

'We have a better punishment than prison for you,' Seth said, taking out an indelible pencil and tattooing over his forehead: 'I am a rapist'. Then all over his chest he wrote: 'I helped Graham Smith to rape and murder and my brother will be the next'.

They then forced his penis into several metal washers and as it became bruised and swelled, the washers cut deeply into the flesh. I know it would have been sheer agony, but so was Janet's agony. He was then tied to the park gate and left to the mercy of the *Express & Star* reporter and the police.

He was too terrified to report who had done it to him and it became another one of those unsolved crimes. He was away several weeks, trying to get the tattoo removed, unsuccessfully of course. He did at least remove the words but he always looked a mess after that.

Jack was sent away for a few weeks after Tim had been dealt with because their father was worried what might happen to his other boy. He didn't realise that the Tremont Street Mob would wait, no matter how long it took.

Chapter 5
Truth Will Out

Whilst Janet was living in the country and my father was at university, the children of the Gough, Wearing, Ambrose and Wilson families made a pact to first, find out what was behind this evil Smith family and second, to take revenge on them, at the same time trying to keep my father oblivious to unfolding events. They seemed so proud that their brother, friend and neighbour was at university and doing so well. It was as though they wanted to protect him and keep him out of things.

However, since Smith Snr had ensured his son was appointed to the firm, things had gone from bad to worse. As I said before, Smith Jnr had spent several weeks in each department learning the business, but now having done so, he was undermining the authority of the department heads and creating difficulties within the workforce, which even caused his father to become aware of the unrest.

It made the Smiths more despised by everyone, to such an extent that more people plucked up courage to openly make comments about Smith Jnr and his father, to whom he was becoming an embarrassment. Several experienced men who had reprimanded young Smith were sacked for their actions. As a result, other workers threatened a walkout which resulted in them being reinstated.

A very inexperienced young man to be throwing his weight around with experienced operatives set him on a course for disaster. Add to this the fact that Smith Jnr had not been prosecuted for any of his crimes and was now treating everyone as though he was above the law. It was all becoming too much for the community. They, together with at least ninety per cent of the workforce, had decided they had had enough, but as so often happens, it was left to the few to do something about it. The few of course were certain senior male family members living in Tremont Street and they were left to find out who was behind the rapid rise of the Smiths and who was protecting Smith Jnr.

They felt it could not be Smith Snr as he was the one benefitting from the actions having been continuously promoted, so it had to be someone higher up the ladder. They also felt Lord Winston Heath would not be involved with such low life as the Smiths, so they came to the conclusion it was Donald Baker, the works superintendent.

However, after they had talked matters over, they decided to speak to Lord Winston Heath himself, put him in the picture so to speak. Their wives objected on the basis they would get sacked which would bring dire consequences for their families.

They had saved the train fare to Sutton Coldfield near Birmingham where Lord Winston Heath lived and set off in their Sunday best, knowing that they were risking everything they had worked for; but as Grandfather said: 'We haven't got much to lose so what we are doing is worth fighting for.'

They hardly said a word to each other until they got to Sutton; the stress of the situation and the fear of what might happen if things were to go wrong was beginning to tell on them. How would his Lordship react to five of his workers mutinying? After all, the unions were not recognised in any of his factories. Would he sack them on the spot, or would he simply take no notice?

They changed at Birmingham New Street and caught the slow train to Oxford which went via Sutton Coldfield, stopping at every station and halt en route. As they neared their destination they began to have second thoughts.

Bert was elected spokesman and managed to pull them together, giving them all a little more courage when he outlined his plan of action.

They arrived at his Lordship's home a little disappointed; they were expecting a huge mansion with an enormous drive to it and flunkies everywhere. It wasn't the case; it was a large house with a beautiful garden and its own entrance to Sutton Park. They were told later that his Lordship did live in the circumstances they believed, but that this was his Midland home; his real one was near Bristol and was how I described.

Anyway, they walked up the drive and must have looked like a bunch of villains as the chauffeur came out from the garage. The two gardeners also suddenly appeared and the front door opened well before they got there.

A young man in his late teens, early twenties stood at the entrance, arms folded, legs apart, waiting for them to come closer.

'What can I do for you gentlemen?' he asked courteously.

'We wish to speak to his Lordship,' Bert replied. 'We are from the Compass plant near Wolverhampton and we are worried that things are not as they should be and his Lordship should be made aware of it.'

'Come on in,' the young man entreated. 'It's all right, you can go now, thank you. I'll deal with these gentlemen,' he said, gesturing to his staff that all was well.

'Well gentlemen, this sounds intriguing. Would you

like to sit down?' he asked, as he took them into the dining room. My name is Jonathan and I'm his Lordship's son. My father is very poorly at the moment and cannot see anyone, but in any event he is at our home in Bristol. Please sit down. I am looking after things for the time being so you can deal with me. However, before we start would you like a cup of tea or something stronger?'

'Tea will do nicely sir,' Bert replied.

Jonathan ordered tea and sandwiches for them and joined them at the table.

'So what's happening then?' he asked.

'Well, sir we have been worried for many years about the rapid rise of our senior foreman, when quite frankly, he is not very good. He stops the men's money for no reason and does not record it, keeping the money for himself. The works superintendent is being sidelined in favour of the senior foreman.

'This was reported but nothing was said. He hires and fires on a whim and only this week he sacked five men who are vital to the production simply because one of them told Smith's son not to fool around and the other four agreed. Yes sir, his son!

'They had to be re-instated as the whole works would have walked out. Us included, sir.

'The boy has been in trouble with the law on many occasions and someone has put the pressure on to get all enquiries dropped. All your employees at the two factories believe your father is behind it, using his influence to get him off. Even the local police make such comments. There was even suspicion that the boy had robbed a local shop and another was paid to take the blame after he had been positively identified. There are stories abounding that he had someone murdered and we all know the investigation was stopped, Even the local paper was silenced and yet this boy is being groomed to run the place.'

'What's his name?' Jonathan asked.

'His father is Graham Smith Senior and his son is Graham Smith Junior. They seem to run it as their own.'

'Yes, I have met a Mr Smith, a man in his fifties, isn't he?'

'Yes sir,' Bert replied.

'Are you sure this is not simply an attempt to ruin a man who was promoted over you and get at him by complaining about his son?'

'Sir, we have been with the company for many years and we hope many more and in all that time have you ever known a senior foreman's son be taken on and have the run of the shop floor and be able to comment at such a young age? He is not well educated; he has never been to university like Evan's son here. Nearly all the workers believe that your father is involved and we feel his Lordship should know what is going on.'

Bert broke off from his little speech when the tea and sandwiches arrived, which were very welcome as they hadn't enough money to buy food.

Jonathan must have noticed they were eating quickly and asked if they had eaten. Of course they had to say no. He immediately issued instructions for more sandwiches to be prepared for the journey home – roast beef and ham.

I remember Grandfather and old Mr Guest talking about those sandwiches for years after. They had never eaten such tasty beef and ham on bread so fresh with real butter.

Jonathan became extremely perplexed and annoyed that they were constantly running down his father. 'This cannot be true. My father does not know anyone like this,' he said angrily.

'Sir! Do you think we would risk our jobs by telling you this,' Grandfather exclaimed passionately. 'Do you think we would pay the fare from Wolverhampton to here when we can ill afford it? No! We wouldn't. We want to protect our jobs and the firm. We don't want your father mixed up in this.'

'Are you sure this is not a ploy to get your own back on the foreman?' he asked again, still with a touch of anger in his voice.

'The boy's father, Graham Smith Snr seems to have the ear of your father and it does not matter what he does, he is forgiven and even promoted. They are getting their money from somewhere, and it's not the workplace,' Grandfather continued.

'Let me give you an example: when they arrived in our street, they used Pickfords removals. No one in our league can afford that. When they moved home to their new house, they used Pickfords again. Their furniture is that of a well-heeled family, certainly not what you would expect.'

'It could have been left to them,' Jonathan replied sharply.

'No sir, this furniture is of the finest quality, not what the likes of us could ever afford and he lives in the same street. We all rent our houses and you own them.

'I don't believe it sir, but there are even rumours that one of your employees from your factory up North had an affair with your father and that Smith Jnr could be related.'

Jonathan stood in silence just listening, but showing no emotion.

'When is this supposed to have happened,' he asked, now becoming angry.

'The boy is about your age sir, so I suppose it was twenty years ago,' Bert replied which annoyed Jonathan even more.

Jonathan snapped: 'I don't like the way this

conversation is going. I want you to leave now and I don't want you to repeat anything we have discussed this afternoon. Is that understood?'

'Yes sir,' they all said in unison.

Jonathan gave them each a packet of sandwiches to take home and two five pound notes between them, to cover their fare.

The men were completely surprised by his generosity, especially as they had so obviously upset him, but none the less they had only spoken the truth. The most surprising thing gained from the meeting was they could all see that Jonathan was visibly upset about the possibility of the bastard child they had mentioned.

As Bert said on the train home: 'That bastard's little son could be the heir to all of this. That's if it's his.'

'Oh, it's his all right,' Bill added. 'Just look at him, He's nothing like our foreman, and did you notice Jonathan's left eye? It's very slightly smaller than his right one. It's the same with that little bastard.'

'No, it can't be. This lad's older than Smith,' Jack said.

'I don't think he is,' Bert replied as the conversation began to revolve round this possibility and helped to pass the time on the journey back home. It's strange but they all saved their sandwiches until they got home in order to share them with their families.

There was no question of silence whatever Jonathan Gremore had ordered. He couldn't silence the entire factory so what the hell. They had started something and now there was no stopping, especially as the factory was rife with the rumours about their visit to see the boss.

They had a great deal left of the money Jonathan Gremore had given them, so the following day Jack Ambrose, one of the Tremont Street Mob was charged by the others to visit Newcastle, to investigate what Grace Smith had eluded to when visiting Mrs Guest and

Grandmother. She had implied she too had been raped. The question now was by whom? They pooled together the money to pay him for two days' lost wages.

Jack seemed the obvious choice to go to the Newcastle Works. Apart from being tall and good looking, he always looked dapper in a suit and tie and he had previously spent a couple of days in the area a few years previously.

The ten pounds from Jonathan came in well and, Jack as an employee himself in Lord Winston Heath's empire, seemed very capable of getting answers to questions quickly.

He went straight to the enquiry office and asked to see Mr Fraser's secretary. Duncan Fraser was the boss of the Newcastle Works and was considered to be next in line to Winston Heath. He was a very close friend of his and it was well known he resented Jonathan, regarding him as a young whippersnapper who would effectively be in command. Like Smith Snr, Fraser was looking for ways and means of securing his future. Tilley Watson was his secretary, still attractive in her early forties, but, so it appeared, was sadly neglected by her husband. She flirted with Jack unmercifully and readily accepted his invitation for a drink, especially as he implied he was working for Jonathan Gremore in an attempt to find out about working conditions at the plant.

It wasn't hard to find the Old George Pub tucked away in a side courtyard away from many prying eyes, especially as Tilley was well known in the area; after all, this factory had over five thousand employees.

Tilley had one of those silly uncultivated voices, a little high pitched but as Jack found out, she was good at her job, except when she had a drink. She also had a phenomenal memory with great attention to detail.

They walked into the pub and to his surprise and delight, he found out she was a half of bitter girl. The money would go a long way.

'Let's go and sit over there,' Jack said, directing Tilley into a secluded corner.

'Cheers,' they both said as the glasses clinked.

'Now Tilley, I know I can trust you so you mustn't tell anyone of our conversation.'

'I won't, I promise.'

'You know his Lordship is very ill at the moment?'

'Yes, Mr Fraser has gone to see him in Bristol. That's where he lives, you know.'

'Yes, I was there the other day,' Jack replied, gaining Tilley's confidence by the minute. 'Gosh that was quick. Another?' Jack asked as the first half of bitter had already disappeared from Tilley's glass.

'Yes please... Jack,' she said, calling him Jack for the first time in a way that someone who wanted to get closer would do.

The second was disappearing as quickly as the first, but the conversation flowed as fast.

'When I first started here I was straight from school. His Lordship, Winston Heath, was nearly always here. He told us the Newcastle Works was his flagship and he was going to make them his headquarters. Duncan Fraser became his valuable assistant. He used to fawn round him doing his bidding until he began to take some of the control of the company. We were all amazed when this happened because none of us thought he was the best man for the job. I don't really like working for him but it's a good job and the money's good for a woman, that is!'

'Why did all this happen and why so suddenly?' Jack asked.

'Mind you, it's only a rumour you know, but I think it was to do with his secretary. Yes, I'm sure it was. She was called Grace, I think. Yes, that's it, she was called Grace. I was only a junior just starting after leaving school. I remember she was a lovely looking woman and many of us girls tried to be like her. She was so... model-like. We all knew his Lordship fancied her.'

'You're not so bad yourself, Tilley.'

'Thank you kind sir,' she said, shaking her shoulders in an appreciative way. 'Grace played along with him,' she continued. 'But she kept her distance as he was her boss, but we all knew she didn't really fancy him. In fact, we thought she despised him.

'We saw him trying to kiss her one day and she was having a hell of a job fighting him off. He didn't see us. There was also a girl called Kate Smithfield, who was sacked. Some of the girls met her in the pub and she told us she had seen him pushing Grace up against the wall in his office, trying to get into her knickers, but it's all a rumour you know.'

'Another one?' Jack asked as the second half had now disappeared.

'Jack, what on earth are you trying to do? Get me tipsy, you naughty boy?'

He returned from the bar with another half and asked, somewhat rhetorically as he knew the answer: 'Does Grace still work here? She'll be getting on a bit now, won't she?'

'Oh no! It was about the time when Duncan Fraser got promoted. We thought that because he was the new broom in, he got rid of his Lordship's secretary and had one of his own, but I know better,' she whispered, getting closer to Jack.

'What's that then, love?' Jack asked.

'Ooh, you have got me tipsy! It's "love" now, is it?'

'You're a mine of information, Tilley. You know everything about everything, don't you?'

'Tilley never forgets,' she added, tapping the side of her nose and taking another huge swig of the beer.

By now, Jack had to stop drinking just to ensure he had enough money in case there were others to see, but there was no need as Tilley was about to tell him just what he needed to hear.

'Come on, Tilley tell me what you know. You're making it sound like a story book.'

'No I'm not, I promise it's true.'

'What is?'

'Well, on this particular day, we all heard a scuffle in his Lordship's office and a stifled scream. About half an hour later, Grace came out of his office very red-faced and looking as though she had been crying. Although she wasn't dishevelled we all knew something had happened, although nothing was said. Many years later Dorothy Phipps – she's the chief engineer's secretary, told me in confidence that Grace had told her she had been raped by his Lordship. We knew it was something like that but who would believe a young woman against the word of his Lordship?

'Grace had a couple of weeks off and came back looking very sheepish, knowing that situations like that cannot be kept secret in a place like ours. The trouble was that the moment she got back he was at her again. That was until she came in one day looking in bloom and every woman knew she was pregnant. We never saw Grace again. She even left the area.'

'What happened after that?' Jack asked.

'Ooh, it gets worse. I was made Mr Fraser's secretary, a very responsible job because Glenys Freeman, his usual secretary was needed by his Lordship. I answered a call from reception one day and was told that there was a Mr Graham Smith downstairs who wished to see Mr Fraser and would not take no for an answer.

'I told the receptionist I would go down which I did. Waiting in the foyer was Graham Smith and I could just vaguely remember him working here. He had been made a charge hand when he suddenly left. I told him that Mr Fraser was far too busy at the moment.

'That's when Smith exploded: "Tell him I am here and I know he will see me." I went back upstairs, knocked on Mr Fraser's door and was almost torn apart for disturbing him.

'There's a Mr Graham Smith in reception and he is being awkward. He says he has to see you and he will not take no for an answer,' I said.

'Mr Fraser went drip white.

'"Well, I better see him," he said, trying to sound casual, but I had never known him do this before. "Go and bring him up."

'I went downstairs, collected Mr Smith and showed him into Mr Fraser's office.

'I went out, closed the door, and began to listen when I heard Mr Fraser say, "Just a moment." I heard his chair move. I don't know why but I knew he was checking up on me so I quickly ran into my office, leaving the door open so he could see me. Sure enough, it was obvious he was checking on me.'

'You clever little devil,' Jack said which encouraged her further.

'I tiptoed up to his door again. It was easy to hear as their voices were raised in any case.

'Well, I couldn't believe what I was hearing. Smith was demanding money and promotion at work. They argued and Smith threatened to tell the world what he knew. That's when Fraser gave in.'

'What was it about then?' Jack asked.

'It's only rumour as I said before but putting two and two together, I think Smith is paid an allowance each month to say the child that Grace had was his but he wanted more. He obviously has a job working for his

Lordship but I don't know where.'

'I do,' Jack interjected.

'Where?' she asked.

'At the Compass Iron & Steel Company in Wolverhampton. What happened after that?' Jack asked, realising he was onto something.

'Well, from then on every time he came, which was fairly regular, I listened and you know it was always trouble and he would always throw his weight around.'

'Just lately that son of theirs is in so much bother it's almost a full-time job keeping him out of trouble,' Jack added.

'Jack, do you know they even leaned on Grace's family, paying them a lump sum to make her leave the area? When I heard that mentioned I really felt for her. How would you like it if your parents sent you away just for the money? It's horrible, isn't it?

'Duncan Fraser has been bleeding his Lordship of money on the pretence of paying Smith an allowance but keeping the majority for himself.'

Jack made a note of this to give to Jonathan as and when they next met.

'I can't say anything or I'll lose my job,' she added, now beginning to slur her words.

Jack could see her wellbeing would not last another half pint so he decided to take her home but not before he had asked her to give him some dates: When did Grace leave? When was Smith transferred to Compass Iron? Who paid for the removal and who paid the rent for Tremont Street and his new house? Who authorises Graham Smith Snr's promotions? When was the boy born?

He also asked her who Duncan Fraser talks to when Smith Jnr is in trouble.

'Can I see you tomorrow?' Jack asked, suggesting he

took her home.

'Yes please, Jack. It's been lovely and it needn't end now. My husband's away you know. We have plenty of time.'

'I have to work tonight. It will be easier tomorrow, especially if you can get those dates.'

'I will,' she replied. 'Mr Fraser will be in Bristol another two days.'

Jack took a disappointed Tilley home. He hadn't taken the hint.

'He works in a colliery and is away two weeks at a time,' she announced again in the hope that he would keep her company, but all he wanted to do was meet her the next day in the hope she could at least get some more concrete information.

On arrival at her house, he kissed her good night on the hand.

'Can we meet in the pub at six o'clock tomorrow?' he asked.

'Try and stop me,' she replied, grabbing him round the neck and kissing him full on the lips. 'There will be more of that tomorrow if you are a good boy.'

'I will be,' Jack replied, relieved that he got away so easily.

Tilley was marvellous; the following day at six on the dot she walked into the pub where Jack had two glasses already waiting for her.

'You naughty boy!' she said, greeting him with another kiss. 'Is this my lucky day?'

'How did you get on?' Jack asked.

'Is this my lucky day?' she asked again, this time in a more suggestive tone.

'Of course it is,' Jack replied after which Tilley gave him all the information he needed. He was right. Tilley had a fantastic memory even when in the tipsy state as she was the night before.

What was surprising was that she knew about the troubles Smith Jnr had been in and that Winston Heath had asked Fraser to deal with these problems direct, paying a small fortune to sort matters out.

'I know there was a lot of money paid out but I never saw any receipts,' she added. 'Now are you going to pay me in kind for all my trouble or am I going to tell the world what you are doing?'

Jack never did tell his mates whether it was Tilley's lucky day, but she did give them all the information they wanted. They now knew Grace was telling the truth about being raped by his Lordship and that Smith Jnr was Lord Winton Heath's bastard son.

His Lordship remained ill for many months during which time Jonathan Gremore was running the business for his father. Within weeks, you could see he was a more enlightened employer than his father. There were small improvements in working conditions at Compass. The toilets were cleaned regularly and a room was set aside for lunch breaks, for example.

Records of pay reductions had to be properly kept and an appeals procedure was introduced for all aspects of discipline, including dismissal. This not only stopped Smith Snr's little fiddle straightaway, but also diminished his power over the workers, especially as the first person he sacked was reinstated immediately after an appeal.

There was a highly positive response from the workmen after this first successful appeal. It was like a weight being lifted off everyone's shoulders. There was even a spring in their step.

One brave employee shouted across to Smith Snr as he passed by: 'You lost that one then!'

Smith turned and snarled, 'It won't last.'

Everyone had been reluctant to challenge Smith

because they suspected he had the ear of his Lordship, but now others began standing up to him and from that moment on they could sense he was trying to undermine his Lordship's son, Jonathan Gremore at every opportunity, simply because he was the one person who was making the changes and the one who could not be influenced by the Smiths.

Smith Snr made one last effort to regain his position by journeying to Bristol to see his Lordship, fully intending to put the poison down, but fortunately for everyone, his Lordship was still far too ill to see anyone and with that, the tables were turned. Jonathan Gremore began to put pressure on him.

In the meantime, Jonathan Gremore, who was obviously taking matters very seriously, began to check on the information received at his meeting with the Tremont Street Mob, in particular the story of an illegitimate child.

He hired a private detective firm from London. When you have money and resources, things can happen quickly and within three or four weeks following their visit to Sutton Coldfield, Mrs Guest was disturbed by a loud knock on her front door. It was still very unusual as few ever used this door. Half the neighbourhood would have heard the loud knocking at number 16. It caused quite a stir in the street, especially as there was a Hansom cab standing outside and a solitary figure was seen stepping down from the horse-drawn carriage.

The door was opened by Mrs Guest. 'Yes, what do you want?' she asked the man wearing a dark suit, bowler hat and white shirt with a winged collar. Her attention was drawn to the meticulous shine on his black shoes.

'Mrs Guest?' he asked.

'Yes,' she replied, raising her eyes to meet his.

'Is your husband in?'

'No. Who wants to know?' she asked haughtily.

'I'm Arbuthnot Townsend from Townsend, Featherstone & Phipps. We are a firm of lawyers acting for a Jonathan Gremore, the son of Lord Winston Heath. Now... is your husband in?'

'I've already told you he's not, but he will be back in about ten minutes if you would like to wait?'

'Yes, I would. Thank you.'

'Come in then.'

'Wait there, please,' he shouted to the driver. 'I don't know how long I'll be.'

'Right you are sir,' came the reply.

Arbuthnot Townsend followed her in through the front door, directly into the parlour which was, of course, the best room in the house but seldom used. In fact, the last time was many years before when they laid her elderly mother out for everyone to see before the funeral. It was always very cold as the door opened directly onto the street and they couldn't afford to light the fire.

'Please sit down. Would you like a cup of tea?' Mrs Guest asked.

'No thank you.'

'Is there anything I can do?'

'No, no, I'll wait for Mr Guest.'

The pregnant pause lasted a few seconds, so she excused herself and left him sitting alone in the front room.

Eventually, Mr Guest and Grandfather arrived back to meet an anxious Mrs Guest who could hardly contain herself with her news. The two men walked into the parlour and introduced themselves, with Mr Guest insisting the lawyer joined them in the dining room, where at least it was warmer.

'Mr Gough will be staying,' Mr Guest suddenly announced. 'So whatever you have to say, it will be all right in front of him.'

Arbuthnot Townsend nodded his acquiescence.

Incidentally, Mrs Guest collected Grandmother and the pair sat in the scullery, listening like two excited school girls.

'Before we start, Mr Townsend, I have got to have a cup of tea. Will you join us?'

He had little alternative and in spite of his upper class resistance, he enjoyed it.

'I'll come straight to the point,' Townsend began. 'It would appear that this young man, Graham Smith may have a claim to Lord Winston Heath's estate, which has come as a great shock to his son Jonathan, his legitimate heir, as he is six weeks older than him. Knowing them as I do, I am sure he would make a claim to the estate, should anything happen to his Lordship, whom as you know, is not at all well and–'

'Young man! He's a bloody animal,' Mr Guest interrupted. 'He has raped my daughter and got away with that. We all believe he has got away with murder and we all know he must pay for his crimes and one day he will. So don't you give him any credit.'

'I must be honest with you, Mr Guest, since you and your colleagues visited Mr Jonathan, we have employed a private investigator – not Sherlock Holmes, I would hasten to add,' he said, hoping to get a laugh, but forgetting that no one had a clue who Sherlock Holmes was. They had no money for books. 'This private investigator was employed to look into your allegations, your claims, so to speak–'

'We're not making allegations or claims for that matter. We are telling the truth!' Mr Guest interrupted again. 'We have also done a lot of investigating of our own and have heard things straight from the horse's mouth that would even have you shocked.

'Jonathan's father, the Lord Winston Heath, raped a young woman, his secretary, Grace and paid an employee, a Graham Smith, to take the responsibility for bringing up the child, giving him an allowance and full employment at the Compass Works. Since then his mother, Grace has lived a life of sheer hell. She has been beaten, bullied and treated worse than some animal and your client's father has condoned all this. Furthermore, that bloody bastard son of his now works at the Compass and is worse than his stepfather and–'

This time, Townsend interrupted, openly saying: 'We know you were, and are telling the truth, and of course it has come as a big shock to his Lordship's son. After all, he has been brought up believing he is the rightful heir. However, we do need to know what you intend to do. We know your daughter had a son by Graham Smith Jnr and that should anything happen to him and I'm sorry to say, he is his father, he will then inherit the estate.'

They were all flabbergasted, including the two women eavesdropping in the scullery.

'You might as well come in,' Mr Guest called out to them.

'We do not know where your daughter is at the moment and would like to contact her.

'She's living–'

'Wilf? Ida said sharply, stopping him in mid-sentence. 'You know she doesn't want anyone to know where she is.'

'It's only a matter of time before we find out,' Arbuthnot replied flippantly.

'Then you better start looking,' Wilf added, getting up from the table.

'I'm sorry,' Townsend replied, realising his error. 'We really only want to do the best for your daughter's child.'

'Or for yourselves and your client!'

'No, Mr Guest. He is already second in line to the title and will get all he is entitled to, which in itself is a considerable sum. Jonathan Gremore is a very fair man and has asked me to inform you he would contest the title, but he will ensure the little chap has sufficient for his needs. In this connection he has asked me to give your daughter whatever is necessary.'

Mr Guest was obviously aggrieved at the attitude of Townsend and simply said: 'I am sure my daughter would not want anything for her son that was not really his entitlement and there would, I'm sure, be no need to contest anything. However, a little support for her would be helpful.'

'We will speak to her when she comes round,' Ida said, winking at Grandmother.

'Here are my details. I would ask you to contact me should you need assistance and not Mr Jonathan or his Lordship because matters could become embarrassing for them. Will you do that?'

'Of course,' Wilf replied.

'I'll take my leave now. It was my intention to make contact with you and your family and I have done that, but also I want to assure you the exploits of the young Graham Smith will be thoroughly investigated as well.'

Arbuthnot Townsend took his leave and they all watched as the Hansom cab disappeared down the street, turning left to Wolverhampton and away.

They sat in silence for a few minutes, obviously shocked at the revelations, before Ida made the inevitable cup of tea again and they began to discuss their situation.

'I don't want Janet to touch any of this filthy money and the bloody father of her child should face the gallows,' Wilf began.

'Wilf?' Ida called out. 'A little money would help her,' she added, trying to emphasise Janet's needs, which in that day and age was very important, bearing in mind people were allowed to starve to death.

They discussed matters, joking that they would have a lord in the family and that they could all have a comfortable life, but Wilf always brought matters back to reality. The child's father was a criminal and he wouldn't want his daughter to receive tainted money.

Chapter 6
Sadness as War Beckons

It was the end of the term at Birmingham University. My father, Noel arrived home with the world at his feet, having been told he would do well in his BSc Mathematics degree. It was at this point that Mr and Mrs Guest's troubles were just beginning as they knew that my father would not take no for an answer and would want and wait for an explanation as to Janet's whereabouts.

It was only natural that the first thing he wanted to do was to see Janet; but it was though she had disappeared from the face of the earth. No one had been told where she was or when she went or why. In fact, apart from my grandmother and Janet's family, no one knew anything at all.

In those days no one would take the word of the woman that she had been attacked; everyone without exception would consider it a self-inflicted wound.

I remember my father telling me when he knocked on the Guests' door, he knew immediately something was wrong. He felt sick to his stomach and could hardly speak.

The Guests wouldn't and couldn't tell him the truth, which on reflection I think was cruel, but they genuinely thought my father would do something to Smith and land up in prison himself, or one of his brothers would. He could not understand the situation when her letters had been full of love and longing. Then suddenly, they were no more. What explanation could there be?

My father told me later, the moment he first saw Janet he wanted to be with her throughout their childhood and more so as teenagers and as young grown-ups. He had never looked at anyone else. You cannot imagine how he felt when he came home to find her missing, and no one to tell him what had happened. He began to hate the world and everyone in it and there was no way he would go back to university.

***

'Noel, I'm sorry, she's gone away,' Mrs Guest said, almost unable to say the words.

He stood for what seemed like minutes, dumbfounded. 'Where to?' he blurted out.

'Noel, I'm sorry. I really am sorry,' she repeated, tears now rolling down her cheeks.

She took his hand in hers. 'She doesn't want to see you.'

'Why? What have I done?' he asked in total desperation.

'Noel, she's just gone away and won't ever be coming back.'

Grandmother heard some of the conversation and came running out to rescue him from the trauma.

'Noel, Noel, come here, my love.' She wrapped her arms around him, in total disbelief at what was happening to him. 'Come on in, love and I'll make you a cup of tea.' He staggered into the house supported by Grandmother and followed by Ida who was still tearful.

'It's not Ida's fault, Noel. Janet has gone away and she doesn't want to be found.'

He heard nothing else; it was as though his heart had been cut out and everything else was failing to operate. He struggled up the stairs, lay down on the bed and stayed there for almost two days; no amount of coaxing from anyone would shift him. Grandfather decided to call the doctor, in spite of the cost.

When the doctor arrived, he too was at a loss to know what to do. However, he felt Noel should be told the truth, not necessarily where Janet was, but at least what had happened to her.

'It will help him to rationalise and possibly overcome the situation,' he said, confusing the family even more.

I must admit it was what Grandmother had originally thought. She had wanted to tell my father that Janet had been raped but went along with the Guests.

After a great deal of soul searching they decided to tell my father what had happened to Janet, but in doing so, they insisted that he wasn't told who the rapist was. Neither would he be told that there was a child. Furthermore, they were to let it be known that the man hadn't been caught yet, but he would be.

Everyone, including my grandmother, reluctantly went along with this and perhaps on reflection they thought it was the wisest thing to do as the bastard Smith was still very influential with his father at the Works. They knew that all the Tremont Street families would suffer the consequences if more so-called rumours were spread.

My father was never a violent man; it was not in his nature. I think Grandmother's motive was to keep her prodigy out of trouble, thus allowing him to continue his education at university.

My grandmother told me it was one of the worst moments of both hers and my grandfather's life when they told my father of Janet's demise, but omitting details of the baby.

It was left to our two families to shoulder the burden of this decision. My father now seemed like a man without a purpose in life. They knew he would accept Janet's little boy and bring him up in spite of the circumstances, but they also knew Janet wouldn't want this.

My father had almost become a hermit, not wanting to go out, not wanting to meet people, and in fact not wanting to do anything at all. He had even started drinking to drown his sorrows, which could not be drowned. Finally, the Guests decided to tell him almost all of Janet's plight, at which point he was able to understand that her departure had not been his fault and that she had done it for the right reasons. I believe Grandmother was glad that Graham Smith Jnr had not been mentioned, otherwise she felt my father would have killed him.

***

The Balkans was a hotbed of trouble and expected to be a cause of future chaos in Europe. Although nothing had yet happened to involve Britain, preparations were underway to strengthen our defences, not only at home but abroad.

The Compass Iron & Steel Company and Compass Castings were naturally a big part of that process and were working flat out on production. Little else seemed to matter; in fact everything else was sidelined, including safety, to ensure nothing interfered with the war effort and the profit going into his Lordship's pocket.

It was this lack of safety and care which caused the central building in the Compass business block to burst into flames. The administration department was on the top floor, whilst on the third floor flammable materials were being stored to support the production process. On the ground and second floors they had installed several new heat processes. It was, to use a modern term, an accident waiting to happen.

When Jonathan Gremore took control of the business he realised the necessity of installing fire escapes to each floor and began work in earnest. However, work was only completed to the first two floors before Lord Winston Heath decided that any further installations were a waste of money.

Of course, the fire had to start on the second floor, which was the most dangerous, and where the fire escapes stopped.

Furthermore, there were neither any fire doors nor alarms. Someone had to be detailed to go round the site clanging a bell in the hope of warning a few people; another was detailed to run to the various sections to tell them there was a fire, usually a young apprentice.

This was the first time there had been a major incident for several years and it became a grand spectacle; the workers ran out of their sections simply to watch and in fact, there were so many they were in the way.

Smith Jnr decided it was his responsibility to run round looking important, telling some of the employees to stand further back. Others he admonished for wasting their time as their section was not on fire and sent them back to work.

The fire quickly spread to the third floor, which could have cut off escape from the fourth floor where there were three young women still working and at that point, oblivious to any danger. Ironically, because of the noise from the lower levels they had not heard the man clanging the bell. The employees from floors one and two escaped without any difficulty, immediately joining the other onlookers to watch the fire,

'Has anyone called the Fire Brigade?' someone asked Smith Jnr.

'I suppose so, I'll go and check.' Even in those days, they could not believe the crass stupidity of the management that no one had called the Fire Brigade and possibly now it was too late to save the building as the third floor was now alight.

There were intermittent explosions which naturally caused everyone to look in its general direction, when suddenly above the noise, they heard the screaming. Three girls were standing at one of the windows on the fourth floor.

They continued screaming to let everyone know they were there, which made the women watching also scream in panic.

'Do something!' they were shouting at Smith, who continued directing activities as if he were the Chief Fire Officer. The onlookers continued to point out the danger the girls were in but Smith seemed to ignore them.

In the meantime, some of the onlookers were trying to gesticulate to the three women to make their way to the lower floors. Some were shouting: 'Get to the second floor!' It wasn't clear whether they could be heard above the pandemonium.

The arrival of Fred Wearing on the scene immediately put Smith Jnr on notice that something would happen.

Smith decided to race into the building, taking his jacket off as he went. He was unaware that Fred was following him, but like all bullies, he was a coward. Instead of going to rescue the girls, Smith hid under the staircase on the ground floor, too scared to try.

However, when Fred entered the building he saw a movement in the space under the stairs; it was Smith who was obviously too frightened to race up to the fourth floor and was hiding in the hope of making an impression that he had, at least tried. He was unaware that Fred, who was now running up the stairs, had seen him hiding.

A few minutes later, Smith came out of the building covered in smoke dust. He waved his arms in the air to suggest it was too late, but at least he had made the effort to rescue the girls.

'Where's Fred?' several shouted.

Smith was shocked. 'What do you mean?'

'He followed you in,' someone said.

Just then there was another explosion as a paint canister blew up, which caused a few of the women to scream.

I was told you could almost see a smile on Smith's face when that happened.

'He must have had it. The flames are too fierce. No one would get past that,' Smith announced to the watching crowd.

A few seconds after that, Fred came running out. 'Get some sheets. Throw them in the water butt. Quick.' he yelled. 'And give me one of the crow bars, or that axe,' he screamed, pointing to a fire axe on a wall.

'The axe will be better. Quick,' he shouted like a Regimental Sergeant Major, sending several onlookers scurrying around to get the stuff.

In less than a minute, Fred was running up the fire escape to the second floor, where he had to break the window as the fire escape door adjacent to it was one of those new push bar escape doors, opening only one way, Within seconds, he was through the window and into the second floor.

The crowd were deathly quiet; every eye was glued to the second floor window. It seemed like minutes before Fred pushed the bar to open the door and release two of the girls into the arms of the waiting crowd.

Little did anyone know until then that the girls had managed to descend the stone stairwell, past the third floor and onto the second. The doors onto the stairs had remained closed which at least for a short while prevented the flames from engulfing the entire third floor.

Fred immediately went back in and once again there was a deathly silence while they all waited in morbid anticipation. The third girl was nowhere to be seen, which caused many to fear the worst. Then suddenly there was another even bigger explosion which took out the window where Fred had helped the girls. There was no escape from there this time as the flames were leaping out as though they too were trying to escape out of what was fast becoming an inferno.

Several women noticed the look of glee on Smith's face, nudging each other in disgust. It was as though he was enjoying the difficulty the young girl and Fred were in. It was as though he wanted them to perish.

There was still no sign of Fred and with more and more windows on the second floor bursting open, releasing the massive pent-up flames, the whole floor was now ablaze. The third floor, holding its highly flammable materials began to go, causing further and bigger explosions, taking more windows out, now from the third floor. The flames were leaping out, licking at the windows before they caved in.

It was a catastrophe with every eye watching where Fred had entered. It was too late, there was no escape; the stores on the third floor had also caught fire and within seconds a further explosion sent the onlookers scurrying to safety.

One or two of the girls now realised there was no chance and began weeping at the loss of their friend. Seth who had just arrived having heard that Fred was inside, was also very upset and could not believe he too had lost a friend.

'Which way did he go?' he asked anybody and everybody. They all pointed at the fire escape, but he could see any attempt to rescue would be useless.

He looked at Smith with hate in his eyes and shouted: 'You've done this, you bastard!'

'I told him not to go. I told him it was impossible,' Smith shouted back with fake concern.

'He didn't, he's a liar,' several of the others also shouted, adding their voices to the growing unrest.

Thinking there was no chance Fred could survive, let alone the young girl, the spectators began to turn away. Many were crying, others silent, unable to take in what they had witnessed.

Less than a minute later there was an enormous cheer as some of the crowd saw Fred appear at the entrance of the building, carrying what looked like the body of the young girl over his shoulder. She was wrapped from head to foot in a wet sheet which was steaming from the heat.

Seth immediately ran over and took the girl from him, peeled back the sheet to reveal the girl alive and well. The sense of relief was felt through the whole crowd as though a huge weight had been lifted from their shoulders and they began to cheer.

Fred walked towards the crowd to rapturous applause and together with Seth, they walked over to Smith and with that cheeky smile which says it all, Fred simply said: 'I saw you.'

Smith was devastated and it certainly showed in his demeanour.

'Mr White, it was pure jealousy.'

Fred was certainly the hero of the hour and everyone joined in his adulation.

The Fire Brigade at last arrived but it was too late to save any of the building and suggested that the other buildings be evacuated so that they could cool down the other buildings, but the Smiths would not allow that. Finally, to rub salt into the Smith's wound the *Express & Star* ran a story, highlighting the courage of Fred Wearing.

Graham Smith hated Fred for taking away his moment of potential glory; it was a hatred which would fester. It seemed to him that every time there was danger or difficulty, Fred was there to sort it out. But what really set

Smith on edge was the smile. Fred always gave him that knowing smile every time he helped him out of trouble. Smith would often mention it when he was in a drunken morbid state, something which was becoming more frequent as time went by.

Chapter 7
Off to War

It was August 1914. The Gough family were having their best year yet. All the children were working and in better jobs than their father. Graham had married his Eileen; Frank was becoming noticed by professional football teams; Jess had been made a charge hand at Benchmans and without doubt would do well for himself. Grandmother's favourite, my father, was becoming used to life without Janet and doing well at university, having now passed the first two years of his Mathematics degree and was already assisting the War Office, whilst still at university.

Nothing lasts forever though and when, on the 28th June 1914, Arch Duke Ferdinand was assassinated in Austria, everyone could sense trouble was brewing in Europe, especially with all the treaties that had been signed and agreements made. War seemed inevitable and would start in the powder keg of Europe – the Balkans. The only question to be answered was: When?

The British Government began gearing up for war with armament production and preparing the Army and Navy for action. In August 1914, the inevitable happened and Britain declared war on Germany.

The Government needed volunteers for the Army and the propaganda started. Posters appeared everywhere featuring Kitchener with the words: 'Your Country Needs You'. There were recruitment rallies in almost every corner of every town and city in the country and even in the factories the cry was heard. When you consider Britain had the biggest and strongest Navy in the world, a powerful Army and the industrial might of the biggest Empire, 'How could we lose?' were the slogans shouted by almost all.

The factories of Lord Winston Heath were working flat out; it was almost as if he enjoyed the fact there was a war. All he was interested in was increasing his personal fortune. His constant posters stuck up in the factories demanded that the entire workforce double their efforts without any incentive. If they did, where did that money go? In his pocket! This was more apparent when the young men, believing war would be almost a game to be played, and in any event, would be all over by Christmas, started enlisting in their thousands.

All age groups enlisted. Children as young as fourteen were trying to look older, so they would be accepted. Ex-servicemen from the earlier campaigns wanted to get back into the action, refusing to be considered too old.

The young men were tempted with the promise that their jobs would be theirs when they returned.

But as I said, Lord Winston Heath was only interested in money, not people, and all the young men who left were replaced by women at half the salary of the men but were still made to produce the same work or lose their jobs. Double the profits for his bloody Lordship!

September 6th, 2014 was an important date in the Tremont Street calendar when all the males, old enough to join up, held a meeting to discuss what they should do. Their employers had already told them their jobs would be open to them when they returned and even my father was told he could resume his degree course when the war was over. It was now a matter of talking it over with their respective parents although they were all old enough to make their own decisions. However, it was par for the course for close families to become involved in all matters.

Evan had already tried to enlist but was told he had too many employees to be able to go to war and in any event he had become a supplier to the Military. It was a terrible evening; Grandmother was devastated and did not want to lose any of her lads, in particular Noel as she wanted greatness for him. It wasn't that she loved him any more than the others; it was simply because he was the first of all of them to fully benefit from further education.

I suppose for my father the declaration of war with Germany was a blessing in disguise as it made him do something and gave him a purpose, even if was only to fight.

Their minds were made up. The following Saturday all the boys together with Fred and Jack Wearing, Bobby Guest, Seth Ambrose, were ready to march to the Recruitment Centre, which had been specially set up in the Town Hall.

There was much bravado; they had no idea what it was all about, but they were following Frank who held the Union Flag on high, causing a stir as they marched through the centre of Wolverhampton, accompanied by their sisters, who also wanted to join up. Janet's absence was still a thorn in the side for my father, but he had to grin and bear it.

A number of other lads joined the march and by the time they reached the Town Hall they numbered twenty-five. However, when some of the lads realised what they had done, they soon disappeared. Of course, when the girls were seen, it was suggested they joined the nursing corps, which many of them did.

The boys were given a starting date two weeks hence and told to report to Whittington Barracks to be kitted out and to have their eight-week basic training before being sent to France.

They tried to cajole Smith Jnr into joining, but of course they had already made plans for him to be excused as his job was more important to the war effort than actually fighting for his country, Ironically, he was not seen at the factory for some time as comments about white feathers were being thrown at him frequently, and the more people heard about the appalling death toll, the more vociferous they became.

Graham Smith Snr had heard that the Government was going to start conscription and that all young men would be called up. Smith Snr also found out that because he was the boss of the works, his son could not use the works as an excuse not to fight because he was not the immediate boss. His father was certainly not going to take his place; he was not that daft.

It was then agreed it would be better if Smith Jnr joined up quickly before being forced to enlist.

You would have thought he was going to win the war all by himself, the fuss they made of his signing up. He even gave an interview to the *Express & Star* saying how he was looking forward to the fight. They hadn't yet learned he was a bloody coward. He, without doubt must have been special because within three or four weeks of training, which he apparently sailed through, he was immediately put on the officer training scheme.

It was amazing because he was made an officer after only nine weeks in the Army; either he was that brilliant or someone somewhere was pulling a few strings. I think it was the latter.

Frank was the lucky one; he was so fit he found training easy. When they heard of his football skills, he was hurried away and within a few weeks, he became a physical training Lance Corporal. Within six months, he was a sergeant in recruitment and training.

Graham's skills were put to use in the engineering field as it was his job to keep all the Army vehicles on the move. He was continually on the Front Line in large vehicles and therefore vulnerable to attack. He won the Military Medal for preventing the Germans from capturing one of our heavy guns by driving his lorry fo the Front whilst it was being overrun by the Germans. He hooked the gun to the back of his lorry and drove it back to his lines, under heavy fire; at the same time his lorry carried seventeen men out of danger.

As for all the others, it was the good old infantry and trench warfare.

They finished the eight-week basic training and were allowed a week's leave to go home, reporting to Wolverhampton Station to catch the troop train to Dover at the end of it.

Thankfully, they had been given their carriage number so at least they all knew where they were going, but there was still pandemonium at the station as there were hundreds of men all trying to say goodbye, with hugs and kisses from their loved ones, their mothers, their sweethearts; none wanting to let go until the last minute, rushing to get to the windows to wave their last goodbyes, which for many it would be. All of them were anxious because for most they had never been far away from home and for the first time, anxiety hit them. Of course, the bravado was on show with shouts of: 'See you at Christmas!' which belied the real truth.

The train pulled out of the station with almost everyone trying to steal that last kiss or hug, followed by the latecomers racing down the platform carrying their new kit bag, only to find they missed the train. How dejected they looked when they found they had!

My father remembered that fateful journey until the

day he died. He said he could sense a foreboding. No one talked for the first hour of the five-hour journey; they just looked out of the window, staring into space until Fred could stand it no more.

'Come on, we've made our bed. We've got to lie on it and make the best of it. We are going to be all right, I know it.'

There were a few forced smiles until Fred began to talk about Smith Jnr and then they seemed to get it together, chatting and laughing, and discussing what they would like to do to him. The worries soon disappeared at least for the moment as their purpose was temporarily forgotten.

They arrived at Dover and had an hour to spare before boarding the troopship SS *Hantonia*. In that hour they found a little fish and chip shop not far from the port and ate the most delicious fish they had ever known – a memory that became a lifeline when they were at the battle front later on when rations were short.

There were more than two thousand troops on the SS *Hantonia* when it set sail that day, all of them trying to put on a brave face, many reading letters given to them by their sweethearts before leaving, simply telling them how much they loved them and missed them already. Others would be looking at the photograph of their loved ones, daydreaming of the times spent together. Sadly, many of them wouldn't be coming back, but at least for the moment that was far from their minds. They were not told of their destination prior to sailing so it was a surprise when they landed in Belgium. Their battle was to be on the Western Front.

Thank goodness it was fine and warm because some of them had to march forty or fifty miles from Zeebrugge to the battlefield over two days, sleeping ten men to a bell tent. The march took its toll, some already feeling the pain of badly fitting boots. Blisters on blisters popped and bled; several men were already incapacitated and were in a field hospital without a gun being fired. Most of the kit handed out was poorly fitting. If it was near enough that was good enough, with the obvious consequences. On the third day, they were now only ten miles away from the Front and for the first time they heard the sounds of battle as the big guns pounded the Germans.

'Those are our guns! We are showing them who's boss,' the regular Sergeants yelled, encouraging the enlisted men, who immediately gained that extra confidence from the words. Little did they realise that guns fired both ways and it was their side taking the pounding.

They were each given their rifle and bayonet, a supply of ammunition and food rations and off they marched nearer and nearer to the Front. The noise became louder and louder until they could not hear themselves think. Finally, they were there in a trench, at the ready to climb out and charge towards the enemy.

Two and a half thousand of those men were killed on their first day. Many were shot as they were climbing out of the trench, their bodies falling back on the lads behind them.

Three quarters of the men that went with them that day were either killed or injured. What a waste, don't you think?

Fred soon began to show his ability not only on the battlefield but also with the men. He had that natural ability to rally their spirits and encourage them – a trait which soon became recognised by his commanders who subsequently offered him a commission, which he refused. My father's caring nature was apparent; he wanted to look after the men. He had several other offers of a commission over the years, but refused them all.

Things began to change for the worst when Second

Lieutenant Graham Smith came back on the scene. He never generated any respect from any of the men but achieved obedience by bullying and adopting the same tactics he used in the workplace. None of these tactics worked. The men were not beholden to him for their current employment and his reputation remained in tatters.

Everyone could feel the animosity he held for them, especially as it was always them that were given the dangerous jobs, or the worst jobs, so much so that a Captain Harmsworth who had been given command of this group told Smith to ease off. The one thing Smith had forgotten was the presence of Fred, who had the philosophy of whatever you were told to do, you could always work it to your advantage; it was just a case of spending a little time thinking about it.

On one occasion, Smith had the idea of ordering a Corporal to march a group of men down to the nearby village where there was a nursing station. The Corporal was to leave them outside the station and return to his command.

Smith was heard to say: 'I'll collect the men shortly as I have a little job for them.'

That was good enough for the Corporal; he instructed the men to wait for the Lieutenant at the nursing station and then returned.

This was manna from heaven for the men, especially Fred. They were still there at midnight; Fred posted lookouts every two hours to check for approaching officers. The following morning the barrage went up and still no one came to see where they were. The nurses even gave them their breakfast. Harmsworth ordered an immediate investigation into why so many men had deserted their positions. The Corporal reported to Major Tenant that he had been ordered to take them to the village on Smith's orders. Thereupon, the Corporal was ordered to go and fetch them.

The lookout saw the Corporal coming and as pre-arranged, the men were to stand in line and look tired.

'What have you been doing for God's sake?' he asked.

'You told us to wait for the Lieutenant. That's what we have done, Corporal,' Fred replied.

They could see the Corporal squirming, particularly when he began to blame Smith. 'Come on, we've got to get you back. Fall in,' the Corporal ordered.

Fred continued: 'Corp, we've had no sleep and we're knackered.'

'All right, come on. Quick as you like.'

The Corporal took them back and they were immediately hauled in front of the Major. 'What's the meaning of this?' he asked sternly.

Fred took over... 'We were ordered by Lieutenant Smith to march down to the village and then to stand and wait for him. We believed it was a punishment order and did not want to risk disobeying. Sir.'

'How long have you been there?'

'Sixteen hours, sir.'

'What was the punishment for?'

'I don't know sir, but we are considered by the Lieutenant to be the lazy squad. Sir.'

'Corporal!' the major shouted, 'Get these men some food. They are off duty until nine hundred hours tomorrow, and send Captain Harmsworth in to see me.'

'Thank you, sir,' the men said in unison as they saluted and marched out, following the Corporal. To make matters worse Smith was nowhere to be found, especially when there was fighting to be done.

I understand the Major was told to give Smith a rollicking and it was to be recorded on his record, as he had cost the unit eleven men from the battlefield.

Shortly after, Fred and Seth were walking towards their tent when they crossed Smith's path. 'Where's the salute?' Smith bawled.

Fred turned round, pretending it must be someone else Smith was talking to.

'You – Private Wearing, I'm talking to you.'

The two men stopped and looked at him in disgust. 'What about, Lieutenant?' Fred asked.

'I'll have you for that little scheme of yours.'

'Yer not big enough,' Seth said, almost snarling the words.

'What did you say?' Smith bawled.

'You heard.'

Smith's raised voice caused a number of men to appear from their tents, 'Any trouble, Seth?' one asked.

'No, just a stupid little runt throwing his weight around.'

Smith scurried away, leaving the men laughing at him.

It dropped lucky for the men as the Regiment was stood down for three days' rest and Fred decided they should have a rabbit stew as rations were beginning to get a bit tight, even though they were only in the first few months of the war.

He disappeared for about an hour and came back with one hare and two rabbits, enough to feed quite a few men.

Fred purloined a large pot and two of the others went into the village for some bread. The scene was set and the smell of the cooking brought onlookers from everywhere including Second Lieutenant Smith Jnr.

'Where did you get that?' he demanded.

Everyone to a man ignored him.

'Wearing, I'm talking to you,' he yelled again.

'No you are not sir, you're shouting.'

'What did you say?' he asked.

'I said pardon sir, I didn't hear what you were saying,

but I am now going to say bugger off and let us enjoy our meal.'

'Private Wearing. Stand to attention!' Smith yelled.

Fred ignored him which caused him to go absolutely mad, turning red in the face and almost unable to speak.

Smith shouted again, but still Fred ignored him. He stood and stared at Fred, not knowing what to do.

'Lieutenant?' Fred said very calmly and quietly.

'Yes Wearing,' Smith replied, taken aback by Fred's manner.

'Private Wearing, sir,' Fred added insolently.

'I asked where you got that and now I'm taking you in for disobeying an order.'

'What's the Brigadier going to say when we tell him you were trying to steal our meal and there are *nine* of us?'

Smith turned and marched away in time with the slow clapping of the men. They knew they were in for it as Smith would find some excuse to get his own back; but the rabbit stew was like manna from heaven.

It's amazing how brave people can be when there are no family pressures, when livelihoods are not at stake. Smith actually thought he could carry on in the same way as in civilian life, forgetting that the battlefield was a different place where men would not care about anything other than each other's wellbeing. They were from all walks of life, many from rough and tough backgrounds where life was cheap and where one little officer could disappear in a flash and many certainly wanted Smith to disappear. You would have thought with an enemy like the Germans, no one would be stupid enough to fight and threaten their own side.

Chapter 8
Henry's Demise

Little Henry was still in Haworth with his mother, but had developed a very nasty cough, which the doctor said would not go away until the child moved to a healthier climate. Haworth was a woollen town with many dark and dank mills, their filthy chimneys blasting out black, acrid, sulphur-laden smoke which, together with the area's cold, damp conditions that were necessary to produce top class wool, was also a recipe for ill health. Poor Henry couldn't cope and neither could many residents; the lifespan for many in that environment was only about twenty-four years of age.

The doctor feared Henry was suffering from consumption and should move away. This revelation startled all the family and although Stanley didn't want Janet to leave, he realised that it was the little lad's only chance and, speed was of the essence.

Mrs Guest took it upon herself to contact Mr Arbuthnot Townsend, the lawyer, to apprise him of the situation and ask him if he could help Janet find another home in a healthier area. Within a few days, Townsend visited Janet in Haworth, explaining that he had already met her mother, but as speed was necessary, he asked if she would prefer a place of her own or to live with someone.

For some unknown reason she preferred to be on her own and within two weeks, she was leaving Haworth and heading south to a little village called Chipping Sodbury not far from Bristol, right in the heart of the Gloucestershire countryside where the wool on the sheep's back was clean and you could see through the air for miles. A world away from Haworth when even on a fine day, you could only see a glimpse of the sun if the wind was blowing and moving the fog and filth over to Bradford. The only downside to the move was that the accommodation was within a few miles of Lord Winston Heath's home. She made a pact with Townsend that her whereabouts would be kept secret.

It was a sad day for Janet after her experiences over the last eighteen months. The time with her uncle and aunt had been a happy one, but it had to be. Henry would not survive if she stayed.

They had been like a close-knit family and very supportive of Janet in her hour of need. She was of course, older and as such perhaps more experienced. She had helped the family prosper and had an ability to organise. Her cousins were now able run the place without her and still leave Uncle Stanley time to further develop the business and deliver all the orders.

Uncle Stanley carried Henry to the station whilst she walked hand in hand between Primrose and Iris with Aunt Ada bringing up the rear, pushing the empty pram.

'I've decided to call and see Mother on the way. It will be a lovely surprise for her and Father of course and it will be the last thing they will expect,' Janet whispered in her uncle's ear. He simply smiled at her.

There were tearful moments as they walked along Belle Isle Road and over the footbridge to Haworth Station. She could still see the young line of poplar trees in Stanley's garden and imagined what they would be like in a hundred years. She could still hear the engines steaming up, getting ready to join the main line, but most of all she could still see her aunt and cousins trying to hold back the tears and failing miserably. After all, a year and a half is a long time to be staying with anyone. Despite her uncle Stanley's attempts to remain casual about the whole affair, Janet could see the stifled tears slowly caressing his cheeks.

The train arrived, the luggage was loaded aboard and finally, Janet took little Henry from a reluctant Stanley and stepped into the carriage. The door slammed shut, the whistle blew, the green flag waved and in a huge cloud of steam, the train slowly began to move away. She lifted Henry up and both leaned out of the window as the train picked up speed. They waved frantically until they were round the bend of the track and out of sight before slumping down on the seat, exhausted with the sadness of the occasion.

The train only stopped at Oakworth, Ingrow and finally Keighley station, where it was a quick change, catching the train to Leeds. This was another short journey, passing the massive Salts Woollen Mill which employed over three thousand and following the busy Leeds Liverpool Canal, an area of the country with the most beautiful scenery. Janet and Henry watched the passing barges carrying their wares to and from Liverpool.

It was then a quick change at Leeds for Birmingham and Wolverhampton, where she had decided on that moment's whim, to stop off and see her family and friends for the first time in eighteen months.

Janet now had money of her own and took a Hackney cab down to the end of Tremont Street. She knocked on the front door only to find more than she expected. She was unaware that her uncle had sent her parents a telegram warning of her arrival and in consequence, half the street was there. Even the cab driver joined in the spirit of the moment as he carried her bags in for her, leaving her to pick up little Henry. Thankfully, my father was not there as he was now in the Army and fighting in France. The Guests had such a lot of catching up to do with the daughter they thought was lost to them.

The Guests had a wonderful two days with Janet and little Henry. She wanted desperately to stay, but even then they could see the little chap had little chance of survival, particularly as Wolverhampton was in the heart of the Black Country, a name which conjured up what it was like. The numerous coking plants, iron and steel works, the massive railway repair yards, all belching out acrid black smoke said it all. They could not have stayed; it would not have been fair to Henry.

Two days later, Janet boarded the train to Bristol and took a cab from there to a little cottage in the village of Chipping Sodbury in Gloucestershire. The climate was perfect, the conditions for Henry were sublime and the frequent visits from her mother and father, paid for by Arbuthnot Townsend, really made a difference.

Little Henry showed signs of a slight recovery but was still a sickly child.

The poor little lad looked constantly pale, never ate a full meal and always looked under nourished; all this in spite of the love and care he was given, plus the better climate and fresh country fruit and vegetables.

His condition never improved but at least his deterioration slowed down a little. Despite his ill health, he was a happy little chap.

The money Janet now received from his Lordship's estate certainly made her life easier not only from the financial point of view, enabling the Guests to visit more frequently, but more importantly, it also contributed towards Henry's welfare.

This was very important because after several months, the little chap was still not showing signs of improvement. Janet could afford the frequent doctor's visits and of course his bills. Should more money be required, she only had to contact Arbuthnot Townsend, the lawyer and further funds would be sent. That said, she never asked for anything other than Henry's health.

It was an Indian summer in 1916; Henry was being very tenderly nursed, but even with the now daily visits from the doctor, there was still no improvement. In fact, on the contrary; his pallor was changing, his weight loss quickening and finally, he was unable to support himself. I will always remember Janet telling me how he seemed to recover slightly for a day or so but then slowly drift into slumber, with her always at his bed side. One evening she was there reading him a story when suddenly he opened his eyes and with a lovely smile she would never forget, he simply drifted away. That was on the 10th October 1916.

My mother told me she held him in her arms until she could hold him no longer. There were never any thoughts of hatred towards the beast of a man that had caused all their troubles, only thoughts for that poor little chap who had suffered all his life and never ever complained.

The hardest thing for her was to contact the vicar, knowing that she would soon be unable to hold him again.

The following day when all the arrangements had been made, she contacted Townsend and told him Henry had died, expecting to be given notice to leave the cottage.

Townsend immediately contacted Jonathan Gremore to tell him the news. The next day Janet received a visit from Townsend who was warm, kind and sympathetic, and genuinely concerned for Janet's wellbeing.

First, he insisted on sorting out all arrangements for Henry's funeral and for all the family and friends to be there. Finally, he gave Janet the assurance that she would not lose her home and that it was there for as long as she needed it. Furthermore, Jonathan attended the funeral and paid the cost for all their family to be there.

Of course, Janet's only thoughts at that time were for her little Henry. He had had a rough little life, albeit short and now he was to be in Chipping Sodbury's cemetery all alone.

He had known very few youngsters his own age as he was always too poorly to go out and play with them. However, some children from the kinder families would call in and bring something for him to read or play with, or call in for a quick chat. Janet said it was lovely when they did as his little face used to light up, especially when Emily, the vicar's daughter used to call; she was really kind.

But now even in death, he was still to be alone without another member of the family or any of his friends from nearby. Now all he would have was the occasional visit from Janet.

Until the day she died, my mother made the trip to Chipping Sodbury as often as she could, just to be with Henry. She would tell him all the news, all the happenings, how his cousins were getting on etc.

I went with her once or twice and she would introduce me to him and tell him all about me. I thought it a little strange, but in essence it's not, if you believe in the presence of someone being there and my certainly mother did.

The funeral was a terribly sad affair because it was just for a little boy starting out in life which was cruelly cut short.

The moment the service ended, Jonathan went over and talked to Janet for some time before offering a lift to her and her parents. He took them home and confirmed what Townsend had already told her, that the cottage was hers, rent free, until she no longer wanted it, or until she got married. Also if she ever needed any support or advice, she was to contact him or Townsend. She would also be given a small allowance which was just enough to live on, but which made her comfortable for the rest of her life, but I'll come to that later.

Mr and Mrs Guest returned to Wolverhampton a few days later, leaving Janet alone in a situation which was not ideal for such an emotionally scarred young woman. However, Janet realised the need to work, not just for the money as she was now provided for, but for her own wellbeing. She needed to have company, women of her own age and have a purpose in life. To this aim, she decided to visit Tremont Street to see Charlotte and talk to her, not realising she was nursing the injured men in France. With just her suitcase full of clothes, she locked the house and set off for Wolverhampton to see her friends.

It was a wonderful reunion seeing all those who had remained – the Wearing and Ambrose family and of course, our family, the Goughs, but it was an odd time as none of her close friends were there. All the young men and women were away in France, either fighting or helping the war effort in whatever way they could and she didn't expect the answer she received from my grandmother when she asked after my father, believing he was still in Birmingham at university.

'He's fighting in France along with the rest of them,' she replied and then added, 'Charlotte has joined Queen Alexandra's Imperial Military Nursing Service and she too is in France.'

Janet stayed with her parents for a few days, realising she could not go back to Chipping Sodbury and be left on her own. Within a few weeks she had made contact with Charlotte and joined up to do her bit.

She and nineteen others were sent away for six weeks' initial training at a Birmingham Hospital, during which time they had a very enlightened training Sister who laid down several important rules, For her, the most important point was to be clean and tidy; the second was that all nurses needed to be cheerful and to learn the Christian name of the patient and use it.

Thirdly, nurses should not become romantically inclined towards a patient and lastly, they should not take the job home with them, as it becomes too depressing; they must wash the smell of blood from them, go out and try to enjoy themselves. The training left them in no doubt what to expect, but without actually being there and facing the real thing, none of them could truly imagine what it was like. That was until the day they actually arrived and were thrown in at the deep end. Several, including Janet were transferred to the Western Front where the war was very bloody at the time, causing one or two to leave as they were unable to cope with the situation.

My mother told me it was difficult, but she got it into her head that without her help these men would die; they would not have a chance. Her little lad didn't have a chance and she wasn't going to let another miss out.

It wasn't long before she met up with Charlotte and the old friendship resumed, but the war kept them apart much more than they would have liked. She did however confess to her why she had gone into hiding and was shocked when Charlotte told her she already knew and that the entire neighbourhood also knew; everyone knew except my father as he was at university at the time and that's when the families decided not to tell him.

Charlotte was a forthright little woman who would tell things as they were with the bark off. She laced into Janet and told her she was wrong to walk away from Noel and that he would have understood.

'He would have never forgiven me.'

Charlotte nearly lost it. 'For God's sake, it was not your fault. There's nothing to forgive. Noel would have understood and we all know he would have stood by you. You should have seen him when he thought he had lost you. Locked in his room for two days, wouldn't eat or drink and joined up as he had nothing left to lose. I just hope he has survived along with the rest because they have all been out here since 14th August. Yes! Since it started.'

'I didn't want him to see me like I was.'

'Janet, he would have understood, so let's forget it,' she snapped, becoming more annoyed; but in spite of that they remained friends throughout the war and, in fact, till the end.

Chapter 9
Intrusion

Janet threw her heart and soul into her new career which began in the main field hospital, away from the Front, getting to know the ropes and the systems, adopting all the rules learned in the training. She was always very willing and as such was being noticed by the hierarchy; but it was that little bit of business experience she had gained with her uncle Stanley that really paid off, particularly her organisational ability. This quickly began to reap dividends as her ideas improved the efficiency of the administration and a simple matter of moving certain patients from part of the hospital to another saved hours of time.

You cannot believe what happened to my mother, yet again with that animal Smith. He was sent by a senior officer to check for malingerers at the hospital and whilst questioning one of the patients, he bumped into Janet.

'Well, well, well, what have we got here? If it isn't my little girlfriend. And how is my little girlfriend? Have you forgiven me for leaving you and going to fight for my country?' Smith asked, in his supercilious way.

She tried to ignore him for the sake of the patients, but he continued:

'Have you seen your little Noel?' he asked, not waiting for an answer. 'I have. He is one of my little Privates. He is under my control.' He continued showing off, which she could see was affecting the other patients.

She was still trying to ignore him and continued treating a severely injured man when he moved towards her and put his arm around her shoulder.

Janet snapped; she swung round giving him an almighty slap across the face which jolted him backwards. The patients were in uproar, cheering as they saw him stagger back.

Then at the top of her voice, she shouted: 'I am not that shy little girl you dragged into the men's toilets and raped with those two other Black rats, and then got away with it.' Did Daddy bribe the police again?' she asked, almost snarling like a cat protecting its young.

'The knocks I have had in my life have made me stronger, better, and now I'm no longer that weakling you *raped*,' she screamed, as she lashed out again, catching him on his right eye.

'Now get out, you *rapist*. This is a hospital full of very brave but sick men. You are not fit to be in here with them, you dirty filthy *rapist*,' all the time accentuating the word rapist.

There was a cheer from those casualties able to rouse themselves. 'Good old Janet, good old nurse, give it to him,' they shouted.

He was becoming very embarrassed and tried to calm the situation down, when again she shouted at the top of her voice, causing others to come in to see what was going on.

'Get away from me you dirty, filthy animal! You vile creature, you evil, evil creature. This evil snake raped me and got away with it.'

'I'll get you for this,' he mouthed as he turned to leave, cowering like a whipped dog.

'That'll be a shiner in the morning,' one of the patients shouted, having watched everything intently. The noise had attracted the attention of the Matron who called her into a tent, adjacent to the field hospital, which was used as an administration office.

'What's all this about, Nurse Guest? We can't have your private life upsetting the patients, can we?' the Matron asked. 'Come on.'

Janet broke down, sobbing uncontrollably, but thankfully the Matron was sympathetic and felt as sorry for her as the troops did.

'Take an hour off. Have a cup of tea and come back refreshed,' she said.

'I'd rather not, Matron, we are short-staffed and there are several that need urgent attention.'

'Very well. I'll come with you to see what damage has been done.'

As they entered the hospital tent there was a huge cheer from some of the men and a wave from all the walking wounded.'

'I needn't have bothered, Nurse Guest. You seem to have enough support in here.'

Matron later met Captain Harmsworth in a social capacity and suggested that Lieutenant Smith did not return to the hospital as his behaviour towards the nurses and patients was not that which one would expect from an officer; effectively he was banned and it was placed on his record.

However, that was not the end of his interference as he continued to plague Janet when she was off duty. It was always little aggravations and nothing worth reporting although she did advise the Matron and even Captain Harmsworth that he was constantly annoying her, just for the record.

News of this reached Tremont Street, but once again not my father.

Smith had been hanging about the nurses' quarters which consisted of several bell tents marked with crosses to signify it was part of the hospital section. Each tent housed four nurses and each nurse was supposed to have at least six hours of private time each day which included rest time. This never really happened as they were on call all the time due to the vagaries of the war; but they were clearly out of bounds to all ranks. However, it appeared not all ranks agreed with that order, as Lieutenant Smith felt he was immune from authority and continued to hang about until he found Janet on her own.

Since the débacle in the hospital, Janet had felt she was being watched or followed and she knew it was Smith, so much so she was a little scared to go to her tent by herself when her shift had finished. Normally, one or other of the nurses would walk with her and when they arrived at the nurses' station there was someone about, whether in her tent or in the next one which was only a few feet away.

On this particular day, the battle had gone badly and there were hundreds killed or injured and in consequence, the nursing teams were working flat out. In fact some, including Janet had worked for almost thirty-six hours nonstop. Matron had visited the hospital and suggested that several went back to their tents to rest, Janet included.

She was too tired to think and too tired to notice that Lieutenant Smith was following her at a discrete distance. She entered her tent, not having the energy for anything and simply fell on the bed and into a worn-out sleep.

He allowed a few minutes before bursting in. 'You should not have done that,' he shouted, referring to the previous incident in the hospital. He sat astride her body and pressed his hands on her shoulders, holding her down firmly. 'I said you should not have done that, you little whore.'

It was a few seconds before Janet knew what was

happening and then let out an almighty scream. 'Get away from me, you rapist,' she shouted and just kept screaming at the top of her voice. Smith then tried to cover her mouth, but her teeth bit into the flesh of his hand, drawing blood which became a torrent within seconds. He desperately tried not to scream whilst her teeth were still holding on. A slap across the face made her let go but the screaming began again.

Smith now thought better of it and ran out of the tent and back to his quarters.

It was only few seconds later that her colleagues, hearing the screams, ran in to help her. Seeing she was in a dreadful state, they tried to comfort her but to no avail.

She was taken to the Matron where she once again broke down in front of her. 'I don't how it happened. I was so tired after the last shift I just went to my tent, fell on the bed and went fast asleep, I was too tired to wash or change. I just went to sleep.'

'Was it the same man?'

'Yes.'

'How long were you on the ward?' Matron asked.

'I think it was thirty-six hours, Matron.'

'Well, we must do something about this man. I'll report matters to his senior officer.'

Later that day Smith was called in to be interviewed by Major Fortesque.

'Second Lieutenant, this is the second time we have had trouble with you and this nurse. What have you got to say for yourself?' he asked angrily.

'Sir, we have been old friends for years and known each other since we were children, rather like brother and sister actually, sir. I arranged to meet her coming out of the hospital and to walk her back to her tent where she invited me in. We chatted for a few minutes and unfortunately had an argument, which resulted in her biting my hand. I then left.'

'This is not what I am hearing from the Matron. I am advised that Nurse Guest was left screaming "rapist" and that you were then seen running away.'

'That's not true sir. I did not run away. I was calm but disappointed that we had fallen out again.'

'Look Smith, I don't believe a word of your story – not one little bit. Now let me warn you, Second Lieutenant Smith, rape is a capital offence in wartime and you could be shot. Now if anything like this happens again, I will shoot you my bloody self! This incident will be placed on your record,' he shouted. 'Now get out and I don't want to see you in front of me again.'

Smith left sheepishly and that was also marked on his record.

Interestingly, he did leave her alone. I suppose it was the warning he received, but in any event he was transferred sometime after.

Within a few months, Janet was promoted to Sister and transferred to a forward Nursing Station, which was probably the hardest job of all because all the injured were taken there to be treated if possible or to be assessed as to whether or not to send them on to the main hospital. Often they had to carry out urgent lifesaving operations such amputations and removal of shrapnel or bullets. It was the bloodiest job in the world and many of the nurses couldn't cope with the stress; but Janet equipped herself admirably, undertaking under supervision of course, some very delicate surgery.

She remained in the nursing sector for the whole duration of the war, moving around from place to place, eventually becoming second in command of the nursing staff in the main hospital. The occasional visits and days off with Charlotte brightened what was very hard and mentally draining work. Just seeing all the results of the bloody war, torn and lost limbs, gaping holes in men from shrapnel wounds was enough to finish many brave women. To see the bravery of the men who knew they were dying, just wanting a few moments of comfort in the arms of a woman they perceived to be their dream and the others who just wanted their mothers or sweethearts with them in their last moments. Saddest of all were those that thought it was their mother or their wife telling them how much they missed them or how much they loved them. Hardest of all was the nurse who had to pretend, answering as though she was their mother or sweetheart. It was heartbreaking for the toughest of them and when it was all over, some often cried for several hours, whilst still preparing for the next arrival and repeat the same routine all over again.

'My mother told me those girls were angels not nurses. A human being couldn't do such a job. Janet, my mother stayed on the Front Line throughout the war, but I'll come to that later on.'

Chapter 10
Christmas Comes
and Goes

'It will all be over by Christmas,' was a statement made so often and by so many, but now it seemed a long way off especially as it was nearly the second Christmas with no sight of an end to the gruesome war. Britain had already lost many thousands of its young men, but thankfully the men from Tremont Street were still in one piece.

As I've already mentioned, the generals believed that they could simply throw thousands of men at the enemy and they would just capitulate, but they had forgotten to take into account that modern weapons were now being used and they were still fighting an old-fashioned war.

It caused an even bigger problem as we the British had lost so many young men that the numbers still available were drying up. Also the sheer brutality of the war was stopping the young men of the time from volunteering. The Government therefore decided to introduce conscription, which meant that all eligible young men and older men too would be called on to fight.

This was interesting as Smith Snr received his papers and all in the factory knew he had, which resulted in a quick visit to Winston Heath. His call-up was cancelled on the grounds that it was vital for the war effort for him to remain in the factories. This was cowardice as his actual job was not specified except by title. He was simply his Lordship's informant and looked after discipline and wages which enabled him to cheat the workforce.

The women in particular used to whisper behind his back and would often put a white feather on his back as he passed by. There was always one placed surreptitiously on the desk in his office.

***

In the meantime, the war went on and Fred, having already built a reputation within the battalion for his so far unrecognised courage, began to show great leadership particularly in the heat of battle, with the result he had a number of followers. Several just wanted to be in his company, but one or two just seemed to tag along. Two of these, a Peter Frost and a Tony Price became really good mates. It was the 19th December, the same day as my father's birthday. There had been a standard bombardment followed by the standard infantry attack, only this time the Germans had beaten the British back. The order to retreat was given and what was left of the men retreated back to their lines.

Fred was one of these and whilst he was running back, he saw Peter lying injured on the ground. He stopped in spite of the continuous fire from the enemy and picked Peter up, carrying him back to their lines. On the way he saw Tony was also injured and shouted: 'Hang on, I'll come and get you.' He offloaded Peter and immediately ran back for Tony who had lost a leg; his war was over. There followed an amazing scene depicting an element of chivalry rarely witnessed in modern-day warfare. The Germans stopped firing when they saw what Fred was doing and began again when he was safe. Believe it or not, in such instances, Fred would wave at the opposing side as a gesture of thanks. That's the sort of man he was and you can imagine what his status was with the men. He won the meritorious award of being mentioned in Dispatches.

For the next few months it was more of the same.

The glamour of what they all did, marching through the streets of Wolverhampton and enlisting had long gone and every man woman and child who had done the same now felt the same – it was a waste of time and a sheer waste of lives. They were all cannon fodder for the generals to use at will. Few had any confidence in what was being done and what was being achieved by them.

All were subject to appalling conditions, day and night in trenches that were always deep in mud. There was little or no shelter from the rain; their clothes were never dry; their feet began to rot in the constant wet until eventually they couldn't walk. Gangrene was common, with limbs being lost as though it was some normal event. This was a ticket home and with all the hardships that it would bring to some, it was preferable to what they were suffering.

The winter arrived and with it, the freezing cold. Then the snow, but at least when that fell in quantity, the scarred landscape became picturesque; shell holes became covered with a white blanket which momentarily covered up the death, dirt and disease, all of which prevalent at the time. A barrage would start and then the bloody generals would order another charge. They would all race across No Man's Land shouting and screaming, hoping to frighten the enemy, slipping and sliding into the covered-up shell holes in the process, churning the ground as they went into thick mud and more wasted bodies would be left where they fell.

***

'I hope I am not boring you, Clive. You will see I am trying to build up a picture which will show you the reason why things happened as they did.'

'Not at all, Irvine,' I replied. I am finding all of this interesting, but I would like to hear what happened to Smith Jnr.'

'I'll come to that. Fred was a wily character. You will remember I told you how as a boy he was always first over the wall to the playing field, first on the stadium roof. Somehow he had the ability to find and quickly assess the easiest way to do things. In fact, he was always first to try anything.'

***

Well, it was the same throughout his life and particularly during the war. He was a born leader, but would never take the responsibility of actually being in charge. My father thought he had that innate fear of causing others to suffer from his decisions and he simply wanted to be with his friends; he wanted to look after them, make sure they were safe, as though it was his duty.

However, I remember my father reminiscing. He said: 'We all seemed to follow Fred's lead without question and didn't realise why, but we knew it would be safe to do so.'

The Army could see his potential and offered him promotion not only in the other ranks, but they also wanted to send him for officer training, which he again refused. He would never accept official responsibility, no matter how many times it was offered.

'I'm sorry Clive, I'm digressing, but I wanted to make sure you realised how and why Fred became so important to them, which I hope will become clearer later on.'

'No that's fine,' I replied. *'I understand and I'm getting the picture. Please carry on.'*

Irvine continues:

It was a dreadful war; it was hailed as the war to end all wars, but fortunes ebbed and flowed. The Germans would charge from their trenches, race across No Man's Land, screaming and shouting as they ran. They would overrun our trenches and claim a victory and the following week, the British would do the same and claim their victory as they recaptured the trenches, both sides losing hundreds of men in the process. For months, the two sides would simply be fighting over a couple of hundred yards of bombed-out dirt.

'How do you know all this?' I asked Irvine.

'My father would tell me stories of their exploits, but he was an avid diarist and from a little boy he would make notes of his and others' activities but also as I grew older, my uncles and their friends would tell me what it was like. Now I believe they told me if only to keep Fred's name alive, but I'll come to that.'

'Can I see your father's diaries?'

'I don't know. There are many of his thoughts down on paper, how much he missed and how much he loved my mother. Earlier, he describes when he fell for my mother. There are all sorts of personal things written. I may show them to you later.'

'OK. Please carry on.'

At this point, the British were having a torrid time. Thousands of lives had been lost and the generals were behaving as though it was a game. Lives seemed unimportant to them. What was the loss of another thousand men? They were still fighting the Napoleonic Wars where numbers of men (superior forces) could win battles, or for example during the wars in Africa, Eastern Europe, India or Asia, when there was the thin red line and they thought raw courage would suffice. They did not realise they were now in a modern-day battle, where the old methods could not win and where modern superior weapons could change the result in the blink of an eye.

The Germans unleashed mustard gas and as long as the wind was in the right direction, they could decimate the British forces within minutes and did so, to great effect. Not the case if the wind suddenly changed because obviously they would get a taste of their own medicine.

The morale of the British forces was at an all-time low. Charge after charge had been beaten back, and the men were still being ordered to attack without any thought for their safety. They would be waiting for the order to charge, pressed against the front wall of the trench, ready to go over the top. They knew what their fate would be; some would accept it, but others simply obeyed, knowing what the consequences were if they refused. Some of the men would pray, some talk to their wives or sweethearts and many to their mothers. My father always told me how they would call out for their mothers if they were injured or dying – never their fathers.

Fred was one of those extraordinary people who accepted his lot and always tried to make the best of things. He never ever thought of himself, only those around him, in particular his friends, all of whom had survived two years of battle. Conditions were filthy in the trenches where they were never dry and where men often lost control of their bowels, not only because of fear, but also because of disease, dysentery and injury. The smell of death, shit, trench foot, stagnant water was everywhere. Then there were the shortages of food and fresh water, but here again Fred came into his own as he had learned certain skills as a boy and was able to trap the odd rabbit which he always shared.

Fresh meat was always welcome at the Front Line, especially on rest days and here Fred would once again be in his element as he would sneak into a nearby farm and steal the odd hen and a few eggs, cooking them away from the battle scene on an open fire. It was a very rare moment of peace which gave them but a short time to reminisce.

However, Fred realised the Germans could read the minds of the British tacticians simply because they were so predictable. It was always a barrage of shells, hoping to blow the German defences away, followed by a charge down the middle, often the best defended parts of the German lines. Hence they were losing so many men. The

Germans also knew when the next attack was coming because everything on the British side would go quiet during the preparation for the attack. In fact, the enemy was sometimes less than fifty yards away and both sides could actually hear each other talking. Anyway, the silence was the dead giveaway and the enemy would stealthily beef up their lines.

Fred noticed that the British tacticians ignored the fact that the German outer flanks were often less well defended and could be a great weakness should they be attacked vigorously. He had also noticed the officers always conducted the preparation of the attacks in the same way and therefore made it obvious to the enemy that something was about to happen.

Fred called a few of the men together and explained what they should do. By following a certain procedure there was less likelihood they would be injured and possibly, be able to capture the area more easily. He could see that a certain line was less defended and that there was better cover when they advanced. He told them they should all stick together and veer off to the German right flank when the order was made to charge.

They were all ready, lined up in the trenches, waiting for the whistle and from where Second Lieutenant Smith would make sure he was in the safest position at the back when the order came. Fred however, kept his eye on the German right flank to ensure all was still safe. The German lines had been pounded by the British howitzers for a good half an hour in the hope of weakening their defences, but they all knew the moment the whistle blew, the Germans would appear from nowhere.

The bombardment stopped, leaving an eerie sound of silence, which lasted just for a few seconds before the whistle blew. The shouting began and the men climbed out of their trenches and charged. Many were simply killed or injured as they climbed out, leaving the others to climb over them. It was horrific.

Fred led his group, charging to the left, whilst the main group charged forward and was being cut to ribbons. Apparently, Lieutenant Smith Jnr was nowhere to be seen.

Fred's unofficial group only had one man down as they reached the German right flank. Fred as usual was the first to jump into the German trench, quickly followed by the others, firing at the enemy as they did so.

They ran along the trench shooting at any sign of movement and immediately, were making inroads in their defences. There were some elements of panic appearing on the German side, as they could see one or two of them climbing out of the trench and retreating. Fred would have none of it; he too leapt out of the trench and chased after them, killing and injuring several and capturing two. He brought them back to the others waiting in the trench and told my father who was with them, to take them back to the British lines for questioning. My father was sure it was simply a means of getting him out of the battle as Fred knew skirmishes along the trenches were always messy.

Fred immediately began a further charge along the German line, followed by the others, realising quickly that the various twists and turns in the trench could conceal a few of the enemy. When they approached the first bend, Fred stopped and told the others to wait whilst he crept out of the trench and crawled along the line, lobbing a few grenades which he did so at each bend from then on. The others, realising what Fred was doing soon ran along, dispatching the few enemy soldiers that were left on their way.

Fred was now moving along cautiously, looking in all directions when one of his group suddenly fell to the ground. 'Sniper,' he whispered loudly and they all hit the ground. 'Keep your eyes peeled,' he whispered again. He rolled back into the trench, then binoculars at the ready, began searching the forestation at the rear.

It took several minutes before he called out: 'He's over there. Large tree. About two hundred yards in front of us and just over to the right. I saw a puff of smoke from his rifle about twenty feet above the ground in the centre,' he said, pointing him out to the others. Then with several rounds from a few Lee Enfield 303s the man fell out of the tree where he was lodged, to the rapturous cheers of the group.

'Shut up and get down. Don't let them know where you are. That's if you want to live,' Fred commanded in as low a tone possible.

'Now get Dick over to the medic,' Fred said, ordering one of them to take an injured man back to their lines, 'and the rest of you, follow me,' he continued, acting as though he was in command.

But that was the man. Everyone knew Fred's ability and trusted his judgement.

The Lee Enfield was a very useful rifle in its day and pretty accurate, but of course, when they had to carry it everywhere it soon became heavy.

Fred and the men continued along the trench, throwing a grenade where there was a likelihood of a trap, followed by rifle fire as and when the enemy were in their sights.

The Germans were now in a state of confusion, although they were putting up considerable resistance in the well prepared part of their line, but even so they were now being attacked on their right flank with some ferocity. Several thought they were being cut off and were surrounded. Fifteen German soldiers surrendered in total and were taken prisoner, including a junior officer. They were escorted back to the British lines but two men were lost in the attack.

This tactic was working as they were soon close to the German main defences which were now being attacked not only from the front but hard on the right flank. They had been outwitted by Fred and his men and were forced to take up new positions some hundred metres away, with elements of the British taking up the positions in the captured areas. The battle calmed down except for occasional sporadic fire from trench to trench.

They returned to base where Fred was immediately arrested and charged with disobeying a direct order by none other than Second Lieutenant Smith Jnr.

Fred was accused of leading a group of men away from the main force, depleting the effective fighting force, endangering the lives of the men, thus causing unnecessary casualties. Fred was taken away and locked up, pending his court martial which in those days was quick, due to the war.

It was the most ridiculous thing anyone had ever done and the incident only lasted about an hour. Captain Harmsworth had been told by all the men what had happened, that it was a decision made in the heat of the battle, which not only saved lives but also led to the advance and the capture of fifteen prisoners.

Fred was hauled in front of a Brigadier for the initial questioning, but was soon released when Harmsworth's story was told. Harmsworth actually recommended Fred for the Military Medal which was duly endorsed by the Brigadier. It was awarded at a ceremony a week later, when the South Staffs who had battled hard for several days without a break, were at last withdrawn from the Front for twenty-four hours' rest. However, they had one duty to perform and that was to salute a brave man receiving his Military Medal. The cheers from all present could have been heard all over France. My father said everyone noticed Smith's seething jealousy.

Fred was once again offered a commission, which he again refused but at least they had the pleasure of knowing that Smith was severely reprimanded.

Fred undertook many independent actions during the course of the war, all of which proved valuable to the British, but whilst never actually accepting any sort of command, his talents as a tactician were being more and more recognised and he was often called in to meetings with the officers to give his opinion and input on the next course of action. My father could see from Fred's demeanour that he was flattered by these requests. Needless to say, Smith Jnr's jealousy only grew at the inclusion of Fred in the planning operations.

Three full years of fighting had achieved little; the numbers on the battlefield were the same, but most of the faces had changed. They were simply younger, fresher, but not as happy at the prospect of war as the Tremont Street lads had originally been. These were not the happy volunteers – they were conscripts. The population no longer believed anything the Government told them about the war; they had all seen or heard of the hundreds of thousands that had been killed or injured. There was hardly a family in the country that had not lost someone, so you can understand why few men wanted to go and fight.

They first conscripted all young men and a few months later, married men were included. Once again these raw recruits were simply thrown into battle. In one sense, they were lucky as they had the battle-hardened men to teach them the ropes, something the earlier ones didn't have. They just had to live and learn or die.

The conflict was never easy, even when in April 1917 the Americans, with their economic power and a new impetus of enthusiasm and bravado, joined the Allies. Of course, the Yanks came over with the attitude they could win the war for us and I know my father didn't care who helped as long as it was over quickly and everyone could go home. He realised that many of the men from Tremont Street, had been very lucky to have remained still unscathed, tempting Fate perhaps even though they had Fred looking after them. Theirs was not to reason why.

Chapter 11
The Death of a Hero

I remember my father telling me about the day Fred was killed. He began with tears in his eyes, hardly able to speak for the first few seconds as he told me the story...

It was now May 1917 and nearly dawn when the artillery opened fire to soften up the enemy and prepare the way for the attack. The rain was torrential; the shell blasts appeared as bright blurs until they wiped the wet from their eyes. The noise seemed endless and even with their hands against their ears it seemed to percolate through their heads.

The first wave, to be led by that bastard, Second Lieutenant Smith Junior, were all ready and waiting in the trench, which was now at least one foot deep in water and mud and stained in places with the blood of those who had fallen the previous day. It stank like some sewer and morgue rolled into one. The air was also filled with the smell of death; but most of all, the smell of fear pervaded; it was impossible to explain, yet it was there. They could see the fear on each other's faces as they waited in total silence, some praying to themselves that they would be spared; some prayed out loud, asking for God to help them, but He wasn't in the trench for many that day. Some of the men would be clutching photographs of their loved ones, taking with them what was to be their last look at someone they cherished. Others would be talking to them as if they were with them and would answer their imaginary questions. They would kiss their image before placing the photograph back in their tunic, next to their heart and patting the outside as if to suggest they would be safe in there.

The barrage stopped and now the eerie silence was deafening. The rain continued its ferocity. They waited for the whistle to blow and the command to go over the top and charge. This was a death sentence; none of them had a chance. Over one thousand men were killed in less than ten minutes. There were less than five men left on their feet. They could hear the screams and cries of the injured and dying; it was like hell on earth. The barrage had missed the German lines, falling some hundred yards behind their lines; their defensive line was still intact.

The order came to fix bayonets, the whistle blew and the officers, revolvers in their hands signalled the charge, waving their arms for the men to follow them. They watched as the first wave went over the top, screaming and shouting, hoping to terrify the Germans as they did so. They were never scared of a few shouting men and our side were the same. What was a bayonet to a rifle or machine gun? It seemed so ridiculous as it simply identified where they were. It's not as if they were still fighting with spears which I am sure the generals thought the bayonets were. They were all looking at Smith Jnr, hoping he would cop it. He was one of them blowing his whistle and waving; but he didn't rush over the top and always seemed to be hanging back until dozens of men were in front of him, taking the bulk of the flack off him and giving him a better chance.

When the first of the men were within fifty yards of the enemy lines, two machine guns opened up, cutting them to ribbons. There was hardly a need for the Germans in their trenches to raise their ugly heads above the parapet, as those guns did it for them.

'We could still see that bloody man,' my father said through gritted teeth.

They continued watching Smith Jnr but within a few seconds they were distracted by a few mortar shells and lost sight of him. They knew he had jumped into a shell crater for protection but couldn't prove it. This turned out to be one of the tragedies of the day.

The second wave with all our family members in it was due to follow within a few minutes, but they were trapped in the situation; every time a man raised his head over the top to look around, it was met by a hail of machine gun fire. Men began raising their helmets to pretend they were looking and those too were met by a hail of bullets. It was certain death to attempt attack with those guns operating. The officers, realising the predicament, were frantically trying to get the orders changed or at least wait until matters could be properly assessed.

They saw the two heavy machine guns on either flank; they had a full view of the battlefield and they knew there would be no chance for any of them if they were ordered to charge.

Fred, just like he was when a boy, always a leader, always daring to the end, seeing the predicament he and his friends were in, went to see the Captain with a plan of action. He felt one man could go unseen and disarm their positions. He convinced Captain Harmsworth it was worth a try and that he was the man to do it. All he wanted was a couple of minutes' covering fire, some noise, a bit of shouting and he would be away. 'Then give me half an hour to get back,' Fred said.

The Captain, aware of Fred's previous valour, agreed to give it a try, He, on his own initiative, would stop all further actions until Fred had either been captured or killed in the attempt. 'I'll give you one hour and no more,' he replied.

As I said, the Captain agreed that he should try and promised him covering fire in five minutes, the time when Fred was to go over the top. Fred was his own man when it came to the daring bit. Armed with several grenades, bayonet at the ready, he immediately ran down to the end of the trench and actually scrambled over the top before the covering fire started. He began crawling along the ground, dropping into every shell hole he could find, searching for every weak point in the German defences. He found himself making it to the end of their line when the covering fire started, which was perfect as the Germans concentrated their attention on where they believed the assault would be made.

This gave Fred the edge and his men could see him scampering into scrubland which would take him behind the enemy lines and nearer to the machine guns.

The Captain was unable to see where he was, but Fred's friends all had their eyes skinned on his position. The group were sharing one of the trench periscopes and the Captain hurried towards them.

'Can you see him?' he asked.

'Sir!' one of them replied, pointing in the direction of Fred's activity. The Captain looked through his binoculars and sure enough, he saw Fred on his mission.

'Good God! How the hell did he get there?' he asked rhetorically.

They all lost sight of him for well over ten minutes and even my father thought he had had it, when suddenly their attention was drawn to the position of the one machine gun on the right flank. They had just been subjected to a grenade attack and the machine gun now appeared to be out of action. That was until it suddenly turned and began firing at the Germans themselves. Fred was actually using it against the Germans until it ran out of ammunition; there would have been no time for him to reload by himself. He simply dropped another grenade into the ammunition boxes and ran like hell for cover.

They could see the pandemonium in the Germans' trenches and hear the confusion as the ammunition blew up, spewing bullets out in all directions at them. Many thought it was a massive attack and began retreating. The firing stopped, following another explosion near or on the machine gun's position and everyone thought Fred was a goner.

The Captain ordered all those near him to scour their lines for any sign of Fred. It was a good ten minutes before someone shouted: 'To your left, sir, past that huge tree.' All heads turned and within a few seconds the Captain had seen him.

'He's there!' the Captain exclaimed, lowering his binoculars. Suddenly he shouted: 'Corporal, am I dreaming? What the hell is he doing?'

The Captain quickly passed the binoculars to the Corporal. 'He seems to be tending to a German soldier, sir. I can't quite make it out, but it looks like he's giving him something.' He looked intently for a few seconds and then shouted: 'He's on the way again, sir,' passing the binoculars back to the Captain.

'That's what I thought,' the Captain mumbled loudly to himself, which was heard by several others. Once again, he followed Fred's progress until he was hidden from view. A further fifteen minutes had elapsed with no action or sighting of Fred which caused much concern for the Captain as there was only twenty minutes of time left for him to get back.

The other machine gun suddenly opened up, firing at everything, spraying their lines as if to say: 'I'm still here.' They knew it and didn't have to be told. The Captain was now in a dilemma as he still had his orders to charge, but he had also given Fred that hour during which he had miraculously removed one of the guns.

A few minutes later, there was a huge explosion near the other machine gun's position. One of Fred's grenades must have hit the ammunition boxes as the bullets were going off in all directions. Once again there was pandemonium in the German ranks but this time Fred was glimpsed making his escape back to our lines.

The Captain immediately ordered the second wave to go over the top which they did, all shouting and screaming as they charged. Without those machine guns, the German positions were overrun inside fifteen minutes.

There was heavy fire from the retreating forces as they began to reposition themselves for a counter attack, which caused several in my father's platoon to run to the nearest crater as they were ordered to retreat. They jumped into this crater and were astonished to find Fred lying in the mud, badly injured, having been shot in the back of the neck What was worse was that Lieutenant Smith was there with him, hiding from the battle. Only now, in the company of others, he was his brave brash self again.

'Come on, get forward,' he shouted at them and added.' It will be easy for you now I've got rid of those machine guns.'

'You what?' one of the men shouted. 'That was Fred and we all saw him, you lying bastard.'

'Who said that?' Smith yelled.

No one replied.

'I found him snivelling in this hole, too frightened to get out and fight,' Smith said. 'Now get forward or you'll suffer the same fate as this coward. Move it.'

They all stood still to a man.

One man refused to leave Fred and told Smith he was going to get a stretcher.

Smith drew his pistol.

'Are you going to shoot all of us then?'

'You lying, cowardly bastard,' another shouted. Smith took aim at Henry but was knocked out of the way by one of the others. The pistol fell to the floor and dropped in the mud, which made it impossible to find at that moment, particularly as they were all deliberately treading on it.

'I'll have you all on a charge, assaulting an officer and... cowardice.'

'Go on then, hero,' another shouted sarcastically. 'Put us all on a charge.'

'You know what penalty that will be, don't you?' Smith shouted in desperation.

Henry ran back to our lines, zigzagging to avoid the sporadic German fire and sought the help of a stretcher bearer. We could hear him shouting 'Stretcher bearer! Stretcher bearer!' He found one and grabbed hold of the stretcher, forcing the bearer to follow him back to the shell hole where Fred was still clinging on to life.

'Move out of the way and let us through,' he shouted as the men were crowding round Fred. 'Get away from him. We need some room.' Fred's body was almost lifeless.

'Come on, let's get him out of here,' Seth said. 'We can't waste any time. He's in a bad way.' They gently put him on the stretcher and carried him to the field hospital. He was still barely alive, but at least he was safe now.

'The rest of you get forward,' Smith shouted.

'Shall we kill him now?' one of the men yelled as they rejoined the others charging back into the German trenches. It was safe now, particularly as Smith himself joined the charge this time without his weapon.

Henry rejoined the group almost an hour later, giving them the news that Fred was still clinging on to life, but also that he had Smith's revolver. 'And guess what!' he asked excitedly. 'There has only been one bullet fired. That bastard has shot Fred.'

'Let me have it,' Seth asked,' I'll make sure the bastard never uses it again.'

The Germans had retreated back sixty or seventy yards and there was once again some normality in the fighting, when the Captain, seeing the men bunched together, became concerned. 'What's going on?' he demanded.

'Nothing sir,' the men said in unison, as they walked away and went back to their positions.

'Good. Go on then. How's Private Wearing?' he added, addressing Henry.

'Not good sir. They don't think he will survive.'

'Thank you, Private.'

'Now Lieutenant Smith, what has been going on to capture all this interest?' the Captain asked.

'I managed to knock out those two German machine guns and on the way back, I noticed Private Wearing hiding in the crater. He was a coward. I told him to get forward but he refused and started back to our lines. I told him to stop but he clambered out and was shot by the enemy.'

'You utter moron! He has just saved the lives of hundreds. It was you who shot him.'

'No, I didn't. I ordered him to go forward, but he was a coward and climbed out of the crater at the back and was shot by the Germans,' Smith replied, beginning to raise his voice.

'Second Lieutenant Smith, remember who you are talking to and don't raise your voice to me. Now I want your report of the entire incident handed to me before 16.00 hours today. Do you understand?'

'Sir!' Smith answered and with that, the Captain walked away.

Out of the Captain's earshot Smith suffered a hail of abuse from the men, but he remained arrogant and continued throwing his weight around.

The Germans finally left their present positions and retreated to a previously held trench, some hundred yards further to the rear.

The second wave succeeded with the loss of only fifteen men and eleven injured. It was a tragedy when you realise with all that loss of life, the British only gained about 150 yards of wasteland which was full of shell holes, and a trench which the Germans had previously occupied and one which they would probably lose the following week. All thanks to Fred, our family and friends were saved.

The men were regrouping after the battle and were being spoken to by Captain Harmsworth when one of the men, a Corporal Slack, asked for permission to speak to him.

'Certainly Corporal,' the Captain replied and paused for a second or two, waiting for Slack to speak.

'In private please, sir.'

'I don't like this Corporal, but come in,' he replied, as he led him into the newly captured underground bunker.

'What is it, Corporal?' he asked.

'Well sir, I don't like telling tales, but you saw Private Wearing scampering round the enemy lines and knocking out those machine guns.'

'Yes, a very brave action and I am going to recommend him for a gallantry award above and beyond.'

'Well sir, we found him in a shell crater. He had been shot in the back of the neck at close range. He's still alive but I don't think he is going to make it. Sir, the problem is Lieutenant Smith is claiming he disabled the guns and not Fred. Sorry sir, I mean Private Wearing, sir. We believe that Lieutenant Smith shot–'

'That's enough Corporal,' the Captain interrupted. 'That's enough. For talk like that I could put you on a charge.'

'But sir!'

'Enough Corporal, and... I do not want to hear any more about it.'

'Private Wearing saved many of us and he's not a coward,' the Corporal added as he was turning to leave.

'I said enough, Corporal!' the Captain shouted again. 'And not a word of this to anyone, Corporal Slack. Do you understand?'

'Sir.'

The Corporal saluted, turned and left the bunker feeling aggrieved and believing the old adage that the officers would stick together, come what may. He told all of them what he had tried to say and how the Captain had shouted him down and told him not to talk about this to anyone, which caused the entire platoon to be disgruntled.

This incident made the platoon determined to tell their story to which ever officer would listen and when and if that became impossible, they would tell everyone else. This was the very start of their campaign for justice for Fred but they didn't realise it at the time.

Fred was taken to the field hospital where he made a slight recovery but was still unable to speak or move. The men were desperate to see him recover. They received an hourly bulletin as one or another would come and give the latest: 'Still the same,' or 'Seems a little better.'

In the meantime, Smith Jnr put in his report, claiming in detail how he destroyed the two machine guns and managed to escape back to our lines by jumping into a crater, only to find Private Wearing hiding in the crater, having lost his nerve. He tried to climb out of the crater to run back to our lines but was shot in the back of the neck from the German lines.

The men were in a state of near mutiny and it took all Captain Harmsworth's skill to calm down the situation. Even he, along with his men, was hoping that Smith Jnr would be killed, if only to save the embarrassment of him going against another officer – something unheard of in the Army at this time.

Smith handed in his report to Captain Harmsworth who in turn handed it to the Brigadier who interviewed Second Lieutenant Smith in front of Harmsworth. Smith related his story to them as per his earlier conversation with Captain Harmsworth and I think from reading the Captain's later notes, Brigadier Reed was not sure of the veracity of the situation. The machine guns had been put out of action and as Fred was too ill to counter these allegations, the Brigadier came down in favour of Smith.

'Congratulations, Second Lieutenant. You deserve a well-earned rest so I would suggest you take some leave. Captain, make the appropriate arrangements.'

'Sir,' he replied.

There were no special words for Smith. The Brigadier simply said, 'Well Lieutenant, you may go.'

They weren't quite sure why Smith was sent on leave, but the Captain thought it was to let matters cool down. It doesn't take long for officers to suss out trouble and the reasons for it. But it was a big mistake to give Smith leave. He came back full of the joys of spring and shortly after, the Army made him a First Lieutenant. There was to be a fuss made of him as they presented him with the Military Cross in a battlefield presentation to several medal winners with the appropriate applause for all except Smith. The officer corps held ranks and cheered, but again it became necessary to transfer Smith elsewhere to protect him.

It has always been an anomaly to me that officers receive the Military Cross for the same level of bravery as other ranks but they only receive the Military Medal.

Of course, everyone knew Smith Jnr returned home to see his father, who in turn went to see Lord Winston

Heath. Boy o' boy was there some pomp and circumstance emanating from that quarter.

The newspapers were informed and there were pictures of him on the front page in his new uniform as First Lieutenant together with the story of how his bravery had saved many lives. *The Daily Mirror* published the citation and what he had supposedly done to achieve the medal and were of the opinion he should have received the Victoria Cross.

There were many officers and men who had won decorations in proper circumstances and yet no one put a finger up to stop this débacle.

What was certain, although there was no proof at the time, was that there were rumblings in the Army of the real situation; they knew of Lord Winston Heath's interference, particularly with all the publicity he had generated in the press where his sphere of influence was felt. The problem was it had caused a great deal of embarrassment for the Army and the politicians and they had ordered a general tidy up, which could only be conducted one way: 'Get rid of everything and everyone involved.'

Without any explanation, Captain Harmsworth, who was a first rate regular officer was sidelined and sent to Army administration, away from the Front.

'However, I'm sure Clive that any person who had carried out an action without any thought for his or her own safety, which had undoubtedly saved the lives of hundreds as Fred had done on that day and survived or not, would have earned the very highest gallantry award. I'm sure when Smith's report was accepted, followed by the rumoured comments from the men, this was downgraded and Smith was recommended to receive the Military Cross. The problem was the Army made the mistake deliberately or not of accepting Smith's report.'

The war battled on, but at least there was hope in sight,

thankfully for the Tremont Street bunch, as they were now lost without Fred and simply became part of the main group, anonymous to all. I think it was this change in circumstance that caused my father to be shot. It was the usual barrage bombardment which again missed its target and then the infantry charge which was expected, followed by the inevitable casualties.

My father was in the first wave along with the others, charging towards the German lines when he was shot. The bullet ripped into his side on the fleshy part and thankfully went straight through. I remember my father telling me it was like someone sticking a red hot poker into his side and leaving it there. It felled him and for a short time he thought he had had it. That was until one of the men came up to him and told him he was a lucky devil as there was a gorgeous looking nurse in the forward Nursing Station and that everyone wanted to get there, just to see her. No such luck for him as he was quickly whipped off to the Forward Station. However, because they were very busy due to an unexpected German counter offensive, they thought it better he be transferred to the field hospital for treatment. This made him feel worse as only those with really serious injuries were transferred quickly.

My father was asleep when the Sister came along with the nurse who introduced my father to her. 'This is Noel Gough, Sister. He has just been transferred here as they have a rush on at the Forward Station.' There was no reply from the Sister. Just total silence.

'Sister, are you all right?' Again, no reply. 'Sister?'

'Yes, umm yes... I'm just shocked to see this patient. He's my beau.' She staggered backwards, needing to hold on to the foot of the bed. My father was beginning to lose the effects of the morphine given for the pain and post-surgery and didn't know exactly where he was.

'My darling, I'm so sorry. I love you,' Janet blurted out. 'You're going to be all right.'

Well, of course the poor nurse didn't know where to put herself. 'I think I will leave you to it, Sister. Sister?'

'Yes... yes, thank you,' Janet replied hesitantly.

My father came round to the realisation that it was his beloved Janet standing over him. It was the best cure he could have had. He didn't care what the past had held; he was only concerned with the future – a future with Janet.

He was soon back at the Front, and spent what spare time he had with her; just being near her was good enough. It was as though they had never been parted.

She did, of course, tell him the full truth of her situation and it was never mentioned again, save to say he went with her to Chipping Sodbury several times over the years. He did, as did all the others, bear a deep concern that Smith Jnr was getting away with murder for the second time.

In the meantime, Fred was transferred to the larger military hospital away from the Front, but the specialists held no hope as they realised that the bullet that hit Fred was still at the base of his skull and they knew that if it was removed he would surely die; it was therefore decided to repatriate him back to a hospital near his home in Wolverhampton.

Fred was a fighter to the end and clung onto life for another six months. His father and mother and in turn his friends, apart from those in France, visited him regularly, but in early January 1918 he died and was buried in a Wolverhampton cemetery at Penn Fields. It was a family plot and he was laid there without any honours or any fuss even though he had already won the Military Medal, mentioned in Dispatches. Family and friends were all there and despite the expense, many had donated money to the family to help with the cost of burial. He was dressed in his uniform and his gallantry medals were pinned to his chest. His coffin was made of the finest English oak and draped with the Union Flag as he was laid next to his mother.

'Clive, I could shed a tear every time I think about it.'

I must admit that the way Irvine had described events even brought a lump to my throat.

All the families in Tremont Street and dozens in the area thought the way Fred's situation had been handled was a disgrace and many vowed they would do something about it. But like everything in life, people who are not closely involved soon lose interest.

It was appalling the way Fred was treated. He had been a very brave man and yet he was designated a coward.

Uncle Evan was a member of the Council and he put forward a motion that Fred was a man of exceptional courage and should have his name inscribed on the War Memorial. However, he had one problem: he was a Labour Councillor. The Council as a whole was controlled by the Liberals and the Tories; and the leaders of the parties were rumoured to be in the pocket of Winston Heath.

In reality, this was inevitable as all councils where Winston Heath had factories were controlled by people in his pocket. We discovered his influence was as strong at the top as it was at the bottom of the political spectrum.

Several Council members did question the legitimacy of the awards given to Fred.

'However, Fred must have known his fight for life would give him the last laugh as he was buried with the bullet still in his head, but I will come to that, Clive.'

'Irvine, I feel I should warn you this is a very important human interest story and I really think it will attract a lot of interest, particularly if we prove that Smith murdered Fred. It will attract attention from everywhere and you will be badgered from pillar to

post. I will try and keep you out of it, but you know the press. At least you ought to by now. They will find out who and where you are. Are you prepared for this?'

'I have to be. I promised my father I would try to get justice for Fred and if that is what it will cost, it is a small price to pay, considering Fred gave everything.'

Chapter 12
Things Begin to Change

Irvine's story was beginning to enthral me. However, we both needed a break so I decided to take him out for something to eat. He took me to the Star and Garter in Wolverhampton where we had a lovely meal and a chat about the area and the Grand Theatre which was adjacent.

We bade our farewells and I returned to my hotel, where I immediately phoned George Stevenson, my editor.

'Clive,' he began with a flourish and we always knew from the way he tried to sound pleased to hear from you that he was far too busy, 'how is it going?' he asked, trying to sound enthusiastic.

'George, it's amazing and you're not going to believe it, but I rang you to tell you I will be another couple of days with Irvine Gough and then I have to see a few others, so it will be at least another week before I can get back.'

'Come on, whet my appetite,' he insisted, suddenly taking an interest.

'I think we will be able to prove the Army covered up a murder and awarded the killer the Military Cross. It really is a scandal of immense proportions.'

'Are you sure you're not getting carried away with things?'

'No George, I'm not. It's becoming more interesting by the hour. There are far too many witnesses which gives it credibility.'

'Can we start the story and run it as we investigate?' he asked, getting a little excited at the prospect of a juicy story.

'I don't think so, not yet at least. Let me get one piece of concrete evidence which I'm sure I'll find and then it will work. There could also be a lot of opposition to any investigation, so I would rather keep the powder dry. There are also a lot of inexperienced people who may know something and again I don't want to scare them off at this time.'

'How long do you think you'll need? We're a bit short here.'

'At least another week, but it will be good, I promise you.'

'As good as *The Two Old Dears*?' he asked with a laugh.

'Better, but far too serious to be treated lightly.'

'Okay, take as long as you need but keep me informed, particularly if you get the concrete.'

'Oh, by the way, Irvine wants some payment,' I added.

'Use your loaf. Pay what it's worth and no more.'

'OK. Bye.'

George was satisfied and I almost had carte blanche to get to the bottom of the story. Like any reporter with an interesting story, it is hard to concentrate on anything else. I needed to complete my notes and it was well after 2 a.m. before I went to bed. Even then the excitement of it all kept me awake for another hour.

I returned to Tremont Street the following day, where Irvine was waiting with a box of papers and two mugs of Sergeant Major's tea, which I will say I enjoyed whilst getting down to business. There was no socialising with Irvine this time as he could sense that I was more than a little interested and he knew I had the bit between my teeth.

'You were telling me about the day Fred died,' I began.

'I want to leave it there, Clive. There is much more to this, but first of all, I would like to tell you what happened when his unit found out he had died.'

Irvine continues...

Everyone believed that something was not right about Fred's demise, even the Army Chaplain, and as the war was going the way of the Allies, there was not that urgency as previously. The officers were not initially surprised and did not expect there was anything untoward despite the numerous requests to attend a Sunday Service. However, it was an enormous surprise when half the battalion turned up to what turned out to be Fred's memorial service. Captain Harmsworth made a special journey, so did the Brigadier, who was now a General.

The General spoke of Fred's continual bravery and how he had saved the lives of many of his men. Several others stood up and gave thanks and made short speeches. My father finally stood up and began to speak, but broke down and stood there sobbing. The congregation simply watched in deathly silence. Suddenly, as though they were part of an orchestra, the entire group erupted into applause. My father's tears had said it all.

It was a fitting end for a very brave man whose life was so wickedly cut short.

Needless to say, the Army criticised the officers for allowing the service to take place. But as there were so many, they could not discipline them all.

However, it caused a few feathers to be ruffled and the powers that be began to make sure there were no witnesses. By making numerous transfers, promotions and promises of careers after the war was over, those in the know were distanced from each other. The end of the war was in sight and it was hoped memories would be short-lived.

'At the end of the war, Fred's service medals were sent to the family in a little box. It seemed an unfitting end to the story, but that's where you come in, Clive. Will it end here?

'You will remember I told you how Fred won his first gallantry award and then his second and there were many other examples of his courage and everyone knew it. It was so unjust for the bastard Smith to take the credit for this latest action, especially as Fred really was one of those special people who had no concern for his own safety; his mates always came first.'

***

The war had been a bloody affair, but apart from some minor injuries, most of Fred's friends and colleagues came out of it physically unscathed. It was Fred's untimely end that left them mentally scarred. None of them could get him out of their minds. How could anyone commit a murder in front of so many witnesses and get away with it? Although none of them actually saw the shooting, there could not have been anyone else involved.

'Clive, I'll quickly mention what happened to Frank and Graham when they returned from France as they were involved with Smith later.'

Frank was the first to be demobbed even though the war had not yet ended, but the need for massive recruitment and training was over, so he really missed the fight and all the trouble there and I think this made him more anxious to do something about Smith. In fact, he was incensed over Fred's death. He talked constantly about Fred and what he would like to do to Smith.

However, Frank's football skills kept him in good stead. He returned to his job with the LMS Railway company, still in the foundry, where of course he was no longer the foundry man's apprentice. He was five years older and very fit and strong. Of course his Saturday job was safe as he was still under contract to play for the LMS as and when needed, He was given a pay rise of ten shillings a match plus five shillings for a win.

It was obvious that interest in this type of competition was waning. People were being drawn to the Football Association League which was fully restored after the war with towns playing towns as opposed to firms playing firms. Their gates could be fifty or sixty thousand where now the LMS could only manage two or three thousand. These clubs became rich and employed scouts all over the country to search for talented players. I believe Accrington Stanley approached the LMS to buy Frank's contract, but they refused.

Frank's contract still had three years to run and he still had to work in the foundry. In fact, he was made foreman with extra money as an incentive, but it was obvious to the family that the moment his contract ran out, he would be away.

***

The war was over. The British and their Allies had won and demobilisation was underway, but by the time many returned, the celebrations were long over. 'Peace at Last' replaced the Kitchener Slogan: 'Your Country Needs You'.

My father doubted if there would be peace especially for those who came from Tremont Street because they all knew Fred Wearing would have survived had he been given that chance and they all knew that First Lieutenant Smith with his Military Cross had murdered Fred and survived. It was a situation they were not prepared to tolerate.

Janet was effectively demobbed from Queen Alexandra's Royal Army Nursing Corps early, as the worst in her area had been over for some time. This resulted in her being on the quayside at Folkestone when my father arrived back from France. He was welcomed back at Birmingham University where he soon finished his degree, and went on to complete a Master's Degree in

Science and at the same time took an interest in politics. His mother, my grandmother and Uncle Evan had always instilled in him the need to help others that were not as fortunate and he carried this on throughout his life.

He now had the world at his feet. He had once again met the love of his life and they were never to be parted.

'As an aside, Clive, my mother Janet, loved nursing and became a nursing Sister at the Dudley Road Hospital in Birmingham and eventually became Matron. She carried on long after she had had her children, which was unusual in those days; it was her management skills that were recognised towards the end.'

What was most important was that my father and Janet were together again and they were married in 1922.

Graham returned home to resume his life with Eileen and Guy Motors; his skills as an engineer made him useful to the Army and being a Lieutenant, he too received the Military Cross. He became one of the country's experts on gearing and his skills were called upon in the next war to come.

Chapter 13
Justice Plays Its Part

On the political side, my father was aware of the anger brewing amongst the local population and not just the five Tremont Street families, who felt they would never rest until they got justice for Fred. There was discontent everywhere as the Government had promised all the troops they would have their jobs back the moment the war ended, but this didn't seem to be the case for some in Tremont Street. Someone appeared to have put the poison down.

My father, with his far superior education and manner and who I will hasten to add, was not known to Smith Snr, went to speak to him, to demand that the jobs were given back to the men.

'Why should I do that?' Smith Snr asked in his arrogant manner which he seemed to have cultivated during the war years.

'Well, if I had a son who had murdered another on the battlefield, which was witnessed by many and I had the addresses of all these people who will swear to that, I would certainly be inclined to give four of them their jobs back, which will at least protect your little chap, don't you think?'

Smith went pale. 'This is not true,' he stammered.

'Oh yes, it is. And unless these men are employed by 7 a.m. tomorrow morning, your problems will start.'

'Who are they?' he asked nervously.

My father reeled off the names and addresses of the men which surprised Smith Snr. 'I know these men. They were my neighbours.'

'That's right. I know them too and I can promise you your son will be arrested and charged within forty-eight hours and... I am not bluffing. Some were witnesses to the crime. All they want is their jobs back. Do you want to take that chance? And remember, if your son is hanged, I am sure Lord Winston Heath would not send you a penny more for looking after his bastard son.'

Smith Snr sank back into his chair, absolutely devastated that others knew of this affair. 'How do you know that?' he asked, his voice breaking up.

'Well, do they?' my father asked angrily.

'Do they what?' Smith asked again. He was totally unable to take anything in.

'Do they get their jobs back? I'll tell you this, Smith, I would sooner see that son of yours hanged and you with him, than work for you or that bastard son. But these men want to work.

'I want to know the answer *now*,' my father said firmly.

'Yessss. Tell them to report to the works foreman. I will notify him now.'

'Thank you, Mr Smith They will be extremely grateful.'

'You didn't say where you are from,' Smith said in a questioning tone.

'That's right I didn't, but that doesn't matter now. All is settled,' my father replied as he left the office.

There were many others that weren't so lucky, returning from the fighting to find their promised jobs were not there. Many found that their jobs had been taken by women, who naturally didn't want to lose the money. It was a problem for the bosses, or should I say, the owners of the factories, as the women were cheaper labour, so it was in their interests to keep them and not re-employ the men. If they had the courage!

Graham Smith Jnr came home a hero and was welcomed back into the business by no one; he was a pariah with power. It was interesting that he went back home to live with his father, but had the same relationship with him as with his mother, in that he treated him like a dog, not only at home but wherever they were, and as the drink became significant in his life so did the treatment of his father. He was also becoming a creature of habit, spending nearly every night be in the Fighting Cocks till closing time with all his hangers on, or until he managed to get a bit of skirt that didn't know him; very few didn't know he was a woman beater. His reputation followed him everywhere. He had beaten up his mother so many times since being a young boy, having seen his father do the same. In consequence, he thought he could treat all women in a similar vein.

He had to resort to violence if he wanted a woman and then had to pay her not to press charges. It was a simple remedy in those days when everyone was short of money.

Winston Heath, although still very ill, was hugely unpopular in his behaviour which brought discontent and near uprising in his factories. Even his son, Jonathan couldn't get him to see sense. It was becoming common knowledge that there was a huge rift opening up in their family.

Finally, things took a turn for the worse which was inevitable as the war had ended. There was no longer a need for ships, guns, military vehicles, military uniforms and even aeroplanes, although there were very few of those. All the contracts with the Military and all those for the war effort ended, bringing factory closures with it.

The numbers of unemployed began to rise sharply and people actually began to starve on the streets. Soup kitchens opened up, mostly run by well-intentioned women serving queues which would be almost half a mile long.

It made matters worse when everyone discovered that Graham Smith Snr who was now the works superintendent, gave his stepson, as I will now call him, his job back at the factory. To rub salt into the wound, when Graham Smith Jnr resumed work at the factory, the fawning underlings at the works gave their hero a very big welcome back, at a special get-together outside the factory. He even turned up in his uniform – all this in spite of the rumours that were being passed around about Fred's murder.

A leopard in the guise of Smith Jnr could not change his spots and he was soon up to his old tricks. There was another rape, several sexual assaults and still the police would not do anything as the girls, none of whom became pregnant, were bought off. Any bit of money was king in those days.

Furthermore, the Smiths still wielded power and both were up to no good especially when unemployment was rife. Again as with pre-war situations, people were being fired on a whim. Money was stopped from a worker's pay on a whim with no record of any reason, but they all knew where the money was going.

I remember my father telling me there was so much discontent everywhere that people were joining the new unions and gaining confidence from each other. It was this courage that caused almost the entire Compass Works to rebel as they had endured enough of Smith Jnr's bullying. They began shouting abuse at him in their numbers.

'How did you win this one, Graham?' one shouted as he was shown a model of a large medal. 'Did your real daddy give it you for raping Diane?' That was one of the girls in the factory, who had suffered at his hands.

Whenever he was on his own the women used to give

him stick. 'How did you win that one then or were you given it for telling tales about Dorothy because she wouldn't, would she?'

His foul reputation was being spread wider and wider and his only friends were cronies. Women hated him and wouldn't go near him, not even for his money, which caused him to react violently towards them. His only salvation in that direction was prostitution and even then there were rumours that several had been beaten up by him and that they too had been bought off.

He was becoming more like his father every day, spending more time in the pub; but unlike his father who spent his time in the Rose and Crown, he spent his in the Fighting Cocks. They were both very lonely souls and had become alcoholics.

I suppose Graham Jnr was fortunate as he was one of the first to have a company car. His new position was as a roving manager, reporting on all his Lordship's factories. God knows how he managed to drive as he was often drunk at the wheel.

However, he used his new position to great effect and immediately began to undermine everyone he didn't get on with, which were many. It was so easy in those days to find an excuse to sack someone and he did that with relish. It was a strange situation because now a number of men from Tremont Street were actually protected by Smith Snr.

'The Smiths were given so much power it was unbelievable, Clive. Whether or not this was due to Winston Heath having a touch of conscience over his bastard son in his old age or that he was too old and ill to really know what was going on, is unclear. My father said Smith Snr seemed to gain more and more influence over his Lordship himself, especially as directive after directive was rescinded and Jonathan's good work was being undone.'

Anyway back to the story...

At the time, the economy was getting worse; unemployment was rising and jobs became even harder to get. Therefore, it wasn't long before the Smiths were once again in full control. There was bribery, corruption and bullying – all the things that were happening before the war. Smith Jnr once again had plenty of money in his pocket, which according to rumours, was made up of a personal monthly allowance from Winston Heath. Once again, they were cheating the employees out of their hard earned money and nothing was recorded but now they began to get their comeuppance. People would turn their back on them if they were walking down the street, No one would talk to them. There were undercurrents of strike threats in the factories, not just at Compass but at all the factories where the Smiths' influence was felt.

It was bad enough when half the population was out of work but having to cope with the Smiths as well was becoming too much to bear.

**

After the war, the Gough brothers and one or two others from Tremont Street had vowed to meet once a week just to keep in touch with each other. Graham was now working for Guy Motors, Jess with Benchmans and Frank was still with LMS. He had moved up from foundry man's apprentice to foreman foundry man. He was still playing football for his work's team but was rising to fame in being offered a position with Portsmouth Football Club starting in four weeks' time.

The return of Smith and to the bad old days was the last straw for the men; they decided to do something about him. It was at this point that Frank and Graham came back into the picture.

They would regularly meet at the Heath Town Working Men's Club, as it was Frank's favourite place. It was where he used to change into his football kit as a boy when he began to play for Heath Town. The pitch was next door to the club. It was also a place not frequented by the Smiths as they were not welcome. I remember Uncle Evan telling me on one occasion, Smith Jnr had tried to enter but was refused by the steward. He began to threaten the steward but was soon surrounded by at least twenty of the men and was told in no uncertain terms what would happen to him if he visited the club again and particularly if any harm came to the steward. He never dared show his face at Heath Town again. It just showed what could happen when the silent majority stood up to be counted.

Anyway, they were all there except my father who was back at Birmingham University where he had just received his BSc (Hons) in Mathematics and was going on to take his Master's Degree in Science.

They ordered their drinks, sitting in their usual corner away from the bulk of the activity. Seth began by outlining the Smiths' latest misdemeanours and getting more annoyed with every syllable spoken. Then it was back to Fred.

I think even the world had had enough when Frank first suggested they should get rid of Graham Smith Jnr.

'He's now raped three women and got away with several assaults. He murdered or arranged to have killed that poor sod in Bridgnorth and... killed Fred. What else will he do before someone does away with him? No one would shed a tear and no one would miss him,' Frank said, leaving the others to ponder over what he had said. 'Think it over. See you next week,' he added, getting up to leave.

That was the first time they had actually had a proposal on the table; previously it had always been the drink talking.

It was at the next reunion when, as always they began

reminiscing about Fred, the war and the bastard Smith, when Frank asked:

'Have you decided on what I said last time?'

'What was that?' Jess asked.

'You bloody well know. Is there any chance of sorting him out yet?'

'There's no chance. He's too well connected. Someone is always pulling strings for him.'

'I'm not talking about all the people he knows. Most of them wouldn't give him the time of day, anyway. I'm talking about getting rid of him, What if he just disappeared?' he asked rhetorically. 'We could do it!' he added for good measure.

They all looked taken aback.

'Look, we are always talking about him and how he gets away with this and that. We know he murdered Fred and–'

'Yes, he did,' Seth interrupted.

'Well then, who's going to miss him?'

'Are you serious?' Graham asked.

'Of course I'm serious. He should be put down like a rabid dog. Well, why don't we, instead of just talking about it all the time?'

No one answered; they just looked blankly at each other.

'How would we do it?'

'Kill him, and as I only have two weeks left in the foundry we could shove him in the crucible and there would be nothing left. No trace of him, whatsoever. Next Thursday would be the best day as we have no production, so no one is working, but I have to be there to keep the furnace going. The only others on site are the two stokers and they have to stay there until they change shift, but anyway, they are in another part of the building and never come to the production area.'

'A week next Thursday? That's only a week from now.

Doesn't give us much time to plan, does it?' Graham said.

'There really is not a lot to plan,' Frank added.

'It's the hangman if we get caught,' one of the others pointed out, the seriousness of the situation suddenly dawning on them.

'We won't. They need a body and as long as we put everything in the crucible, and I mean everything that could be traced to him, we should be all right. And let me say this, I will take the responsibility if we get caught. None of you need be involved.'

They all sat in silence for what seemed like minutes. Graham broke the silence:

'Frank? Why the rush?' he asked.

Frank chose this moment to break the news about his new job: 'Well, I've been offered a contract to play for Portsmouth, starting in two weeks and it will be our last chance to get rid of the bastard.'

Immediately, a cheer went up from all of them. News of Frank's rise to fame spread round the club like wildfire. He became the centre of attention with congratulations all round from everyone in the club.

It took a while before they were alone again and Frank was able to bring them back to the main topic of the evening – that of Smith's demise.

'We need time to think. It's a big decision,' one of them remarked.

'We don't. It's simple. Next Thursday,' Frank replied before going to get another pint for all of them.

They no longer had Fred's guiding hand. He was the most eloquent and bravest of the bunch but also a forward thinker; in other words they were lost without him. Seth felt they should ask my father for his opinion as everyone respected a man with his education. Graham joined in supporting Seth. 'Yes it's a good idea. Let's ask Noel for his opinion.'

Frank was now getting angry. 'We don't want Noel involved with any of this as you know very well. He would immediately come under suspicion, as the police would believe he has a very strong motive. Don't forget Smith raped Janet.

'Anyway, I am away in two weeks. I have no ties and have offered to take full responsibility but you cannot make your minds up. What the hell is the matter with you? We have moaned about Fred's murderer for over three years – our best friend, and now we have one chance where I know I can get away with it and you are still talking about it. Unless you make your minds up now, you can forget it.'

The conversation went round in circles with no one really wanting to begin again until Graham asked: 'How on earth would you propose to do this?'

Frank, who had obviously been thinking about this and planning for some time replied:

'All I need is for you to get him to the foundry between eleven and midnight next Thursday. Dead or alive. No one is ever there. It's too dirty, too hot and too late. Get him there in whatever condition and leave the rest to me. I won't need any of you there to help.'

He paused for a minute or two to allow things sink in. They simply stared at each other in total silence and then he added: 'You lot fought for your country and hundreds, *no, thousands* of you never came back. I was lucky. I did come back, unscarred not only from the battle but from the trauma. I have felt dreadful from the moment I went into the training corps. I took the easy way out...'

'We would have all done the same, Frank, if given the opportunity,' Graham said. The others mumbled their agreement.

'No, but you weren't. Let me finish. I need to get this off my chest. Many of our friends were killed and you were very lucky you didn't join them and we all know in part that Fred helped you all. Time and time again, he risked everything for you and the others and now I want to risk everything for my own piece of mind, and in particular for Fred. You did your bit. I now want to do mine. Please don't try to understand. This one is for me.'

They were dumbfounded and sat in awe of him, again in total silence, only broken by Seth who asked if someone could lend him thruppence.

'I need another drink,' Seth croaked.

'I'll get them,' Frank replied and left the table.

'What have you lot been plotting then?' the publican asked. 'Huddled together and all that whispering.'

Quick as a flash Frank said, 'I'm thinking of having a few drinks and a bit of a leaving do and didn't want to let it be known at the moment.'

'In here, I hope?'

'Of course, Bill. Where else?'

Bill smiled and began pouring the pints. 'I'll bring 'em over Frank.'

'Thanks.'

Frank returned to the others and sat down somewhat surprised at the publican's comments. 'He's just asked me what we've been plotting. I told him my leaving party, but you see how careful you have to be. You have to be disciplined. You cannot talk or even hint to anyone what we have talked about, not even to your families and friends especially. We simply forget it. No regrets, no conscience, no feelings. We will simply be getting rid of one of nature's vermin.'

The beers arrived and they all sat in silence while Bill passed another freshly poured pint to each of them. 'Well, what have you plotters decided then?'

They looked agog and already guilty of the crime they hadn't yet committed. Frank came to their rescue: 'Yes, and it's a pint and a pork pie for thirty of us, a week next Friday from seven. Is that all right?' he asked.

'Of course it is. I'll put it in the book.'

'You see what I mean?' Frank remonstrated with them. 'You have to be so careful as it will be my neck on the line this time. Even the look on your faces made Bill suspicious.'

'It was as simple as that, Clive. I think Frank would have done it by himself if they hadn't agreed to help. None of them had realised that he was feeling very guilty about his non-combat role and very determined to put matters right, at least in his own way.'

The rest of the evening was taken up with the plan on how to get Smith Jnr to the foundry and who would do what. It was decided that Seth and Graham would go to the Fighting Cocks as Smith Jnr was always in there with or without his entourage and ninety per cent of the time he would leave in a drunken state. They would look after him for the evening, offering the occasional bit of flattery, which would always keep him attentive. Then, when it was time for Smith to leave, they would see him off the premises, walk him a short distance away from the pub and hand him over to the others. They were to return immediately to the bar and wait until after closing time, making sure they flashed the odd few shillings around, declaring it was gift from the 'boss' for them to have a drink on him.

This was simple; it gave them a cast iron alibi. However, they had to leave the pub somewhat worse for wear.

'But not too worse,' Frank added.

Bobby, Janet's brother and Jack, Fred's brother would walk Smith around the back streets whilst making their way to the LMS yard with a bottle of whisky in hand, just in case there was a danger of him sobering up.

***

Thursday evening arrived and Seth and Graham escorted Graham Smith off the pub's premises into the waiting arms of Bobby and Jack. Smith was worse for wear and quite oblivious to what was happening.

The next part of the plan proved more difficult than they had imagined. Bobby and Jack had assumed that because the LMS yard was empty, the streets would be too. But no! It seemed to them the whole town was out that night. They were dodging in and out of alleyways and worse still, at one point they saw a couple of policemen in the distance, walking towards them.

They hopped into a front garden, hiding behind a privet hedge until the policemen had passed. The difficulty was keeping Smith's mouth shut, and plying him with a few more mouthfuls of the whisky just before they arrived was a mistake; he was becoming very maudlin and loud. It was Jack's arm around his mouth in an attempt to shut him up which caused the main problem as he began to cough and splutter. Finally, Smith's own jacket did the trick. They pulled it over his face and silence was restored.

They sat behind the hedge for a few minutes just to ensure the coast was clear, by which time Smith was crying and in a very drunken state, slurring his words and almost incoherent. 'You're my friends, aren't you?' Smith asked, half crying, half stammering, his head lolling on Jack's shoulder.

'Of course we are, Graham.'

'You two are great. I don't know what I would do without you.'

'You're the boss. We have to look after you,' Jack said. 'You're very special,' he added, giving him a few more sips from the bottle. Then out of the blue, Jack asked, 'Why did you shoot Fred?'

Bobby was furious. Something like that has a knack of

sobering people up very quickly. But to the astonishment of both of them, he replied:

'He was always the leader and I wanted to be. He was always the bloody hero and I wanted to be. He would always smile at me and I hated that smile because I could tell it was his way of mocking me, so...'

The last few words were spoken with such venom you could actually imagine Smith killing him there and then.

They looked at each other in total amazement. For the next few moments they were both unable to take in what had been said to them. They had just heard the confession of Fred's murderer. There was no equivocation; he had done it and had received a bloody medal for it.

Jack wanted to kill him there and then and it was only Bobby's strength and powers of persuasion that prevented it. 'Don't change the plan. It has worked so far.'

For a few minutes the two of them were so shocked at Smith's revelation they did not see the small crowd of people walking in their direction.

'Bloody Hell! Half of Wolverhampton is coming!' Jack exclaimed and immediately pulled Smith into the first alleyway between the houses. They failed to notice the half dozen steel rubbish bins which the three of them fell over, making a hell of a din. This caused some of the residents who were trying to sleep to open their windows to see what was going on. Thankfully, the Wolverhampton crowd had crossed over the road and were too intent on their own enjoyment to bother with them.

They picked themselves up. Jack helped Smith to his feet, securing his arm round Bobby's shoulder whilst he restored all the bins to their original position, shouting, 'Sorry!' to the two women still looking out of the window.

Jack looked up and down the street. The coast was clear as they left the alleyway and Jack felt justified in taking his revenge for his brother. He found a new lease of life as he transported his brother's killer to the crematorium.

It was just before midnight when they arrived at the LMS. Frank was waiting like a mother hen, worried about the time they would get back home at night. He had prepared everything and from the moment they arrived, he took over. He immediately sent Jack and Bobby home and began to finish the job. No one ever knew directly from Frank himself what he actually did to Smith, but they all knew the murderer simply disappeared.

However, Frank turned out to be a worrier, not about the murder itself, but how the outcome of his actions might affect his family and friends should he die an early death. Once the Smith case reared its head, the residents of Tremont Street would probably be questioned as part of the investigation. It would not be difficult for any one of the four of them involved to slip up, no matter how minor it would be, and that little slip could lead to the rope.

He therefore decided to write a full description of what happened in the form of a confession, which was clearly designed to protect the others. He had actually changed the modus operandi which totally exonerated the others and had his signature witnessed by Randall, a cousin who was a solicitor

It wasn't until many years later that he gave my father a letter to be opened after his death. Sure enough, when Frank died, my father duly opened the letter. It was his confession, but most important of all were his reasons why he carried out the deed. It too gave details of Fred's actions and what Graham Smith Junior did to him but it was not the truth. The other four assisted in the murder.

'Can I see the letter?' I asked Irvine.

'Of course, but this one is not for publication. It was written purely for certain people's protection.'

Irvine searched in his box of papers and duly found the letter. It

was very descriptive of the way Smith was finished off, with Frank emphasising he was not cruel and vindictive and did not, in spite of everything, make Smith suffer. The letter reads as follows:

I left the yard about ten thirty, feeling dehydrated with the heat and needing my liquid intake. The pubs were closing so I hurried to the off- licence in town, as I knew the local ones would be shut. I then saw Graham Smith Junior staggering down Brickiln Street towards the railway yards, obviously drunk.

I wanted to punch him there and then and would have done so, but there were too many people around, so I followed him as he was obviously trying to make his way home. I suddenly had the urge to dispose of this monster. He walked to the bottom of Brickiln Street under the railway bridges where I saw my opportunity. The moment the coast was clear I ran up to him, knocked him out, picked him up and carried him over the bridge. I was going to put him across the lines when I had a change of plan. As I was walking over the bridge, I saw one of the coal trains coming and decided to throw him over into one of the wagons. I did just that and to make sure I had succeeded, I ran across the road to look over the other side. I think the fall would have killed him as his head looked loose. I didn't know whether he was alive or dead and quite frankly I didn't care.

I saluted the First Lieutenant and shouted: 'Good bloody riddance,' and then went home.

He had stunk of alcohol and I was sure that if he were found they would think that was the cause.

We all knew that there was nothing truthful about Frank's letter but at least he made sure he would be the only one to be accused of being involved with Smith's death.

I would have loved to have used Frank's letter in my story, but Irvine wouldn't allow this. Also, from the story point of view, it didn't get us any further as it was just about a man in his later years trying to protect his family and friends.

***

The relief felt by all of them when the deed was done was extraordinary. It was though a weight had been lifted off each of them, but the moment it was over, it opened up another problem. Fred's name had been left off the War Memorial and this was too much for them to bear. Hence they started a campaign to put matters right.

The first job was to collect evidence from everyone who had been there, even contacting the officers, for example, Captain Harmsworth, who actually lent his support to their scheme; but as for getting help from the establishment or the Army, it was quite the opposite. They were baulked at every turn. Certainly at that time someone still had a lot of influence and did not want this brought into the public domain,

They even tried to talk to the *Daily Sketch* but the newspaper did not want to get involved.

'Interestingly enough, Clive, my father told me that everyone they spoke to was full of admiration for Fred and full of indignation for what had been done to him, but as for getting involved, they had had enough of war and troubles and they just wanted to get on with their lives without hassle. As you know, there were just a few who could not or would not let go.'

Chapter 14
Just Desserts

In reality, I believe that when Smith arrived in his drunken state, Frank, having sent the other two home, quickly used his unarmed combat techniques, learned during the war, to dispatch him and then carried the body over to the furnace, hopefully dead. But no one ever really knew. What was certain was that Smith was never seen again.

Frank was right. There would be nothing left of him except an unusual pile of white dusty ash which came to the top and had to be skimmed off the following day. On the day when my father told me about the deed he said he wouldn't have been surprised if the ash they scraped off hadn't blown to the Compass Works and gone into the eyes of the employees as it was just like Smith to get his own back.

The following week, Frank gave up working in the foundry and left for Portsmouth. They had bought his contract and football had now become his boss. He actually played in the First Division for a number of years.

However, before Frank left they all met for the last time and Jack told them what Smith had said to him and Bobby.

'Do you know, Clive, they were relieved. Strange, but it was though another weight had been lifted from their shoulders. They now knew the truth about Fred's murder. None of them had any feelings of guilt.'

Of course, the next day Smith was missed, but as he was often drunk and didn't come in for work until late or not at all, no one thought anything was unusual about it; but two days later, he was missed. On the third day the papers had a field day: 'Hero disappears' showing pictures of Smith in his uniform and for the next few days, everyone was speculating what had happened to him. It was the talk of the town; even the *Express & Star* ran a favourable story in spite of knowing his past record, but of course they were not aware of his murderous activity on the battlefield.

'Clive, there was the same degree of attention given in the papers to this as there was when Lord Lucan disappeared in 1974. It too captured the nation's interest. Of course you will remember that?'

'Yes I do. I covered it for a few days, but like this one it simply remained a mystery.'

The headlines were full of it. Why has he disappeared? Is he in hiding? What's he hiding from? Where is he? Have you seen him? Then of course there was a £5,000 reward which was a fortune in those days and naturally, the papers were flooded with sightings; someone even convinced them they had seen him in Brighton living with a blonde woman. Then finally he was in Glasgow which drew the headline: 'Our Hero sighted in Glasgow'. He wants anonymity, but of course it was a lookalike who was trying to cash in.

Most of the residents of Tremont Street were unaware Smith had been murdered, and began to tell the papers about Fred, implying that Smith was now ashamed and had gone to the Continent to hide, but they were soon hushed up.

'I have to tell you, Clive, other than myself, you are the only person outside of Tremont Street to know what happened to Smith. The rest are all dead. Frank himself never discussed what he had done with anyone other than my father and they never talked about

the matter from that day on. As I said, there was never any remorse or feelings of guilt from any of them. My father told me to tell the story one day and simply say all they did was to save John Ellis the job of doing it.'

'Who's John Ellis?' I asked.

'Sorry, he was the public executioner in 1923. There is no one alive that was connected to his murder or knew anything about it, except me and now you know, and of course I was too young when I was told. I could not have done anything to stop it. Anyway it happened before I was born.'

Irvine made another cup of tea before getting back to the story. It was as though he needed to refuel.

Irvine continues...

Several weeks passed and the story naturally ran out of steam as the papers lost interest. That was until Lord Winston Heath, who as you are aware had been ill for many months, died from natural causes and the papers found out that Graham Smith Jnr, the hero, was the illegitimate son of Winston Heath, but was also first in line to his fortune.

This really did open up a can of worms in all directions especially for Jonathan, who immediately came under suspicion over the whereabouts of Smith Jnr. It was very embarrassing for him as he was becoming shunned by his so-called friends, as well as being tried and almost convicted by the media. His only salvation was that he was in India and had been for at least eight weeks before the time of Smith's disappearance, but of course that only led to the speculation that he paid someone to do it. He also argued that his father was still alive at the time and he wasn't to know how long he would live, which only brought suspicion and calls for his Lordship's body to be exhumed and examined as to the cause of death. His Lordship's doctor was adamant that he died from natural causes as he had been ill for some time. Matters were left at that and within a year, the newspapers had dropped the story and it was no longer on anybody's lips.

My father and the others for that matter were deeply sorry for Jonathan as he was without doubt a very kind and a forward thinking businessman and it was this latter quality that he put into play in his dealings with Graham Smith Snr.

The firms were in turmoil; they were at this moment headless and rudderless and although still fully operational, they were quickly running into difficulties.

Smith Snr was aware of this, and as my father believed, he knew his days were numbered unless Jonathan was arrested. This resulted in Smith making a systematic attempt to embezzle as much as he could take out and as quickly as possible. What was worse for the Tremont Street residents and the employees of the factories Smith controlled personally was that they were the first to suffer. He stepped up his ruthless methods of stealing money from the employees, stopping money from their pay for bogus reasons. He even used bogus names in the wages book, amassing a tidy sum in a matter of weeks. The mere fact there was a possibility Smith could lay claim to the fortune, or so he believed, meant that he began to throw his weight around, even visiting some of the other firms in the Winston Heath portfolio.

However, this was about to change. In fairness to Jonathan, during the war he was not allowed to join up and fight, as he held a position in the Winston Heath Company, which was vital to the war effort. At this point in time, Jonathan was effectively in control of the companies and had introduced many improvements to the management structure, not only to increase production, but also to improve the lot of the workforce. These improvements were now well ahead of the normal practices and this had earned him great respect amongst the workforce, his suppliers and customers alike.

Despite this, it was crunch time once more. Unemployment was rising, the Military no longer wanted any equipment; people could not afford to buy the simplest of things and all the wartime promises were now being broken by the day. Haphazard rebellions which had started in the factories were becoming more and more awkward and were spreading to the towns and cities. Everyone began to consider whether what they had fought for was all for nothing, especially as the numbers of unemployed grew and grew and with it, the discontent.

The Government was becoming worried about a revolution; street riots were on the increase, plus there was the rapid growth of socialism and the influence of communism, following the Russian example by knocking their Zsar off his pedestal.

Many were also dissatisfied with the Monarchy, remembering they were of German stock and they were still living in comfort. The entire Armed Forces were on full alert in case of trouble. The problem was there were still hundreds of weapons in non-military hands, taken as souvenirs from the war, including, I believe, the one used by Lieutenant Smith to murder Fred.

This was a surprising revelation and a significant one in the scheme of things.

'Who has it and where do they live?' I asked somewhat excitedly.

'I don't know but I believe Captain Harmsworth's family have the key to that answer. I only remember my father and one of the others talking about it, but I'm sure it was Harmsworth they were talking about. Unfortunately, he died several years ago, so I don't know how accurate the information will be. There were many rumours at the time,' Irvine replied.

'Never mind, I'll go and have a scout round,' I added.

Irvine continues...

Jonathan could see what was happening to the companies and what Smith was seen to be doing, which gave him added impetus to go to court and fight for control, showing the court all he had done for the country and the workforce, bringing many witnesses to the court from all sectors of the business, including several employees. The biggest shock of all came when several of the workforce, two of whom from Tremont Street gave evidence as to what Smith was doing and showed the court proof. Smith Snr was devastated and more so when the court gave Jonathan temporary control until the other matters had been concluded.

The moment the judgment was made by the court, Jonathan ordered an investigation into the actions of Smith at the Compass Works. A search was made of his house, which he owned and was fully paid for – by his Lordship, of course. The police found over £300 in cash which was confiscated and held, pending further investigation. Dozens came forward telling how they had been cheated of their wages by illegal deductions. Jonathan would have none of it. He gave Smith the choice of returning the money or facing a police investigation. He chose the former and was let off.

However, Jonathan immediately sacked him from the firm for dishonesty and what was worse for Smith, he stopped the allowance his father had paid him for over twenty years. He was devastated as he now had no income, no job and no prospect of one, not only because of his dishonesty, but also the fact that no one in the area liked him.

It didn't take long before he had to sell his house and move into rented property, simply to live. Whilst he had plenty of money from the sale of his house it soon went and he spent the latter years of his life in the poor house and was often seen drunk, begging in the street. A fitting end for a man who had been so cruel to all those with whom he came into contact.

Chapter 15
Surprising Revelations

Irvine concluded his story and we finished by having our last Sergeant Major's cup of tea and a homemade scone straight from the oven. It was a beautiful and fitting end to the interview, but before I left, he furnished me with his father's papers and all the others he had amassed over the years – except Frank's letter, of course. He walked me to the end of the road and waited with me at the bus stop for the bus to take me back to Wolverhampton, all the time reminiscing about the various buildings around us, all due for demolition – the butcher's, the off licence, the baker's and so on. A little anecdote of what they were like followed and finally, as the bus drew up, I made a promise to keep him informed of my progress.

I spent the whole of the next day in my hotel room, reading through the mass of papers Irvine had given me and also planning how I was going to broach the story. I was now completely sure that there had been a terrible miscarriage of justice and also there had been deliberate attempts by the Army, to not only cover up the truth, but also a major effort by politicians and the like to stop people looking for it.

I have never known so many people, apart from the entire Irish nation be so determined that the truth should come out. Their spirit for truth championed the cause for justice. The Wearing family and their neighbours had spread the word for two generations and their determination for justice for Fred was such that it convinced me that something should be done.

***

My first task was to meet and interview any of those mentioned in Irvine's papers that had either witnessed Fred's murder or knew about it. After talking to George my editor, I decided to whet the appetites of the British public and use the power of the *Mail* to flush out any extra information. We ran this story in the form of an advertisement by showing a picture of Fred, explaining what he had done during the war and asking for anyone with further information to come forward,

In the meantime, it was not too hard in this day and age to find out where people live, who they are descended from and who they are related to and as Captain Harmsworth was the most important person on my list, I began with him. It was an easy start as his family had remained in the Wolverhampton area all these years. His granddaughter lived in Brewood, a lovely little village on the outskirts of that town. Having made the arrangements to see her, that was my first port of call and from the ambience of the place, it was going to be pleasant.

It was picture postcard – roses over the door, flowerbeds filled with Russell Lupins, Delphiniums, Hollyhocks, and many other perennials in full flower – a sight which would grace any gardening book cover.

I remember knocking on the front door of this lovely little cottage to be greeted by a woman, probably in her mid fifties; she had retained much of the beauty she had been blessed with as a youngster and much of the elegance that befitted her.

'Clive White from the *Mail*,' I announced as she opened the door.

'Yes, I know. I've been expecting you. I'm Teresa, Teresa Wall. Please call me Teresa,' she said as she stepped aside to allow me to pass into her home which turned out to be an enormous four-bedroomed house overlooking the valley and hills in the distance. The rear garden was as immaculate as the front and as pretty. She had won many prizes for her garden craft.

It was her attention to detail that impressed me, not only in her garden but also in the keeping of her grandfather's war record.

'Go on in, Mr White and sit over there in the sunshine. I'm only showing off really, I just want you to see the garden. 'Better Homes and Gardens' are coming next week to inspect it and hopefully write an article on it, as we are opening to the public from June to September to raise money for The RAF Benevolent Fund.'

'That's a noble charity.'

'Yes it is. Grandfather was the last of our family to be in the Army. All the others have been in the RAF, hence the charity.'

I don't know how people have learned that I love a cup of tea and am partial to fruit scones, but sure enough, within a few minutes I was enjoying both and admiring the countryside as Teresa began to relate her grandfather's discoveries.

'I'm so glad you came, Mr White. This matter has haunted our family since the First World War. Grandfather was always mithered that he didn't do more to … um... to change history. I spoke to him many times about the situation and on every occasion he told me how the top brass had sabotaged his every effort to right a wrong. Someone very high up in the ranks stopped his every move. In fact, Grandfather was very young to be made a Captain and was told he had a wonderful career before him, but it came to an abrupt halt. Suddenly, the ears of his senior officers stopped listening and he began to be excluded. In the end he was advised to leave the Army, hence all the others joined the RAF.

'I think the smell came from our political masters. I believe that the man they protected was the illegitimate son of a peer of the realm who was able to wield so much power at the time to cover up a multitude of sins committed by this man.

'Grandfather couldn't let it go and unfortunately became somewhat obsessive. He wanted the world to recognise the bravery of a chap called Fred Wearing. See, I even remember his name. Not hard really as my father loved Fred Waring and His Pennsylvanians, a band famous from the forties, I think. His surname was spelt slightly differently though.

'Mr White, I want to show you this before we discuss anything else,' she said as she walked over to the table, picking up a well handled envelope and handing it to me. 'Go on read it,' she added.

I opened the envelope as though I was opening a very old historical document discovered for the first time; I felt as though I should be wearing white dust gloves to protect it. I pulled out what was the original statement Captain Harmsworth had made about the affair and several other statements from members of Fred Wearing's platoon. What was so amazing about the Captain's document was that it was signed as received and dated by a Major Fortescue two days after Fred was shot.

'How on earth did he get this back from the Army?' I asked in complete astonishment.

'Read the back,' Teresa replied.

I turned the document over and again couldn't believe my eyes. Captain Harmsworth had detailed all the reasons why the report had been handed back to him by Major Fortesque, including the off-the-record comments made by the Major, which were made five days after the shooting.

Harmsworth had been ordered to change his mind

about the report and to accept it back. Furthermore, he was requested to destroy all other statements and to support Second Lieutenant Smith's account of the action. He refused; his conscience wouldn't let him and from that moment he was sidelined.

The Major told him, off the record, that this order had come from the very top and that they wanted to make an example of this man's bravery, to show that the officer class was in the midst of the battle as well.

Captain Harmsworth writes:

I said to the Major, this cannot be right. The man was a coward, We all saw what Private Wearing had done, officers and men, and not for the first time. Major, you know as well as I do what would have happened to Wearing if he had been shot in the neck from the German lines. It would have been from a rifle and the bullet would have probably knocked his head off. It was also strange that the Lieutenant's gun had disappeared.

He then told me that this was an order and nothing more was said, except that I was to forget everything I had seen and heard about this matter.

'Mr White, Grandfather often told me he would not support anything concerning that Smith man, He said he knew he had murdered Private Wearing but couldn't prove it and his punishment for trying to rock the boat, Grandfather was transferred to Administration, dumped at the port of Zeebrugge, where he simply kept the stock control. After a few months at that job he uncovered further corruption so they shipped him back to the Front, hoping he would disappear.

'After the war he was eventually sent back to England, where he ended up a leper in an office on his own, supposedly out of the way.

'This move led to the complete ending of his career, but at least it did eventually give him his Captain's pension, so he didn't end up a pauper.

'Grandfather always did things properly. He always paid attention to detail; often minute detail, which I suppose would annoy some people. In fact, as he put it, it was this attention to detail which made the General realise within a few months he had made a mistake by banishing him to the stores.

'I'm telling you this because I want you to know that Grandfather was a strong character and an honourable man and that he would always do his best and you can trust what he has written.'

'I'm sure he did, especially as this,' I said, holding up the document, 'has begun to confirm what I have already been told.'

Teresa Wall continues:

Well, as you would expect, Zeebrugge was a large port in those days as well as having an extensive rail network leading to and from it. It had become the main distribution point for all the armaments and rations sent from Britain and her Allies that were required for the war effort. The British were fighting on numerous fronts: Italy, Turkey and North to South Africa, the Balkans and all of Europe in the North. It therefore meant that goods were transported in all directions from Zeebrugge. It was very easy for a wagon full of food to be diverted to the black market, which is what Grandfather discovered on a routine inspection of the railway sidings.

He noticed one wagon, apparently due for the Somme, had been put on its own in another siding. He immediately tackled the soldiers and the railway officials involved with the movement of the wagons in the port, together with the foreman shunter, the pointsman and the banksman, as well as the office staff. The moment he began to talk to them he became suspicious as their stories tallied like some set piece in a play – not a jot of difference. 'Why would they have rehearsed their statements if they were not fiddling?' he asked himself.

In every normal event their stories may have meant the same but the wording would be their own and obviously slightly different from each other's.

However, Grandfather may have been sidelined, but regardless of that, on the battlefield he was a very brave man himself; decorated three times and had citations for the gallant way he led and looked after his men. Well, that bravery continued as he pretended to accept their story, but decided to follow this wagon to its destination.

It was obvious to anyone with a little experience in the railway business that something was wrong as the wagon involved was eventually connected to the train behind the guard's van – the last wagon. It was also obvious that there were many people involved in this action, from the engine driver right down to the guard and whoever was involved at the other end.

He knew the train was leaving later that afternoon and after studying a map of the railway, he noticed there were several places where sidings or local, almost private lines, were connected to the main line. You know the sort – the ones used by groups of local farms to transport the tons of grain, or the potato crop or even hay during the seasons. Even local factories would use the nearest lines to ship anything bulky by train.

As Grandfather was in charge of the stores, he decided to requisition a new Triumph motor cycle from the compound, which he could do easily and after giving the train a five-minute start to avoid suspicion, he began to follow it.

He set off towards Amiens, eventually catching the train up and continuing to follow at a discrete distance; but when the train was about twenty miles from Amiens the line ran some distance away from the road and he lost visual contact.

However, he raced to the nearest point where he would see it again and thought nothing of the fifteen minutes' wait for it to arrive; but when it did, to his astonishment, it passed without the last goods wagon attached.

Speed was now of essence; he had to find this wagon before it was unloaded and all those responsible before they disappeared. This was a distinct possibility as the organisation seemed extremely efficient.

The Triumph now became a cross-country bike as he rode up on to the track, retracing the train's journey, riding adjacent to the lines. He realised that the wagon could not have been pushed by the engine as it was the last wagon. Also it could not be left on the main line for obvious reasons; it was not possible to use another engine to assist, as all other methods of railway transport had been requisitioned by the Military on both sides of the conflict. Therefore, it had to be dropped off before a set of points and pushed manually onto a siding or a branch line leading to a village or an agricultural depot. This meant the track had to be on the level or at least with a very slight downward incline to facilitate this; it also necessitated the involvement of several people in the movement and unloading of the wagon. Grandfather felt they would be armed for obvious reasons, as everyone knew in wartime, in all countries, black marketeering would mean the firing squad if caught, so those involved had nothing to lose. However, it was here they had made their first real mistake; the lines had been running straight for several miles, which meant one could see in the distance and Grandfather could see the signal was up in the stop position, which meant they had left the points open. He now knew this was the place.

He hid the motorcycle in the undergrowth and keeping out of sight, followed the single track line down to a central loading area which was only used by the farms in that area. France is blessed with many of these, even in this day and age and all of them are in relatively quiet surroundings. This one was no exception.

It had taken him about fifteen minutes to find the place where they had shunted the wagon off the train. It was as he had suspected, pushed onto a local line where there was a very gradual slope away from the main line. Even so he knew they would need several men to move it. He followed the line, creeping along the bank, keeping out of sight until he came to the wagon. Sure enough, he saw a well organised group of men and women removing all the contents and transferring them to a series of horse-drawn carts. He had one problem – they were all well-armed and he knew he would be totally outnumbered if he tried to take them on. Having made a mental note of all those involved he crept back to his Triumph and quickly returned to base.

He could understand the theft of food as many of the local population were going hungry, but the fact it was being taken from the mouths of those fighting for them and all profits were going to unscrupulous racketeers was too much for him and he was determined to do something about it.

The moment Grandfather returned to the port he went to see his Commanding Officer or should I say the Port Controller, as I'm not sure if he was under his control. Anyway, he was the long standing Major Bright, a bit of a rough diamond, having accredited himself very well with several gallantry awards in the Boar War, losing an arm in the process. He was put in charge of the port and stores at Zeebrugge. He had been the Regimental Sergeant Major but had been commissioned as a result of his bravery and promoted several times for the same reason. On one occasion he had taken control of his group as the officers had been killed and led them into battle, capturing an important position.

On the face of it, he was a stickler for doing things to perfection. The paperwork etc. had to be done properly and nothing would be allowed to leave the stores if things weren't, but underneath that facade he was still a Jack the Lad and always ready to make a bob or two if the opportunity presented itself. Grandfather thought it was his security blanket when he was kicked out of the Army. Who in those days would want an ex-Army veteran with one arm?

Anyway, Grandfather explained the situation and to his astonishment Bright made light of the matter.

'You cannot treat this lightly. Our men are dying on the Front and many are going hungry and you talk in this way.'

'Captain, remember who you are talking to.'

'I know who I am talking to sir, and if the man I am talking to does not take matters further, I will.'

'Then do so, Captain but remember many nasty things happen in wartime, so watch your back.'

'Is that a threat, sir?'

'Yes.' Now get out and do your worst!' he shouted.

Grandfather tried to take the matter to the Brigadier but once again no one would listen. The only message forthcoming from the upper echelons was, 'What's a little food if it will help the local population?' No mention of the money being made by all the people in the chain.

Within a couple of days of this incident he was told he was once again being transferred back to the South Staffs for active service and within two weeks, he found himself back at the Front.

However, before he left he carried out a little research to see if any other fiddles were going on and to his horror he found out the corruption was endemic from top to bottom. The Army used three copies of the appropriate forms for the distribution of all supplies whether it was for tanks or butter. The top copy was the one received by the end user, the second was sent to the accounts to pay the suppliers and the third was the stores copy. The first and third matched but the second was often a greater amount with the suppliers paying the difference back in cash or kind. The various departments never checked each document; after all, there was a war on so why worry about detail.

What was so obvious when he looked into matters was that this system worked very well for the companies of Winston Heath and was the reason he could pay out so much to his obedient and grateful officers including General Malcolm Weatherall.

When he discovered these anomalies and saw who was involved, he simply gave up and was happy to go back to the Front to get away from the bad smell.

One consolation for his return to the Front was that Lieutenant Graham Smith had been transferred to Egypt and became involved in the Palestine troubles.

Grandfather always joked that he was happy to see the back of Smith as he may have killed him himself. Actually, I don't think it was a joke.

When he returned to the Front Line, he was sure all those involved were hoping he would get killed, as he was a man who knew too much. I'm also sure they were disappointed because Grandfather survived the war, but became very disillusioned after it. He lost interest in most things, except trying to right a wrong. They tried everything to make him resign, but he stuck it out and retired on a full pension.

He never gave up and made copious notes of all the circumstances; some mentioned a Corporal Slack who tried to make a formal complaint about the Lieutenant, but Grandfather turned him away.

He could have written a book about the war and Fred Wearing would have featured on every page.

This extract seemed to confirm the points made by Irvine when he related the same story. Irvine had never seen or heard of Corporal Slack and yet their stories were so similar they could have been written by the same man.

'I have the original, Mr White, but that's not something I want to let out of my sight.'

'Please Teresa, call me Clive and don't worry, I will not allow anything concerning this story to be ruined. If we need to borrow it sometime later...'

'Of course, Clive. You only have to ask.'

I went through all the other statements, including the one made by the Corporal Slack and he certainly didn't mince words in his report. He too corroborated Irvine Gough's account as did one or two of the others. The most interesting aspects however were they were all formal statements and had obviously all been handed in properly. All had their full names, rank and their regimental numbers, which would make tracing them much easier. It also confirms the formality that was introduced into the complaint and gives it that sense of truth.

In my experience, there was enough verbal evidence to at least confirm a prima face case, but of course Smith couldn't answer for himself, being dead, so there had to be other supporting evidence.

'Teresa, I have been talking to another family, also with close connections to this story and it's turning out to be a honey pot.'

'Have we got a chance then?' she asked. It was obvious this had raised her hopes.

'It's early days yet. But what intrigues me is that Second Lieutenant Graham Smith actually survived the war, in spite of all the animosity he engendered and then, when he returned to Wolverhampton, he suddenly disappeared. I believe he was murdered. Do you know anything about that?'

'Good God no,' she replied, shocked at the question. 'I do remember there was always a lot of talk in the family about a terrible secret, but no one ever mentioned it directly to me. But I wouldn't be surprised. They used to talk about what this man did to all their families. He was evil, Clive, simply evil. The world is a better place without him.'

Another cup of tea and a few minutes' chat about herself and her plans for the future and I was on my way.

***

Teresa had added a piece to the jigsaw and confirmed that others knew and had talked about this evil Second Lieutenant Graham Smith, so I decided to try to contact a few of the soldiers' families who had made statements, assuming the soldiers were now dead.

It was a simple matter to start with as I was near Whittington Barracks, original home of the South Staffs Regiment. Although long gone, having been amalgamated into other regiments, the barracks became my next port of call. A chat with the Adjutant, a Captain Hopkirk and the curator of their museum and records department and I was able at least to find out where the soldiers' last known addresses were, even though it may have been in 1918.

Of course it was a job for one of our researchers and within the week I had the possibility of seven potential addresses with only two lost completely.

A couple of days later, the power of the *Mail* had produced a miracle in the form of a phone call from a Freida Leberfeld in Cologne, Germany. She had just arrived back in Cologne after a visit to London where she had seen the *Mail's* advertisement with Fred's picture featured. The message was taken down verbatim by Sophie, the operator.

'Could I speak to Mr White please?'

'I'm sorry he's not here at the moment. Can I take a message?'

'Yes please. Will you get him to ring me as soon as possible?'

'Can anyone else help?'

'No, it's with regard to the advertisement showing a picture of a Fred Wearing.'

'Do you know him?'

'No, but my father does and I would know that face anywhere.'

Sophie contacted me with her number. I couldn't believe it. What was to be a quick call turned out to be an hour long phone call with me arranging to visit Cologne at the weekend.

I returned to London with a quick update for George and then immediately flew over to Cologne via Dusseldorf where I was met at the airport by Hans, a man in his nineties, with his daughter Freida, the lady I had spoken to. They had decided to take me to their home, via the Florence Nightingale Hospital in Dusseldorf where we stopped to meet Frieda's husband, a radiographer and to sample the delights of their restaurant which was for visitors and patients alike.

Digressing from the story, I must say the restaurant was an amazing place. The food was excellent and à la carte; the service was second to none, and I was told the healthcare was one of the best in Germany, It would have been considered almost five-star, even for a hotel.

Hans was a First World War veteran, who was unable to rest the moment he saw the photograph of Fred Wearing and the article in the *Mail* which his daughter had brought home, following her visit to England.

'It's him, it's him, I know it's him,' he had said repeatedly and immediately gave his daughter instructions to contact me.

Freida had bought the paper when she had seen Fred's photograph; it was a face she would never forget. In my newspaper article I had requested help from anyone who knew or who had heard about Fred and his exploits during the war. She had indicated in her conversation with me that it might be the man who had given her father a photo to hold when he was injured.

Could this be the man Fred was seen bending over on the German lines after the machine gun was blown up? Was it too much to ask, I thought to myself.

We arrived late in the evening at their home in Cologne, where to my surprise they invited me to stay with them for a couple of days. It was a great experience with wonderful hospitality but all the talk from Hans was about Fred Wearing and what he did for him during the war. Freida showed me a pencil sketch of Fred, which Hans had drawn from memory about six years after the war. The likeness to the photos I had of Fred was uncanny.

'We had been worried about Father for a long time,' Freida began. 'He would talk of nothing else and I'm sure bored the pants off all our visitors, so I hid this away. He was becoming obsessive about finding the man who had helped him and it began to worry us.'

'I hope this will bring closure,' I replied before being interrupted by Hans.

'Is he still alive?' he asked.

'No,' I replied, not realising I had been hooked by the investigation, now believing the campaigners. 'He was murdered by an officer who took the glory for what this man had done.'

'What? How could this be?' he asked, deeply shocked. 'He was an amazing man. What happened?'

Hans was in a state; it was as though I had shattered his dream. 'What happened to this murderer?' he asked.

'He too was killed, but long after the war, but I'll tell

you about that tomorrow. I don't want to keep you up.'

'I can't sleep,' Hans replied. 'Let me tell you about this man. I can remember it as though it was only yesterday.'

'Yes all right, of course,' I replied. I couldn't really refuse when I was a guest in his house.

Hans began a very emotional tale; it was as though it was happening all over again – now – at that moment.

'I was manning a machine gun on the right flank, on a mound which gave us a good view of all the surroundings especially in front of us, right up to the British lines. There was another gun about three to four hundred metres to the left of us, which enabled us to cover the entire open area where the British were attacking. They had bombarded our side for well over an hour, but had missed the target and our Front Line defences were still intact.

'The British charged, as they always did after a bombardment and we already knew they were coming so we were ready for them. They could see from the start, when the first wave of men were sent that the bombardment had failed, so we could not understand why they sent hundreds upon hundreds of men to charge at us.

'They hadn't a chance. We just continued firing at wave after wave and the bodies were falling like skittles on top of each other. We were sick at the sight of the carnage and sounds of the dying men and... the smell. You can never forget the smell – the smell of death.

'I remember it was about 2 o'clock in the afternoon. There was a lull in the fighting which was an excuse for all the officers on both sides to get their binoculars and survey the entire area. Often the officers from both sides would see them looking at each other and wave. Ridiculous really when you consider they were fighting each other.

'The officer in charge of the battery suddenly pointed

out some movement on our left flank and told us to keep our eyes open. He then gave me his binoculars and told me to keep my eyes peeled and sure enough, I saw a figure of a man about three hundred metres away, crawling along the ground dropping into shell holes. He was like a fox hiding from the hound and yet hunting at the same time. He was now heading quickly away from us and appeared to be making his way towards the other machine gun. We thought nothing of it and assumed he would soon be shot.

'It was simply interesting to watch him as he suddenly veered to the right of the others, still dropping into holes and clambering out, going in all directions, but eventually going back on his course to the right. One or two of us had also seen him and you could hear a few shots being fired in his direction, but still he kept going. Suddenly, he disappeared and we all thought he had been shot and then I suppose it was about five minutes later, there was an almighty explosion and our machine gun post just blew up with the ammunition blasting off in all directions. We knew it was him who had caused it, but none of us could see him and presumed he was making his way back to the British lines.

'We couldn't believe our eyes when we saw several explosions in our trenches and thought a platoon of British soldiers had attacked during the confusion of the explosion. But no, it was that man; he had an unbelievable way of out-thinking us. We knew he would be after our gun simply by the way he was moving along the trench and creating mayhem, but again, whilst we were all watching the direction he was coming, he outwitted us by going right round and began attacking us from the other side. He threw several grenades into us, killing all but me. I was thrown out of the trench, receiving serious injuries to my chest with blood pouring from the wound. The front of my uniform had been torn off in the explosion and all my personal things were scattered over the ground. I remember I was lying on my side thinking I was dying and looking at my sweetheart's photo lying on the ground, just out of reach. I wanted it near me, and I thought if I am going to die she will at least be with me when it happened. I remember I kept struggling to reach it but couldn't.

'I could not believe the next few minutes – it changed my life forever. The man had again created mayhem, killing many of our men and yet when he came across me, he saw me trying to reach my photograph and passed it to me. He then lifted me up and propped me up against a tree stump so that I could see it. He could see I was badly injured and with that, he grabbed my other hand, pulled a piece of rag out of his pocket and put it in it. He then pressed my hand to the wound in my chest and said, "I must go now." With that, this will-o'-the-wisp as you say just disappeared. Now you can see why I could never forget his face. He saved my life.

'One of our senior officers saw this man's bravery and would not allow anyone to fire at him as he returned to his lines, but again he was jumping and diving, but he was never seen again. I have that blood-stained piece of rag in a tin in my room. It's to be buried with me when I go.'

***

That did it for me. I now knew in my own mind that Graham Smith Jnr had murdered Fred and I had joined the crusade for justice.

I spent the next day going over Hans' story in minute detail, absolutely thrilled at the prospect of a very exciting exposé and although I was delighted with the hospitality, I was anxious to get back to write up the story so far, but not before I had told them what really had happened to Fred and why.

188

Hans was devastated at the news but at least it had brought closure to his obsession and we now had three other members of the campaign able to confirm the story. Hans placed Fred's picture in pride of place, but not before a few tears were shed by all present.

Yes, I was now one of the members; I was now hooked as well and determined to right a wrong.

I left on a happier note with Hans and his daughter signing statements as to their part in the affair and another piece of the jigsaw was set in place. However, I left realising there was another piece of the jigsaw in place, only this one was totally unexpected. Smith, in his statement had claimed that Fred was shot in the head by the Germans and yet here was Hans telling me that there was a senior German officer so obviously amazed and in awe of Fred's bravery that they would not allow anyone to fire at him. So how could a German bullet have killed Fred?

There was chivalry in those days and it was probably the last war when this would manifest itself. You will of course remember the 1914 Christmas truce when the two sides stopped the fight and played football. Well, here we had another case and this time we had a totally independent witness, none other than a German soldier who would confirm the facts. Of course, he would also confirm what others had said in their statements: how Fred had gone from crater to crater and how he had destroyed the two machine guns.

George, my editor was delighted with our discoveries and decided to start the ball rolling with the human interest story about Fred's kindness and bravery. He felt it would bring a few more skeletons out of the cupboard and sure enough, it did. I picked a few out for myself to investigate whilst our entire research department was temporarily seconded to the case.

George also ran the story past a very famous criminal lawyer, James Hayton QC who confirmed he could make a case with the evidence so far but would prefer a little more concrete on the table. This gave George the confidence to fight this to the end.

Chapter 16
Further Investigations

It doesn't take long in this day and age to find out where someone or other is living, unless they are deliberately in hiding. Sure enough, using the resources of the *Mail* and the skills of our researchers, we found David, a member of the Earl family (name changed to protect identity), who was now living in a quiet suburb in Northfield, Birmingham.

Naturally, with the bit between my teeth I quickly went to see another grandchild of one of the participants. He turned out to be an English and History teacher at the local secondary school.

I remember knocking on the door to be greeted by his wife Anne.

'Mr White?' she asked immediately the door opened.

'Yes,' I replied.

She began by excusing David's absence. An incident had taken place at school and he had been detained. I thought I had made the journey for nothing as we suffered a pregnant pause, simply looking at each other in silence for what seemed like minutes before she broke the silence and invited me in, but I'm sure it was only seconds.

The house was typical of the Birmingham suburbs – semi-detached with a small garden front and rear and, like all the others in the area, it was well kept. They were fortunate enough to have a drive with a garage at the rear.

We chatted about this and that with me trying to bring

the story round to my subject, but she was as adept as I was at changing things back to generalities and their two children, Elizabeth and Margaret and how well they were doing at school.

'I would expect that with their father a school teacher,' I said, trying to be clever. The comment went down like a lead balloon as she made it clear that it was her who spent time with the children.

I was thankful when at last I heard a car pull up and looked in the general direction of the sound when Anne confirmed David had arrived.

'David's here,' she said, scurrying off to the hall to greet him and let him know I was there.

'I'm so sorry, Mr White. One of the parents failed to turn up to collect his child and the school became a little concerned, All's well that ends well,' David said the moment he entered the room.

'It's refreshing to know you have this regime,' I replied.

'I'm sure you've waited long enough. Come into the front room and we can talk in there, away from prying eyes,' he said, raising his voice as his two children popped in to see the reporter from the *Mail*.

'This is Elizabeth and this is Margaret and this is Mr White from the *Mail*. He has come to talk about great Granddad Black.'

The pleasantries over, the children were then dismissed, leaving us to begin the interview.

I began by briefly explaining Irvine Gough's part in the story and what I had gleaned from Mrs Teresa Wall of Brewood before asking him to comment.

This was when I found out he was a history teacher. He had been so methodical in his collection of information and so obviously interested in their grandfather's story that he had written a few pages of a story around this affair.

'Our families were all friends from the Wolverhampton, Wednesfield area when they all joined up to fight in the First World War. Amazingly, they all survived, not all without the scars of battle but they lived to tell the tale so to speak, except Fred Wearing, that is. He's the one you are interested in, I take it?'

'Yes he is,' I replied.

'He was murdered, you know,' he announced with conviction.

'I believe so,' I replied.

'No seriously, he *was* murdered, There is no doubt about it in my mind,' he added, walking over to his bureau where he pulled out a loose leaf folder, packed with information, collated and indexed.

'Granddad Slack wrote about this before the Second World War. Everyone knew the war was coming and it had brought back memories. He felt he should record what the officers did to Fred Wearing and quite frankly, I felt he should too. I am appalled at the situation.'

'I can see you are,' I added as he handed me a copy of the notes made about Fred's demise.

'I made it my goal to get the truth published, but it takes over your life, Mr White. It becomes an obsession and you have to know when to let go. It nearly destroyed my marriage,' he whispered.

'Just read the notes from Granddad. I'll call him Corporal Slack. It will save confusion and it won't take a minute and will give you an insight into the situation.' he said, forgetting I had already briefed him similarly.

However, this was a very useful document. Considering this was from memory so many years later, it was almost a carbon copy of the statement made by Corporal Slack at the time of the incident. It was uncanny and when I showed David a copy of this he was flabbergasted. There were many other notes to read and when finished they confirmed Captain Harmsworth's story to the minutest detail – even how Fred had conducted himself on the battlefield, crawling round and destroying the two machine guns. It even corroborated Hans Leberfeld's story of the action undertaken by Fred especially when he was seen leaning over a German soldier, which when you consider he was on the opposite side of the battlefield, was remarkable.

'These are the notes he made in his own hand about the actions of a Lieutenant Smith during the war and these are letters he wrote to my father when he was away at school. You will see the writing is the same. I put this together just to show the story was genuinely written by my grandfather from World War 1.

'Mr White, my grandfather used to go to the Heath Town Working Men's Club as did many of the men from that area. The beer was a half penny cheaper than anywhere else, including all the pubs. It was always packed on Friday night, after pay day. A gang of them would meet up, including Fred Wearing, a man called Ambrose, a Bobby Guest and several of the Gough family, just for a drink and a chat. Then after the war, the routine was the same, only this time there was bitterness in the air about the war and the waste of it all, where many of their friends were killed, injured, or gassed, and all of them angry about Fred. Everyone seemed to know what the truth was, but many were too frightened to say anything as they worked for Compass. That said, all of them wanted to find a way to tell the world the truth about a Lieutenant Smith.

'He had been a dreadful man, unfair to all the people and their families that worked for Compass Castings or the Compass Iron & Steel Company for many years, especially before World War 1. When the war started, he even continued throwing his weight around on the battlefield. You will see they all mention in their stories that Smith was always the last to go over the top and always found a shell hole to hide in. They all knew he was a coward. How he became an officer I will never know.

'All the statements and stories I have received point to the fact that they believed Lieutenant Smith shot Fred Wearing and claimed that he was the one who had saved them and not Fred. They became bitter as no one would listen to them; even so they remained determined to keep telling the story and did so until the end. Fred's name was not on the local War Memorial. After all, he had already won the Military Medal for gallantry and been mentioned in Dispatches and yet he was now allegedly a coward.'

David then went on to relate the story I had previously heard, only this time from two others' point of view, but all were corroborating each other; even down to the fracas in the bomb crater, where Smith had dropped his gun. I could sense a strong case was building, but I still needed something more concrete, and as he had mentioned Smith's gun, I simply asked, 'Did you ever find out what happened to the revolver Smith had dropped?'

'Yes, the men trod it into the mud, which made it impossible for Smith to retrieve.'

'No sorry, I meant did any one find it and give it back to him?'

'I believe it was discretely found by a Seth Ambrose who hid it in his kit and smuggled it out of the war zone and eventually back home to England. The Ambrose family are one of several I have not been able to trace and I know Seth would have a wealth of information as he was very close to Fred.'

I could not believe my ears. Here we had the possibility that one of the most important pieces of evidence could possibly be in the country; stolen by one of the men who saw it all; a man who risked a court martial if he had been found with it and a possible death sentence in wartime, especially World War 1.

I left the family with a huge thank you, as they had opened up new doors and promised to keep them informed of my progress. They too were excited at my enthusiasm and looked forward to hearing from me.

It was now a long phone call to Captain Hopkirk, the Adjutant at Whittington Barracks to find out if they had any records of the small arms issued to their officers. To my astonishment, they had records going back to the 1890s.

'Captain Hopkirk, it's Clive White from the *Mail*. I am trying to check what type of revolver was issued to a Lieutenant Smith in 1914. Can you help me?' I asked.

'I can answer that now,' he replied. 'It will undoubtedly be a Webley and likely to be a Mk IV .455 calibre.'

'You know your weapons, Captain,' I replied. 'I was wondering if there was any further detail you could give me. For example, do you have a record of what weapon was issued and to whom – serial numbers etcetera?'

'Now Mr White, it's my turn to ask questions. What's all this about?'

So began my telephone call which lasted an hour, detailing the whole history and at the end he said it would be messy and thought it unlikely I would be permitted to have such information.

It isn't often I get annoyed with the stupidity of the bureaucracy in the Forces but I was so convinced that there had been a crime committed with the full approval of the Army that I was not going to let go of this one, especially when he told me he would have to ask approval.

'Why?' I asked, 'when the information is in your

museum records. This is ridiculous.'

This made him dig his heels in even more. 'I will write to you shortly with my answer, Mr White.'

'That's fine,' I replied, but I emphasised, 'If I do not have the information within a week, the headline in the *Mail* will be such that the Army continues to cover up a murder.'

'You can't do that.'

'Oh yes, we can. If we feel the Army is being obstructive, we can take whatever action we like in the public interest, and murder *is certainly* in the public interest.'

'But it's not a murder. You only think this could have happened.'

'But Captain, I don't. I have the original statements from the men involved, including the words from three officers and about twenty other ranks. We also have a statement from a Captain, stating that the Army ordered him to change his statement and when he refused, he was pushed aside.

'Now Captain, if you want that headline and a campaign run by the *Mail* to get justice, then you are welcome, but I have a feeling you will ring me at the *Mail* with full cooperation. The number's in the book.' And with that, I rang off.

I should have known that the conversation would stir up a hornets' nest as an Under Secretary from the Ministry of Defence came into the *Mail* with an appointment to see the editor, and of course I was invited. It was a good job he was not in the diplomatic corps because first, he tried to throw his weight around and second, he began to threaten no cooperation with the *Mail*.

Well, that was like red rag to a bull for George and the poor sod went out wishing he had never been born. He also left knowing that George would feature him and his responses in the following morning's *Mail*, which he did. You have never seen such a change of attitude so quick and within twelve hours of that article with its hint of an Army cover-up, Captain Hopkirk rang with all the information I needed and a very sheepish, 'If there is anything more I can do to help, please let me know.'

The results were very enlightening. Smith's revolver was a Webley Mk IV, serial number 198342 and it was reported damaged and lost in battle. His second, a Webley Mk VI, was handed back when he was demobbed in1918.

'Let me know how you get on,' the Captain remarked at the end of the conversation.

'Of course I will. Thanks,' I replied, replacing the receiver. 'At the same time as everyone else. You can buy a damn paper and read it for yourself,' I added.

I now had the impetus to go all out to find that revolver and the first stop was to go back to Wolverhampton to see Irvine.

It was of course the usual scenario, a sit down in the comfortable chair, a general chat, with a cup of tea and because I enjoyed the last one, he included a scone and we were back to business. I was able to apprise him of events so far and told him I was making progress.

'Now Irvine, the next is up to you. After I had seen the granddaughter of Captain Harmsworth, she said that Corporal Slack's family might know the whereabouts of Smith's gun. It gave me the idea to contact the South Staffs to see if there were any records left of who was issued with what in the Regiment and to my surprise they even gave me the serial number of the gun Smith was issued with; the one that he used to kill Fred.'

'You're with me now then, are you, Clive?'

'Yes I'm convinced, but we need more concrete evidence than just words. The finding of that gun would change everything. Corporal Slack's grandson has kept an amazing amount of notes and he believes that Seth Ambrose was the last of them to have the gun and that he smuggled it back into the country; but he cannot trace him. Have you any idea where they could have gone to live?'

'Gosh! They left here in the fifties and I haven't seen them since. Mind you, I did get Christmas cards from them, but they stopped about twenty years ago.'

My heart sank, I thought this was going to be the end of the line and then he said, 'I suppose we could look at the postmark. That would give us a clue, wouldn't it?' Irvine asked.

I could not believe what I was hearing; Irvine actually had cards and their envelopes from twenty years ago. I left him to it and returned to London to organise the researchers with other work.

It was a good seven days later when I received a fax from Irvine clearly showing that a Bill Ambrose had sent him a card in 1973 which was clearly postmarked in Walsall. It was now a job for the researchers. There were twenty-seven Ambroses in the phone book and sixty-three on the electoral register. One hour later, I had the name and address and all those living in the house old enough to vote, that is. It was to be my next visit.

I decided to call on the off chance, as I felt phoning might scare them off. If they had the weapon in their possession, they would most definitely not have a licence and for that, they could face a prison sentence if it was found on them; so the last thing I wanted was them to throw it away for fear of being caught.

My journey to Walsall was a first; it was like most Black Country towns in a state of reconstruction, but I did manage to buy a beautiful leather briefcase from a small back street leather manufacturer, in the old part of the town, for which Walsall was very famous. Then it was out of the town to find Selbourne Grove.

Seth Ambrose had done very well for himself considering his background and the hardship; he had obviously worked very hard and bought this house, a large terraced with a small garden at the front and a large one to the rear, which seemed well kept from over the fence.

I knocked on the front door and immediately an elderly man opened the door to a shout of: 'I'll get it, Dad.'

Racing down the stairs was a young woman in her forties trying to beat the gentleman to the door to meet me.

'I'll deal with it, Dad,' she said, as I was about to introduce myself. 'I'm sorry about this. My dad's had a fall today and he's not himself.'

A very cross elderly man through gritted teeth and with only his lips moving added: 'I'm all right.'

The young woman carried on: 'Can I help you?'

'I hope so. I'm looking for a Mr Ambrose.'

'That's me,' the elderly man replied and before he could say any more his daughter interjected:

'What do you want to see him about?'

I felt like saying his forthcoming wedding, just to lighten the atmosphere but stuck to the business. 'My name is Clive White. I am an investigative reporter for the *Mail* and I have come to ask, what I am hoping is the son of Seth Ambrose, about the murder of a Fred Wearing in 1916, by a man called Smith.'

'Graham Smith?' he snarled with the venom of a cobra.

The elderly man nearly fainted, holding on to his daughter for grim death.

'Are you all right, Dad?' she asked.

'Yes I am,' he said, tears beginning to run down his face.

'Know him–' he began, only to be interrupted by his

daughter inviting me in off the step.

'You had better come in, Mr White. My dad can tell you all about him.'

I walked into the hall of this immaculately kept mid Victorian terraced house, with its beautiful stained glass windows on the inner door and a splendid terrazzo floor. The high ceiling with its moulded plaster frieze, and electric lit chandelier looked absolutely beautiful. I was then ushered through one of the seven doors off the hall into another lovely room with its broad wood upright piano.

'Nice,' I said, caressing the smooth wood on the piano.

'My name's Sharon, Mr White and Seth Ambrose was my grandfather. Please sit down. Her father followed us into the room and sat down opposite.

'I'm William. Bill,' he said. 'Please call me Bill. You have brought an old man joy to his ears.'

'Why's that?' I asked.

'You are the first person outside of friends and family to say that you are investigating the murder of Fred by that evil bastard called Smith because that's what he was.

'Fred Wearing was my father's best friend. He saved my dad's life twice and those of several others. He saw Smith murder Fred and so did many of his friends and others for that matter. But no one would believe them. The officers wouldn't listen and they weren't even allowed to make a report. It was rumoured that Smith was the bastard son of a lord who had to be protected at all costs, so it was an almighty cover-up.

'My dad could not let the matter rest and made me promise that if he didn't succeed in his life time, I would continue. I tried but as time passed, I seemed to become that silly bugger in the corner with a cross to bear. Do you know, Mr White, they didn't even put his name on the War Memorial – a man who in my opinion should have won the VC at least twice.'

'We all have times like that, Bill. I too have become embroiled in this business and could now be considered that silly old bugger, but I at least have the *Mail* supporting me.'

'Would you like a cup of coffee, Mr White?' Sharon asked.

'No thanks.'

'Tea?' she asked.

'I'd love one.'

'You should have said, Mr White. How do you like it?'

'Strong, with a little milk and no sugar.'

'There's my dad rambling on and it's you that have come to ask the questions.'

'No, it's fine. This is precisely what I want to hear and I want Fred's name cleared as much as you do.'

'Is there any chance?' Bill asked.

'Two weeks ago I would have said fifty-fifty. Today, seventy-five, twenty-five and I too will not rest until Fred's name is cleared and a conviction lies on the perpetrator.'

Whilst Sharon made the tea, I briefly told them what I had discovered, raising my voice so that Sharon could hear whilst she was in the kitchen.

'Is Irvine still alive then?' Bill asked. 'I used to see him now and then, until we moved here. Dad bought this house, and the journey from here to Wolverhampton and nearly to Heath Town took almost the morning, so you tend to drift apart and of course we went to different schools. I suppose it's inevitable. I'd like to see him again, just for old times' sake.'

'He's still living at Tremont Street, number 14.'

'No, he's kidding you, Mr White. He's well off, is our Irvine. He lives in Penn and has a big house off Mount Road, Wolverhampton and stays at Tremont Street as he refuses to leave. He now owns the whole row, both sides, apart from two or three. They are worthless but the land isn't.

'He loves Tremont Street and stays there when he has a row with Clara, his wife. His three children are grown up and away now, but he looked after them well.'

'Gosh, you have surprised me. I thought he was content to simply live there.'

'He is. He loves it. I think it is those two leather chairs by the fireplace that he loves. I know if the chairs were removed, the house will fall down and he with it. I don't think he relishes full time with his Clara. It's not that he isn't fond of her – he just loves to be on his own.'

Sharon re-entered with the tea and a box of papers which she handed to me. 'These are my dad's and many are what his dad managed to get shortly after the war – the first one of course.'

I started to read the papers and as with all the others, the message was the same: soldiers saw Fred Wearing shot and whilst they believed it was Smith, it could have been the Germans. The proof was in Fred's grave.

I began thinking aloud, much to the fascination of the two of them who listened intently.

'These papers now confirm that Smith has made a huge error in his statement. He's implied he had ordered Fred to go forward... but why do that when the men had been ordered back to their lines and were waiting for Captain Harmsworth's order to attack again? I'm sorry, just thinking aloud.'

'Don't worry, it's interesting,' Sharon replied.

This was another piece of evidence which I had not expected and one which proved Smith was a liar too, as he would not have gone against a senior officer's orders.

'In the beginning I had a doubt because it was established that Smith was an evil man and in this case, were the men using Fred's death opportunistically to get rid of Smith? No one had said why the men were nearby or how they got there. So far they had all referred to the fracas in the shell crater. Until now! Two of the notes, possibly statements refer to the moment they raced out, apparently regardless of their own safety to help him. A note also refers to three of them trying to get back to their lines as they were well to the fore. This was long after the retreat had been sounded when they heard the sound of English voices and made their way towards them. This to some degree confirms that some of them thought that Fred was in trouble whilst others were there by chance. No one however, actually saw Smith shoot him.

'That's where I hope you come in, Mr Ambrose. I have to be honest with you. I have been told that you have Smith's gun.'

'Who told you that?' Sharon asked, a little shocked at the question.

'It was actually in a statement made some thirty years ago,' I replied, telling a white lie to save my sources and their embarrassment.

'No, Dad hasn't got the gun, Mr White. He wouldn't have anything like that,' Sharon said, now being very protective of her old dad.

'Oh that's a pity, as I've heard from several people that it was smuggled into the country and that that your father brought it in; but of course time confuses reality.' I paused for a moment, trying to think of a way through her fears; she was so obviously terrified that we were talking about a gun and yet for me it was becoming the most important part of the case which could condemn Smith.

'Would you have any idea if he did have it?' I continued somewhat nonchalantly. 'If so, would you know where it may have gone? Perhaps it's mentioned in the papers?'

'I can't remember,' she added nervously.

We sat in total silence for what seemed like minutes, and the only movement was me drinking my cup of tea until I broke the silence:

'Could I possibly borrow these papers just for a few days? I'll return them quickly.'

'Of course you can, Mr White. Dad won't mind. Will you?' He nodded his head in acquiescence.

'Thank you. I am hoping to find the whereabouts of the gun, as it really could be a key piece of the puzzle. On the other hand, it could clear Smith of murder...'

'But not of taking the credit for what Fred did that day,' he added angrily.

'No. There is no question of that. It is quite clear from everyone that Fred did an amazing thing that day.'

It was very rude of me I suppose when someone is talking to you, but I glanced at one of the papers Sharon had given me and noticed it was from a Private Charles Blackledge. He was one of the three that were scurrying back to their lines, but when they heard English voices they made their way towards them. It was the last paragraph that I began reading. Blackledge states he distinctly heard one of the men shouting: 'You're a snivelling coward!' and it wasn't the officer. It was a man with a strong Black Country accent, which Fred had. Smith's accent was a mixture of Black Country and Geordie, which of course would be likely as both his mother and stepfather came from the Newcastle area. He also stated that although he couldn't remember exactly, he thought the officer said the moment they all jumped into the crater, 'I had to shoot him! He was a coward.' This of course was denied by Smith by virtue of the report he put in about the incident.

I handed the letter to Bill and asked him to read it.

'My eyes are bad, Sharon. Will you read it and tell me

what it's about, there's a love?' he said.

Sharon carefully read the letter during which time Bill remained very quiet; in fact, he had been quiet throughout most of the conversation so far, which I thought was unusual for someone with a tale to tell.

He then showed me a copy of a statement made by a Major Fortesque after interviewing a Lieutenant Smith who it had appeared had interfered with one of the nurses.

'It was the notes underneath that made it very interesting,' he said, handing me the papers.

'Good lord, this *is* interesting,' I replied. 'He writes: "I didn't believe his story. To me it was totally untrue and I warned him about his future conduct. I warned him of his possible capital conduct and told him I would shoot him myself if he appeared in front of me again."'

This didn't take the matter further but it was an interesting development which highlighted Smith's character.

'Where did you get this?' I asked.

'I don't know. In the beginning my father looked everywhere for support and met dozens of people.'

This was yet another little piece of evidence which confirmed and added light to Irvine's story.

'Mr White, I have often thought of this moment and so did my father. We thought the gun, it was a revolver you know, would have no real value on its own and we needed to get rid of it. We knew it was against the law and if it fell into the wrong hands it would be deadly.'

My heart sank. 'I can understand you wanting to get rid of it, but this gun would have been of the most importance, as I think I know where the bullet is that killed Fred. I am now fully convinced of Fred's innocence and Smith's guilt and it is my bet that it was fired from the gun you had to get rid of.'

'I didn't say I got rid of it, Mr White. I have a tin box with a lock on it which my son Randle now has.'

'Dad!' Sharon exclaimed. 'What if the children had opened it and found the gun?'

'Darling, they didn't and it was only last year I gave the tin to Randle as I'm getting on a bit. It has not been looked at since my father brought it back. It was his bit of Fred, his best friend.'

'Where is it? Can I see it?' I asked excitedly.

'As I said, it's with my son. He has all my papers, my will, insurance policies. You know the sort of things and I have the key – it's in my room.'

I was absolutely dumbfounded. I sat in the chair, unable to speak. Sharon later described my expressions as that of a clown with a smile from ear to ear. I could not take in what had just been said.

Bill continued, giving me chance to recover: 'He doesn't know what's in it for obvious reasons. It is to be opened in the event of my death. It has all my papers in it, my medals and the gun. I have given a full explanation of why it is in my possession and I have explained about Lieutenant Smith and my thoughts about the gun which has one round fired and five rounds remaining. He was the coward, Mr White and not Fred. How can an officer leading a charge have only fired one round?'

We were left speechless, just looking at each other, wondering what to say or do next.

This was another piece of circumstantial but supporting evidence. According to Bill there was only one round fired when Smith was leading a charge. Furthermore, if he had blown up the machine guns and charged down the trenches, surely he would have fired more than one round?

'Would you like another cup of tea, Mr White? I think we all need one, don't you?' Sharon asked, breaking the shocked silence which had taken over.

'Mr White, where's the bullet?'

'I'm hoping Fred's still got it, I believe it was buried with him and I now think he will have the last laugh. Could you contact Randle and ask him if he could bring the tin over?'

'Yes, of course I can.'

'Don't tell him what's in the tin. At this stage, it's better he doesn't know for his own legal safety... in case anything happens en route.'

'He doesn't live too far away but he's not home till five. I'll ring him then.' Bill added.

'This calls for a celebration,' I said, then made my excuses that I was going to buy a bottle of champagne. I called for a taxi and went into Walsall town centre.

My primary concern was the revolver. Was there anyone alive that would still want this matter hushed up? Would it be safe to give it to the police? How could we protect it? It was such a vital piece of historical and criminal evidence. I called into the Post Office and requested the use of a telephone and was shown to a booth where I had the privacy I needed and rang George.

He was as excited as I was, but like all editors, he had to make sure of the legality of the situation. He rang off, asking me to wait for his response which I did and two damned hours later I was told to take the gun and its contents to a forensic science laboratory in Warwick. Of course, we were advised not to contaminate anything and if it was loose in the tin, to take that as well, complete with its contents. I also had to be careful as the bullets may have been at the end of their useful life and could be dangerous. Whatever we had, we needed to get it there before 9 a.m. the following morning.

All I needed now was the gun.

Chapter 17
Difficult Questions

I returned to Bill Ambrose' home an hour later than I had
intended to find that Randle had already arrived and with
him was that little tin box. I hadn't forgotten the bottle of
champagne, which I immediately asked to be put in the
freezer for half an hour.

That little tin box was not so little; it was a trunk: 2 feet
x 1 foot 6 inches x 1 foot 3 inches, with a very strong clasp
and lock. Bill handed me the key and I placed the trunk
on the table to open it. We were all standing round
waiting for Aladdin's genie to come out as I opened the
lid.

'You do the honours, Mr White. You take it out – you've
earned it. I just wish my dad was alive to see this.'

I started removing many bundles of papers, several of
which were statements which Seth had collected in the
early twenties from friends and the like who had served
with him in the South Staffs during World War 1.

I then removed a little cardboard box containing Seth's
medals; even he was mentioned in Dispatches and had
served in six theatres of the war. The next item was bar of
Army carbolic soap, shaped like and the size of a brick,
stamped with the crown and GR (George Rex) just to
ensure the soldier knew who it belonged to. At least that
brought a titter in the present gloom.

Old Bill was nearly in tears; Sharon definitely was
when I read out the citation for Seth's gallantry award.

Then my fingers touched the material which was wrapped around the gun and I could feel the shape as I carefully picked it up by its barrel. We could all hear a pin drop as I placed it on the gleaming white table cloth and began to peel back its cover.

Slowly but surely the revolver began to show itself – a wicked weapon of murder, not of war and there it was, the first bit of concrete evidence we had, but was it Smith's revolver?

Looking at the revolver I couldn't help thinking about its last moments when Smith attempted to shoot Henry and how the gun was hustled away from him. How it was lost in the mud and now after so many years, it was here on the table. You could still see the mud, the mud that had seen the death of hundreds of thousands of our troops; the mud that had saved Henry; the mud that poor Fred Wearing had fallen into when shot by Smith. Now I could see the bullets in the chamber and one with its empty case, the one which killed Fred. Now thankfully, I could see the innards were clean, the mud hadn't touched them; in fact it had protected the chamber. Could Fred get his revenge even in death?

The revolver lay on the table and we all stared at it in silence, which was broken when Randle moved to pick it up.

'No don't!' I said, almost shouting. 'I'm sorry Randle, but it is going to the forensic science lab and we daren't contaminate it. Believe it or not, Smith's DNA may be still on it somewhere,' I said excitedly, explaining what the new DNA techniques were. 'Especially as your dad has kept it in perfect condition all these years. Come on, let's make sure it's Smith's.'

I put my pen through the trigger guard and lifted the revolver up to the light. Can you see a number?' I asked, everyone's eyes fixed on the gun.

'Is this it?' Randle asked, starting to read slowly and steadily: 'One... nine... eight... three...'

'It's his! It's Smith's gun,' I shouted excitedly as Randle finished calling out the final two numbers – '... four... two.'

No one heard the rest as I was too excited for anything. 'Let's celebrate, Sharon. Fetch the champagne and the glasses.'

Two minutes later, I was popping the cork and pouring four ice cold glasses of Mercier and we were all congratulating ourselves on our achievement. I proposed a toast to Fred which brought tears to Bill's eyes and then he added: 'To my dad's best friend.'

We sat around the table, smiles on our faces until Bill asked: 'Is this enough to do something about it?'

'It is a big step forward. We have to confirm whether it was possible that Smith fired the gun. They have to see what DNA can be traced from the gun, if any, after all this time. Then we have to obtain the bullet and that means an application to the court to exhume Fred's body.'

In fact, the *Mail's* legal team decided that a direct application to the Home Secretary would be the best route as several people mentioned in this débacle included a former Home Secretary long since dead, together with other very high profile people.

'But the first thing we must do is get the gun to the forensic team in Warwick and I've got to tell the police what we are doing as the gun looks to be useable. It may be they will escort me, I don't know yet. One good thing, we do know now that this gun was issued to a Second Lieutenant Smith, but we don't know if any others used it.

'It is possible when all the facts are known that Smith's relatives would object to a court application for exhumation or object to the publication of what we have discovered.

'Think about it. Nearly all the men under his control, not only during the war, but before and after, hated Smith. Was this a way of getting back at him. Farfetched I know, but a good lawyer could make a very strong case.

'We have to play this game very slowly but surely. We must not let any of the possible opposition have a whiff of what we are doing because at this moment, we are not there. We now need the proof that the bullet in Fred's body was fired from this revolver.'

'It is. I know it is. My dad always used to say it was the bloody gun that killed Fred. He hated Smith. He hated everything about him. He could not mention his name without wanting to spit out the words.'

'Do you know what happened to Smith?' I asked, pretending not to know anything.

'I understand he went off with some woman in Brighton or Glasgow and was never seen again. The papers made a lot of fuss at the time. I've got some copies here, Mr White.'

'Clive, please.'

'You can borrow them if they are of any interest to you.'

'Very much so. Thanks.'

I thought I would just tempt a response by suggesting that Smith had been murdered.

'Oh! Don't know anything about that,' Bill said quickly.

My taxi had arrived and it was time for me to leave what had been a very exciting development in the investigation. I could tell after such a short time Bill was sad to see me go, but I could also sense his relief that his obligation to his father had been fulfilled.

We all said our tearful goodbyes and I walked towards the taxi.

'Sharon, I just want a quick private word with Mr White. I won't be two minutes,' Bill said.

'All right Dad, but don't catch cold.'

The moment we were out of earshot Bill whispered, 'You know, don't you?'

I knew exactly what he was talking about and whispered back, 'Yes I do. The LMS Railway repair yard?'

'Yes, that's right.'

'I am not going do anything about that. I think everyone has suffered enough. Smith was an evil man and all they did was save John Ellis a job,' I added, showing off my new found knowledge.

'Who's he then?' Bill asked.

'He was the public executioner at the time.'

'Oh right,' he replied nonchalantly, totally unimpressed with my historical knowledge.

'My father confided in me towards the end of his life and told me everything that happened, hoping I would take over his quest. I found it taking over our lives and had to stop. I know now, I can feel it. It's coming to the end.' Tears welled up in his eyes. 'Thank you,' he said.

I managed to get the gun to Warwick for nine o'clock the following morning. If the tests proved positive, I felt that this, together with the other evidence, would be sufficient enough to warrant an exhumation.

Bearing in mind all the effort we had so far put in so far, it was quite a wrench to leave the gun with complete strangers at the forensic science laboratory but... that's progress.

I took William Ambrose' papers back to the office and left them with one of the researchers to read through, thinking they would be simply relating to the stories I had already heard, but later, when June Davies shouted across the office for me to have a look at some notes, I knew it was something special.

She had discovered several statements and notes made by another junior officer at the time of Fred's shooting and it is very clear that it was a major talking point for many of the lower ranks; so much so, the officers were all becoming very worried and began covering their backsides by writing notes and making statements, witnessed by one or another. By the look of their notes, they were not going to be the fall guys for the generals or for Smith.

In fact, when I read a statement from a Major Fortesque he recounts an interview with a Lieutenant Bakewell, who clearly states that he had interviewed several Privates and they all stated that Private Wearing was shot by Second Lieutenant Graham Smith.

In his informal statement, which was signed and witnessed, Major Fortesque recounts a quick interview with a Brigadier Reed who orders him to withdraw the statements and to forget the whole thing. It was intimated that the order came from above. He also writes that the Lieutenant was dissatisfied with this explanation and shortly afterwards, at a second meeting, it was relayed to him that the other ranks were also troubled. He notes the men were very angry and mutinous.

The officers were ordered not to say anything. It was pressure from the generals and the like, but no one knew exactly where and who from, which made then extremely nervous and feeling vulnerable.

Whilst these findings didn't take us any further, they did confirm what others had said, but with more emphasis, as these were officers that were clearly concerned at the state of affairs that existed at the time. It would seem that some men from other ranks had witnessed the incident that led to Fred's death.

I would have liked to trace one of these men but I knew time would have taken its toll and statements by relatives are worth very little unless properly noted at the time.

This was a surprising revelation as previous evidence

simply related to that given by a number of men from Tremont Street, their friends and all those in Fred's platoon although none had actually seen the shooting, Now we had independent statements from other soldiers and officers from other platoons confirming they had seen the incident. We have to remember that this was indeed possible; the battlefield was large and the troops were in a state of confusion as they had been given the order to pull back; there were also hundreds of casualties being carried back and many could have easily passed by at that moment.

We spent several days trying to trace the regiments these men belonged to, managing to trace only one relative, but unfortunately he was unable to add anything further as he hadn't really known his uncle and, as his only surviving relative he inherited his house, but the search went on.

At this point in time, the evidence from those in Tremont Street could be construed as circumstantial and would only be supported if the ballistic report was favourable to their cause; although it was obvious to everyone that they were sure of their facts.

However, the other statements were a different kettle of fish, as witnesses confirmed they had actually seen the shooting. I now realised that in a modern-day court of law there was enough hard evidence to obtain a conviction without the ballistic evidence, but here because most of the players were very old or dead, we still needed the ballistic report.

The more the researchers looked into the new statements and notes the more astonished I became that the Army was able to cover up all the evidence and prevent all the witnesses from coming forward and telling their stories.

It was apparent that there were numerous transfers of

men, promotions of officers who were then also transferred to other units, as with Captain Harmsworth; even groups of troops were transferred to other theatres of war.

As Teresa Wall told me, when her grandfather was transferred back to the South Staffs, he found that Graham Smith had been transferred to warmer climes away from the troubles, but I know he would have had a torrid time as news travels fast in large companies of men and it would not have been long before his new unit would know all about him. Her grandfather was appalled at the amount of effort which was put in by the top brass to remove all possible traces of the cover-up but also which was most important, to break up all the groups that were or may have been involved at the time.

Chapter 18
It All Begins to Make Sense

I couldn't believe how the pieces were falling into place and if the ballistic report and the DNA investigations were positive as well, we would have had the strongest case possible to convict Smith.

However, George wanted the *Mail* to go further as the story was grossing enormous revenues and our readership was increasing rapidly. He also wanted this story to run indefinitely. It was now time to contact the Army to get their view of the situation and here I was charged by George to personally investigate.

I spent the next week trying to make contact through all the usual channels but seemed stalled at every point. They were refusing to answer letters, faxes and telephone calls. Even threat of court action didn't soften their attitude. From all my conversations with officers down to the secretaries and receptionists I got the distinct impression they were trying to put a block on the story.

In the end I had to admit I had gone as far as I could from my lowly position and had to illicit the help of George, my editor.

George would never pussyfoot around and went straight for the jugular. He telephoned the offices in Whitehall and spoke to a receptionist, requesting to speak to Field Marshall, Sir Willoughby Blackledge.

'Who is speaking please?'

'George Stevenson, Editor of the *Mail*.'

He waited the customary four minutes and was then told that Sir Willoughby was not in the building at the moment.

'Oh, thank you,' George replied, 'but that is not strictly true is it because I can see his car? So would you please give him this message? Take it down verbatim please. Friday's *Mail*, front page headline: Army covers up a murder and a rape by one of its officers. They refuse to comment on the cover-up. Why and who are they protecting?' He paused to let it sink in.

'Have you got that verbatim?' he continued.

There was total silence. 'Hello?' George said in a questioning tone. 'I asked whether you got that message?'

'Er. Yes. Yes I have, Mr Stevenson.'

'Tell him that if he wishes to talk about it I will be in my office between nine and five tomorrow.'

'Can I have your number please sir?'

'Yes. The *Mail*. It's in the book, just ask for me,' at which point he put the phone down.

Within half an hour George received a call from one of Sir Willoughby's aides, wanting to know what it was all about.

'Thank you for your call, but I left a message with your receptionist explaining what it was all about, asking to speak to Sir Willoughby. Now I don't want to appear rude but we have been running an article in the *Mail* explaining how the Army covered up a murder, which we can prove and we wanted your comments. Now if he does not want to make a comment, then the headline I gave your receptionist will appear in Friday's paper.'

The following morning, Peter Pugh, a civil servant plus the Assistant Defence Secretary George Blakewell, the MP for Barkston Ash, plus Sir Willoughby himself arrived in reception to be greeted by George and, of course, the two senior members of the Board with Sir John Plunkett-Ward, the *Mail's* Chairman.

'Come on up, gentleman,' Sir John said, leading the way upstairs to the Board Room. The introductions were made and he invited them to sit down whilst Trevor Pellow, a junior reporter in only his second week in the job was on duty to make tea and coffee. Once the refreshments were dispensed, I was invited in, introduced to everybody and sat down.

Sir Willoughby opened the proceedings; he was clearly old school and thought that he could dictate to anyone and they would immediately oblige.

'I want you to drop this story about Wearing immediately,' he said, speaking directly to Sir John, who already seemed a little out of his depth.

'Why?' George chipped in.

'Not in the national interest.'

'Who says?' George asked.

'I do,' Sir Willoughby said in a pompous sort of way 'and my colleagues do,' he added, receiving nods from the others.

Sir John looked at George as if to say carry on, which opened the door for him to attack.

'What is your view on the matter, Mr Blakewell, as I am surprised you want to get mixed up in a cover-up of a murder?'

'And two rapes,' I added.

'Yes thank you, Clive. And two rapes.'

It was clear that Blakewell was in a state of shock; in fact, he could hardly respond, except to ask: 'What do you mean?'

'Clive, you explain,' George said.

'It's a simple case really. This fellow Wearing was murdered by an Army officer, a Second Lieutenant Smith during the First World War. It was covered up by an Army General simply because the boy's father was a member of the House of Lords and a personal friend of the General.'

'And it would appear that Sir Willoughby still wants to protect that General's reputation,' George added.

Blakewell was again stunned, looking at the civil servant for some guidance but none was forthcoming.

We sat, waiting for someone to at least make a comment, but George had had enough.

'Gentleman, what do you want? We cannot and will not stop this story, as it is in the national interest and we do have evidence, strong evidence as to the truth of the matter, so what do you want?'

Blakewell could see the difficulties for him in the political sense and asked:

'Could I have a word with my colleagues?'

We all left, leaving our visitors to discuss the problem they were facing. It was about an hour before we were called back, only to find on returning we were left with Peter Pugh, the civil servant and the Assistant Defence secretary, George Blakewell to finalise the matter. In other words, Sir Willoughby did not want the embarrassment of losing and after wasting another hour with chit chat, we made a promise to keep them informed of progress.

But one thing it did signify was that they were worried that it would open a can of worms, which perhaps they were unable to deal with and possibly it showed we may be on the right track and someone did know something and wanted it hushed up.

Ironically, whenever there is interference from political sources, especially when civil servants are involved, ninety per cent of the time they are trying to cover up something, either legitimate or otherwise. From a newspaper's perspective, it's worth investing more time to see what's going on underneath. George's trick was to keep ruffling a few feathers to see what would turn up and Willoughby's visit was just that.

Chapter 19
The Beginning of the End

When Irvine had finished his story, you, the reader, may well have been as incensed as I was. I was certainly determined to do something about it. Of course, all the protagonists were dead and long forgotten except a few of Fred's family relatives whom Irvine kept in touch with or at least knew where they were. Add to that all their families and friends, who continued to tell anyone that would listen about the biggest miscarriage of justice in British history and you had a very powerful little band of people who would never give up.

I had to smile at the way Noel, Irvine's father had collated all the information. He had detailed the facts as explicitly as he could and then slipped in a character reference just to back up or confirm that Fred was a good egg. For example, you will remember how Fred rescued a Tony Price from the battlefield after he had lost a leg in a charge. He detailed how Price explained what Fred had done, how he carried him back to the British lines and how he was eventually shipped back to England.

Price detailed how Fred had taken him on a scavenging trip where he taught him to catch rabbits. They would wait by the run, teasing the rabbits out and catching them to bring back to share with the others. He would never keep anything for himself; it was always to share with others.

Fred took Price on an unofficial scout round where they

bumped into a small three-man German patrol.

Price tells the story:

'Wait here,' Fred told me whilst he went around the back of them. Price states he moved out of sheer fear and was seen by the Germans. The Germans called out 'Hände hoch!' ('Hands up!') and Price immediately held his hands high.

'Don't shoot! Don't shoot!' Price shouted which alerted Fred who immediately came on the attack. Apart from a bayonet each they were unarmed and, of course, Price's bayonet was taken from him. Fred approached the group and watched. He made some animal sounds and one of the men went over to see what was going on. The moment he was out of sight of the others, Fred took his bayonet and clubbed the German on the back of the head with the handle and knocked him out.

The other two began calling out 'Freidrich' but of course there was no reply. They began to retrace Friedrich's steps with Price leading the way, a German rifle stuck in his back. It was too easy for Fred this time as he now had the German's rifle. They passed Fred who was hiding in the undergrowth. Price was still leading when one of the Germans spotted their fallen comrade. They pushed Price to the side as one soldier bent over to look at him, whilst the other nervously looked around. That was Fred's cue. He knocked the second German out cold and had the rifle pointing at the other.

'Disarm them, Tony,' Fred said, 'and take off their helmets. Then we'll take them in. Just shove that bike in the undergrowth together with their helmets. We'll get them later.'

Once the Germans had come to, they began to march them the back to our lines. To Price's surprise, Fred had taken them behind the German lines because he knew there were more rabbits there.

...

They managed to avoid the gunfire and eventually they arrived back at the base and turned the prisoners over to the guards, reporting to the Captain.

'Privates Wearing and Price reporting, sir,' Fred announced. 'We have brought these three prisoners in, sir. We found them scouting our perimeter and thought it better to bring them to you, rather than kill them,' Fred added, winking at Tony.

'All right Privates, report to the Adjutant first thing in the morning and give a full report.'

'Sir,' they both said in unison.

'Come on, Tony, come with me. We are not leaving that bike the Huns left behind or their helmets,' Fred said the moment they were released.

'We can't go back there. It's their territory.'

'Come on, don't be silly. I'm not leaving the stuff there.'

This was the trust the men had in Fred's judgement. Price followed him without question.

It didn't take two minutes to find the place and to pick up the bike and the helmets, but also in the scuffle, one of the Germans had dropped his wallet which Fred found and wanted to return to its owner.

The next thing everyone saw was Fred, and Tony sitting on the crossbar, riding into the compound on the German bicycle, with three rabbits held aloft.

The following morning they reported to the Adjutant as ordered. Fred advised Tony to say nothing and leave the talking to him.

He walked to the Adjutant's tent and saluted. 'Privates Wearing and Price, sir. We are ordered to give you full particulars on how we captured the three prisoners. We saw them creeping around and thought we would get them.

'Sir, Private Price was very brave and pretended to

surrender whilst I hit two of them and took their weapons. It was very brave of him as he could have been shot and that's about it, sir.'

'Is that correct, Private Price?'

'Yes sir,' he replied, totally shocked at what Fred had said.

Both of them were awarded the coveted mentioned in Dispatches – a gallantry award.

This was typical of what Fred would do for his friends, but most importantly he was a thoughtful man. He handed over the German's wallet to the Adjutant as he wanted to make sure its owner got it back, simply because it had his family photos in it, which at least gave a bit of cheer to a man whose war was over.

I believed what Irvine had to say and joined him in his campaign. I had the information and evidence which would start the beginning of the end of the quest for justice for Fred Wearing and, most importantly, I had the gun that was allegedly used to shoot him.

Chapter 20
Political Interference

I had almost come to the end of my investigation. All we were waiting for now was the forensic team to finish their research, but we were already pretty sure it would confirm my thoughts, that the gun was the murder weapon. If so, we would then start the last battle to get Fred Wearing's name in its rightful place, engraved on the War Memorial, a place where he would be always honoured and remembered.

I was back in the office when I received a phone call from Dr William Field of the Firearms Section of the forensic science laboratory.

'Mr White?'

'Speaking,' I replied.

'Bill Field.'

'Good afternoon, Bill,' I said excitedly. 'Come on, put me out of my misery.'

'Well Clive, I have read all your notes and as you say everything points to the possibility that this was the murder weapon. All the bullets are in the gun except one, but the casing remains. We have of course, checked the numbers with the Military and this gun was issued to a Lieutenant Smith.

'However, there is another problem that's raised its head. Now don't be worried, it's not insurmountable. I sent the gun and all the contents to the DNA testing section just in case there was some left on it and there was.

There were two samples but they were from different sources.

'One lot is on the trigger, but there are two different sorts on the handle; there is also some on the barrel. We believe the person who fired the gun was perspiring a great deal as his DNA is on both the handle and trigger. The gun has been well preserved and fortunately, the mud was not all over it. Hope that's helpful?'

'Yes thanks,' I replied, sounding droopy.

'Clive, it's not the end of the world. Try and find someone with the same blood line as Lieutenant Smith and take mouth swab samples that will give us their DNA. Also and this is important, take one from every person you know who may have touched the gun. If any are dead, then take them from blood line relatives, brothers, sisters, children, grandchildren and so on. And don't worry,' he added.

'What if can't find anyone?' I asked.

'Clive, of course you can. There are dozens of people who will share the same blood line. Don't worry.'

'I'll need to show George the findings. Can you fax me them?'

'I sure can. Five minutes, okay? Speak to you later. Bye.'

It was a most wonderful feeling to receive the results of the forensic tests on the gun and the bullets. It was absolutely clear the bullet was fired from Lieutenant Smith's revolver. They had even fired one of the other bullets left in the gun and that too was identical. But as Bill had said, it created another problem, having two different lots of DNA on the weapon. Unless we can trace the owners of those DNA samples, we can no longer say with one hundred per cent certainty that Smith was the only one who had handled the gun; and any good lawyer would argue that Smith may not be the murderer.

Whilst the essence of the story was going well, there was still a niggling doubt in my mind as to why all the alleged crimes committed by the individual had been covered up. It had seemed that every voice raised in this direction had been silenced and that every piece of paper ever written about the topic had been destroyed; that is, apart from the personal papers of those involved.

There was nothing left to lead to the top; nothing that would give a clue as to who or why. What in my mind was so strange was that it could not simply have been carried out by one or two people. There had to be a conspiracy with several involved and all with serious influence in their sphere of activity.

I discussed my concerns with George, my editor as I felt these rich and possibly famous people should not get away with a crime like this. But as he said, the *Mail* had now invested a great deal of money into the investigation and if there was no evidence to find we should be thankful for the wonderful story, for catching the murderer and righting a wrong,

He was right about that; the *Mail* had never received such a huge response to a story. People were sending in money to help the families, believing it was happening now. Many were calling on the phone, sobbing their hearts out that this sort of thing could happen; hundreds were saying that Fred should be given the VC posthumously and many wrote in and said Lieutenant Smith should be stripped of his Military Cross. It really had touched the hearts of the British public and you know what that can be like.

One old lady, who appeared to have been greatly touched by the affair, was a Davina Freeworthy. She contacted the *Mail* and asked for me to call and see her. She hinted that she could add a little more to the story without actually telling me anything, but it was enough for me to get on my bike and hotfoot it to Virginia Water in Surrey. The address alone was enough to attract my attention. She was undoubtedly from a well-healed family as the trappings around the house were not to be sneezed at, to coin a phrase.

I walked to the front door, totally unaware of what this was to be all about, rang the bell and waited. I could hear a few raised voices and got the impression I had arrived at an inappropriate time; in fact, I seemed to be waiting so long I decided to walk away, particularly as the second push of the bell brought no result.

I turned to leave when a young boy, aged about eleven I suppose, together with a man in his forties or fifties opened the door.

'I am so sorry, Mr White for our rudeness, but I will explain. Do please come in.'

'I was to meet a Davina Freeworthy here at ele–'

'That's my mother,' the man said, interrupting me. 'My name is Peter Freeworthy and I am afraid we are having a little family dispute.' He led me into the dining room and invited me to sit at the table opposite a lady who I presumed was Davina Freeworthy, his mother. *(The name has been changed to protect family identity.)*

'Good Morning, Mr White. I too am very sorry for wasting your time but I really do not want to go ahead with this. I have been cajoled into it.'

'Granny, you promised!' the young boy exclaimed.

'You keep out of it. You're too young to know,' Davina snapped back.

'Mother, please don't snap at David like that. You agreed.'

'Well, I've changed my mind and I'm sorry.'

Reporters often are put in a situation like this where they have the embarrassment of just sitting, head turning side to side looking at each contestant as they verbally attack each other. Often it can be amusing; this one was interesting as some titbits of information were mentioned that could be researched.

'I gather it's about our story of Fred Wearing?' I remarked, more as a question as I got up to leave.

'Yes it is,' she replied.

'Well, I had better go, I would rather not cause you any further embarrassment, but, if you do have anything to add, please contact me at the *Mail* and I can assure you we would be interested in what you have to say.

'Fred Wearing saved the lives of hundreds of our servicemen and he was without doubt cruelly murdered. What is not yet known to the public is that by the end of this week, the gun he used, which was sneaked back into this country in 1918 will have been forensically examined and I know the bullet will match the gun.'

'How can you tell that without the bullet?' young David asked.

'Ah, but we do have the bullet but this also is not generally known. It was lodged in the back of Fred's head and buried with him. His body was exhumed last week and the bullet was still there in good condition,' I replied, not telling the truth. 'We all want his name to be in its rightful place on the War Memorial.

'You see, we will prove it was murder and there will be an almighty investigation into who covered it up. Lord Winston Heath, of course, is the number one suspect, but he was helped by those high up in the Army and in the political establishment. It won't take long for our researchers to find out who Winston Heath's friends and associates were.'

Mrs Freeworthy went grey and slumped back in her chair. There was a long pause and, as if wishing to put me in my place she suddenly announced: 'Mr White, I don't normally read the *Mail*. It's *The Times* for me.'

'Of course, I can see that,' I replied a little sarcastically.

'Touché, Mr White, I deserved that.' She paused for a moment. 'My son reads the *Mail* and so does my grandson's teacher. They along with the rest of the country, or so it seems, have been following this story, almost living it. I'm almost afraid to say, Mr White that my family were involved with this at the time. In fact when they were relating the *Mail*'s story to me I was ashamed to say that my father was a personal friend of Winston Heath.

'Mr White, I must have anonymity from this story and I will tell you in full what I am aware of.'

'Guaranteed, Mrs Freeworthy.'

She paused for a moment or two, reflecting on her decision.

'Well, it doesn't look good for my father, Mr White. Thankfully, he's been dead a long time now and so has my mother so that makes it easier. She left him years ago. I was an only child and she took me with her.

'Here goes, Mr White.'

Mrs Freeworthy tells her story...

I was born in India and had all the trappings you could imagine. We had a palace of a place and honestly, you cannot imagine the opulence of it all.

My father was Malcolm Weatherall. He excelled in the Army and was sent to South Africa as a young man. He carried out several daring deeds, going through enemy lines to take messages and he also managed a few other brave things which of course got him noticed very quickly. He lived and loved the Army and when the Boar War started he did the same again. He was then sent to India to quell the rebellions, and again made a first class job of it. All this time he was rising through the ranks on a yearly basis and finally, whilst still in India he was made Major General, responsible for supplies amongst other things.

As a Major General, he had all the trappings of wealth, the mansion, the servants, the horses, the grooms, and the adoration, but not the money; at least none of his own and this is where he first met Lord Winston Heath and his troubles began.

Lord Winston Heath was the owner of several armament factories, amongst other things and whilst on a visit to India, to show the Army the latest field guns, howitzers I think he called them, he met my father, in the hope of supplying them. He gave an excellent account of himself as the guns were all that they were claimed to be. However, at the time there was another British manufacturer that gave an equally good demonstration of its capabilities, so the competition was intense.

Dozens of these weapons were required by the Army and my father had to make the choice and organise the purchase. No one else was actually involved, just him. Not the sort of thing that would happen these days but at the time it was one man who was an officer and a gentleman and no gentleman would cheat.

Business was straightforward; my father would invite each of the manufacturers in turn to dinner at our house and on the following day, he would make his decision. The successful one would be invited back to discuss matters further.

My mother hated all of it and wanted no part of it. My father treated her like a second class citizen. He only loved the Army; his wife was a chattel, his little Memsaab and she would be introduced as that, which she hated. Every time she showed dissent, my father would embarrass my mother by referring to her again as Memsaab and then order her to do small errands for him. His attitude towards her certainly did not help their marriage. When I came along I was a nuisance chattel and the moment I was eleven, he wanted to send me away to boarding school.

But my mother would not have it. I was her only ally and friend.

I recall one day, I was sitting on the stairs when Lord Winston Heath arrived, in all his self-styled importance, to be met by my father and not the servants at the entrance. This was very unusual, as he always liked to show off and have his guests announced, whilst he was allegedly engaged in something or another. My father directed him in, whilst my mother dutifully waited to be introduced.

'This is the little Memsaab,' my father said, showing my mother off as if she were some prized possession.

I was then invited to meet his Lordship and immediately scooted off to my room where I dared not come out until the following morning, but as I grew older I used to hide and listen in. I would never stay in my room.

My mother told me all about this dinner the two men had together, saying: 'That was the time when your father became a criminal.'

Both men had lots to drink and were laughing and joking when my father invited him into the smoking lounge, where naturally, they had to sample the best Virginia cigars. My dear mother, the little Memsaab had to stand and light them and then, of course, she was sent to the ladies' lounge to do some needlepoint or something similar.

However, the rooms were adjacent and when they started talking business my father went over and shut the doors, to stop anyone, including my mother from listening. That was a signal to my mother that something secret was taking place, so it was now her cue to listen in, which she did.

Winston Heath, to use modern language, Mr White, was a crook through and through. There was no doubt about it, particularly when you hear such words as: 'I can make you a very rich man if this order comes to us.'

Followed by my father asking: 'How rich?'

'Very,' Winston Heath replied.

'How much is "very"?'

My mother heard them suddenly stop talking. My father got up from his chair and walked over to the adjoining doors. She raced back to her chair just in time to pick up the needlepoint as he opened the door.

'All is well, Memsaab?' he asked.

'Yes dear,' she replied like the dutiful housewife, who was not allowed to do anything, pour a drink, make a cup of tea, wash up or make a bed.

You can understand why the Indian Nation rebelled against the British; they were treated just like my mother, only without the lifestyle.

He stood at the door just looking until he finally said, 'That's good.' And went back to the other room, ensuring the interconnecting door was properly shut and the conversation started again.

'How much is very rich?' my father asked again.

'Seven thousand pounds.'

'Make it ten and this deal is yours and the next one as well.'

'Ten it is. You drive a hard bargain, Major General.'

'I'll want the money now.'

'I'll pay half next week and the other half when the order is signed and deliveries commence.'

'No, all next week in cash or we can forget the matter. I will not renege on the deal. I am an officer and a gentleman. Just a little strapped for cash.'

Winston Heath chuckled: 'That's a hell of a lot of cash.'

'They're a hell of a lot of cannons.'

'I shall put this on the price to cover it. That will be all right?'

'Of course.'

They shook on the deal and from that moment my father was hooked. He was in Winston Heath's pocket as well as that of the Home Secretary, the MP responsible for Transport and numerous members of the House of Lords. Suffice to say this made him immensely powerful in those days.

In fairness, Winston Heath paid for all the help he ever received. What am I saying! He was nothing but a gangster and his vast fortune was used to bribe all of them, and for all these payments made, he expected one hundred and twenty per cent loyalties which he got from them all.

I don't know how the money was paid, but my mother made notes which she threatened to use when they were divorced. He bought a lot of property over the years from payments received and was very sensible as he did things gradually, did not go over the top to make people suspicious; but in any event, no one would ever suspect a Major General in those days.

My father was knighted and I honestly believe that this was influenced by Winston Heath. My mother would not go to the investiture as she believed he had paid for it, or at least his benefactor had.

However, from then on the two men became firm friends – at least that is what it appeared to be, if anyone can be a friend in that situation!

Winston Heath used to confide in my father; he would talk about his sex life and certainly had one great problem; he couldn't keep it in his trousers. He fancied every skirt he saw and on the odd occasion he would force his attentions on them, particularly if they worked for him. My mother actually thought at one stage she was going to be offered to him.

He had sired a son by one of his secretaries, in Newcastle, I think; then hived her off to live somewhere with another man. I remember hearing him say that this man was a bloody nuisance, always wanting more to keep his mouth shut. He remarked on one occasion that he wished he had got rid of the child in the beginning.

He hadn't any children of his own at the time and didn't want to risk losing the ancestral line which he was proud of; but as in many situations like this he suddenly had one of his own, or so they say. They called him Jonathan. He was not like his father and as he grew up, he despised what his father was doing.

Believe it or not, they wanted me to go out with Jonathan but I thought he was far too old. Anyway, Winston Heath was a lecherous person, always wanting to touch you or feel you. I couldn't stand him or bear him near me. Do you know I was not allowed to complain if he did put his hands on me? I had to grin and bear it.

However, as the illegitimate boy grew up, he was the same as his father; he couldn't leave the women alone and always wanted power over them.

My mother heard he was always in serious trouble; in fact Winston Heath would often say: 'I wish that little bastard hadn't been born.' He was never prosecuted for any of his crimes. You can understand why. They, including Chief Constables, were all mates together.'

'I know dozens of people who feel the same even now. The misery he caused,' I added, interrupting her.

'Who?' she asked.

'The little bastard.' We both smiled.

Mrs Freeworthy continues...

The police were involved on numerous occasions, but my father and his political cronies, including, of course, the Chief Constable, all ensured the crimes of this little runt were covered up, making sure that nothing would reflect on Winston Heath or any of his loyal friends as he was always at pains to point out.

They were too deep into corrupt activities which is where Winston Heath scored; there was no way out and had to assist, becoming more embroiled as they went along.

I remember when Father was on leave in England, we received a surprise visit from a very worried Chief Constable; he came to ask my father for his help. It was apparent that he had performed what he called a little service for Winston Heath and had not been paid.

'Could you have a word with him for me?' the Chief Constable asked my father. 'I seldom get the chance to see Winston Heath these days?'

I think it was to do with a rape of a young woman in Wolverhampton. He had made sure that charges were never brought.

'I don't wish to sound rude, Mrs Freeworthy, but you and your mother were very keen listeners.'

'That is rude, Mr White but we felt we had to. The whole atmosphere was nasty and we thought there would be trouble. Mother was becoming so concerned for my welfare and her own; we both began to listen at every opportunity and Mother even made notes. And don't ask me where those are because I don't know.'

One thing I do know is that we were thankful when the war started. Father was promoted to Lieutenant General and transferred to France to assist in organising the war effort, which gave him even more power and, of course, it was a wonderful time for the armaments industry as it enabled my father's wealth to grow and grow, as did Winston Heath's.

I remember just after my seventeenth birthday, despite it being wartime, my father decided to throw a party at our home in Sevenoaks, where we had an enormous house in about twenty acres. Many of the elite were invited, including of course, his Lordship, together with prominent politicians and senior ranking Army officials not involved with the conflict, plus another Chief Constable from where I cannot remember.

I was growing into a right little madam of a lady and couldn't fully understand all what was going on. My father still thought I was that little girl that could be sent to her room out of the way. He also still thought he was in India where he could send the ladies out of the room whilst the men enjoyed a smoke and a port together. He never realised that at times I used to smoke his cigars and drink his port.

My mother and I often talked about that particular party evening. Winston Heath was in a very worried state; we had never seen him like that before. He was desperate for Father to help him out of his trouble. They went into the drawing room, which Father used as his office, away from the other guests. Mother signalled to me to go and listen in. It used to be a game with us and we would get very excited. There were three doors to the drawing room, including one to the garden. In those days there was no such thing as double glazing and you could hear everything outside that door. No one would suspect anything because no one in their right mind would go outside just to listen!

...

'Now then, Winston what can I do for you?' Father asked.

'I really need your help urgently.'

That was the cue to concentrate and listen carefully.

Winston Heath's bastard son had shot a man, who had refused to obey an order. It seems that the Captain's report implied that he had shot the other man for no apparent reason.

'That was obviously Fred Wearing, Mr White.'

His Lordship continued by saying that several other ranks on the battlefield at the time had backed up the

Captain's statement. They too implied it was deliberate and if he were to die it would be murder. He was hardly likely to survive as he had been shot in the back of the head.

'How did you get this information?' Father asked.

'My son came home yesterday with five days' leave. He had filed a report claiming that he had captured two German machine guns. When he was returning to British lines he had seen a man cowering in a corner of a bomb crater. The man was subsequently shot by the Germans whilst trying to retreat. The Brigadier suggested that he take some leave as he deserved it after his bravery.

'What sector is he in?' Father asked.

I didn't hear the answer but my father remarked that it was Brigadier Reed's patch.

'Leave it to me, Winston. It will be all right and don't worry.'

With that, his Lordship left the drawing room and joined the other guests.

I waited as I heard Father ring his bell and a minute later, his Adjutant came in.

'I want you to get Brigadier Reed from Belgium quickly. I want him here in two days. And tell him I want to see Lieutenant Smith's report on the capture of two German guns. He is not to discuss the matter with anyone and that applies to you too. Understood?'

'Understood, sir,' said the Adjutant who saluted and left.

Mother and I were extremely interested in what was being cooked up and we were hoping against hope that the Brigadier would come here and not go to the barracks. As luck would have it he arrived here two days later and a further meeting was held in the drawing room. Unfortunately, even though I was wearing a raincoat, I still got soaked as did Mother who joined me outside. We could not believe what we were hearing. They were conspiring to cover the matter up. At least my father was.

Father had read the reports and even though he knew Smith's report was doubtful he ordered the Brigadier to give the reports back and another one written to confirm that of Lieutenant Smith.

'I am prepared to take the word of this officer,' my father said. 'I know his family and they are of the highest pedigree, Make sure he is decorated for his action. The Military Cross will do. See there is a fuss made; it's always good for the officer class to be decorated in the thick of it.'

He paused for a moment or two, thinking about his next move, when the Brigadier interrupted his thoughts:

'Sir, there is already a good deal of discontent over this matter.'

'Well quell it, Brigadier Reed. I want this sorted within one week and I want all those involved moved away. No. Better still, I want this man transferred to another unit. I am holding you personally responsible for this action and it had better be done. Furthermore, I do not want to hear about this again from any source. Do you understand?'

'Yes sir,' the Brigadier replied.

'There is promotion in this for you, Brigadier Reed,' Father added, trying to soften the order.

We could tell he was very upset at the attitude of my father, not only for not listening to the warning he gave, but also he had been sent from France for less than half an hour's meeting and his Regiment was in the thick of battle at that moment.

It was a week later when his Lordship came to see Father to discuss the matter, and for the first time, it was Father who laid down the law.

'Good to see you, Winston. I must admit I expected to see you earlier in view of the circumstances.'

'Is it resolved?' Winston Heath asked with a touch of

desperation in his voice.

'Yes it is, but you have to keep that bloody son of yours under control. I have been told that half the Regiment is aware of the truth. Your son did shoot that man for no genuine reason and if this man dies, it will be murder. Let me tell you now, if it wasn't for our friendship he would be shot.

'And Winston, this will cost a small fortune to hush everything up. I have already had to transfer him to another unit, just to save his life. I have also got to transfer several officers, some of whom are first rate. It cannot happen again. If it does, he and you will have to face the consequences. I can do nothing else.'

'It won't happen, I promise. So how much is this going to cost me?' he asked. 'I hope this will be enough,' he added, handing him a thick parcel, not waiting for an answer.

'I'm sure it will be, but Winston if it isn't, I will have to ask you for more.'

My father was clever in his dealings with Winston Heath. He always gave the impression that he was using and paying others to facilitate the deals and the influence, but there was never any other person involved. My father was dishonest, but he wasn't stupid. He knew that only one person could keep a secret.

Shortly after the war, I think it was September 1925, my mother and I left my father and came to live in this house. She had been as cute as he was. He had so much cash coming in, he never knew at any one time how much he had. As a result, my mother used to syphon off her share every time a sum of money arrived. It went on for several years, long before the war started.

She paid cash for the house and had plenty to spare. My father never knew where she got the money from and yet on the one occasion when he was curious, she simply said: 'While you are away, which was eighty per cent of the time, your little Memsaab took in washing.'

***

'There you have it, Mr White and you can thank my grandson for this,' Mrs Freeworthy said as she ended her tale. 'I am not proud of what my father did, in fact I despise him for it and my only defence is I could not have done anything about it, even if I had known the full facts. When you consider they covered up a murder witnessed by many, they would have covered up with ease anything I or my mother may have said.

'However, if I had known what I know now, I would have told the world because it is obvious that Fred Wearing was murdered by that man Smith and for what? Just to get a bit of tin on his chest – to let the world think he was a brave man and he's not. Whatever happened to him, Mr White?'

'You must read the *Mail*,' I replied with a smile. 'It will be in next Saturday's edition.'

'If I promise to read it, will you tell me?'

'OK, it's a deal. I think he was murdered by several of those involved with Fred, but the paper will report that several people have seen him in South Africa, so you will have to judge whether that's right or wrong,' I replied.

'I have to tell you, Mrs Freeworthy, I have worked for the *Mail* for many years and never realised our system was so corrupt. It has shocked me. I thought this sort of thing only took place in Communist or African countries and let me tell you, it's not just one murder they have covered up, I suspect there is another one too.'

'I think we better have a cup of tea don't you, Mr White?'

'I'd love one.'

'Mr White, I know that man killed Fred Wearing and my father knew it too and it's wicked. The more I have read and heard about it from my grandson, the more disgusted I feel. I'll go and make some tea now. I also need to stretch my legs. What do you think? Was it worth waiting for?'

'It is amazing, absolutely amazing and it is exactly what our readers will say. They will be baying for blood, saying everything should be confiscated from the surviving members of the family, but you have my word nothing will identify you or your family.'

The tea arrived with my usual buttered scone, which I have to say was not as good as Irvine's. Neither was the tea, but after Mrs Freeworthy's exposé, it was welcome.

Another big piece of the jigsaw had been put into place and we now had a lead as to which of the people in the upper echelons of society helped to suppress any evidence as to the behaviour of Graham Smith Jnr. Thanks to Mrs Freeworthy, we had several other names to research and ascertain whether or not in any way they were involved with Lord Winston Heath. This was a job for our research department. Hopefully, it would not be of the greatest importance as we were expecting the results from the forensic science laboratory, and the bets in the office were 2/1 that the bullet would have been fired from Smith's gun. I wished he was still alive to face his accusers and thus the gallows.

Chapter 21
The Mail's Revolution

I left the Freeworthys shortly before five o'clock and hotfooted it back to the office to write up the next phase. George had been trying to get hold of me all day, as he needed both of us to talk to the company's solicitor straight away. The solicitor had been on call, waiting all day and arrived feeling aggrieved; not the attitude to adopt with George, especially when he is paying for the service. Think about the fee he would have earned.

'Clive,' George shouted the moment he saw me enter. 'Come on into the office,' he continued, half shouting with excitement. It had been a long time since we had a story which was generating so much interest and had increased the circulation by almost half a million a day.

'Clive, I have arranged for Somerville and Price (the company lawyers) to come now. We need to discuss our next move to get an exhumation of Fred Wearing's body and I want them to do it. I don't want us to be directly involved, as it may seem that we are using undue influence.'

'Good idea,' I replied, knowing that he had now saved me hours of paperwork, formal meetings and discussions with Fred's living relatives to get formal permissions etc. They were all for it, but you had to go through the motions, which takes time.

John Perry, a solicitor assigned by Somerville to undertake this work, arrived and we began in earnest. I explained the story of my involvement so far, with George outlining what he wanted to see happen and how they were going to ensure it did happen legally.

'I need an order post haste to exhume this man's body,' George began. 'Our chairman has already spoken to the Home Secretary and explained the situation and in view of the unusual circumstances, he has told us he will deal with it personally.

'We are worried however, that there are several people mentioned in this criminal matter–'

'Alleged,' John Perry interrupted.

I think he was trying to be clever with his legal jargon, not realising I am sure that George had a degree in law. It was a mistake he would never make again as George snapped: 'You obviously don't read the *Mail,* young man. There is no "alleged" about it. We are talking about a murder of a very brave man which was covered up by some very senior people. The corruption even extends to a former Home Secretary, several ministers, senior Army officers and civil servants and there are some witnesses to the fact, albeit getting on a bit but all there, nonetheless.

'So now you go back to your office and don't waste our time until you have read the articles and you can come back with some ideas on how we can get an exhumation with the least fuss and with the paper fully protected.

'One other thing, there are several relatives alive who were aware that this corruption was going on and may try to stop any further action in this case.

'A prima facia case does exist and I don't want these people interfering with justice by trying to stop the exhumation. It's your job to see this happens.'

George then handed him the complete up-to-date file with a parting comment: 'Tell David Somerville that if members of his staff who are dealing with our problems don't at least read the *Mail*, we can always go to someone that does and if you don't tell him, I will.

'Oh and another thing, the present Home Secretary wants our information on Monday morning, first thing.'

John Perry left with a flea in his ear, leaving me and George to discuss the latest findings and my programme for the next few days.

***

My priority was to obtain the DNA samples needed from the various parties concerned and of course my first port of call was back to Irvine's. I suppose it was really to sit in those chairs and drink another lovely cup of tea.

'Good morning Irvine,' I shouted as he was at the top of his garden feeding his hens.

'Hello Clive. You've got some news then?'

'Yes, and it's all good, but I need your help.'

He came shuffling down the garden in a hurry to hear the news but not before he put the kettle on.

'We have established that the gun used to kill Fred was issued to Smith Jnr. The Army have confirmed it.'

'How do you know that?' he asked.

'Forensics have proved that the gun issued to Smith has been handled by two people because it contained two different samples of DNA, and we now need to find anyone with a similar DNA so we can eliminate them from the enquiries. Would your mother have kept anything that belonged to Graham Smith after she was attacked by him? Did she keep any of little Henry's clothes as a keepsake?'

Unfortunately, he couldn't think of anything, so I asked if he would contact his relatives in Haworth, just in case they had something.

'Anything at all, Irvine. We have to make this one stick.'

The following day, I joined our researchers working flat

out trying to trace the relatives. In fact, even George was involved, emphasising the importance of speed on this case. I then received a phone call from Irvine.

'Clive?'

'Speaking.'

'Clive, it's Irvine. I've been reading up on the DNA system and it says DNA can be taken from hair.'

'Yes, that is the case, Irvine.'

'Well, my mother left a gold locket when she died and in it was a lock of hair from little Henry. That would do, wouldn't it?'

'Irvine, that's brilliant! I'll have it collected by special delivery.'

'No need, I'm outside in the telephone box.'

I looked out of the window and sure enough he was there waving.

I raced down the stairs to meet him with the locket and the lock of hair, untouched since that little lad died.

'Come on up,' I entreated, 'and meet George, my editor.'

'Good morning Irvine, I've heard a lot about you!' George said as we entered his office.

'I've heard a lot about you too,' he replied, 'and I'm very thankful you believed my story. My father knew it would come out one day. I only wish he could have been alive to see it. Also Seth, Frank and the others. That bastard tried to ruin all their lives and he will get his just reward. He will go down in history and always be known as the First World War murderer forever.'

'You're right Irvine, but we have yet to finish the story. We need this sample DNA tested quickly, to keep the ball rolling.'

'Do you know something Clive, since you told me about the dangers of DNA identity I have been looking it all up and do you know what? That locket of hair is going to prove that that bastard Smith raped my mother and someone deliberately covered it up.'

'What's this?' George asked, sounding very surprised.

Irvine chipped in: 'Smith raped my mother and she knew it was him. They lived in the same street and had known him for years. The police covered it up, making the excuse that there was no conclusive evidence. It was his word against hers.'

'And I know who that may be,' I said, turning to George, who signalled me, with a nod of the head to follow him out of the office.

'Excuse us a minute Irvine, I need to talk something over with Clive.'

We were a discrete distance away from the office when George laced into me. 'Why didn't you bloody tell me about this before?' he demanded.

'I thought it was insignificant to the main story, but it's not too late and it does show the police were involved with more cover-ups to protect this animal. She was raped and subsequently had his illegitimate child – a son, who was to inherit the Winston Heath estate. Smith denied it was him.'

'Good, we will run this story in the next issue. It will add more to this individual's character and generate more antipathy from the public. This will put more pressure on anyone who wants to hold up our investigations.'

We returned to George's office and continued our research, constantly being interrupted by Irvine who would suddenly remember something else.

'Tell him about the robbery in the shop where he was again positively identified and yet the police were told to drop it.'

George lost his patience. 'Look Irvine, I am sorry but we have to get on with this and we are rather pushed for time. Would you like to have a look round the place?'

'Yes please.'

'Lucy,' George shouted and within seconds, this lovely strawberry blonde walked in.

'Yes Boss.'

Lucy was then instructed to show Irvine round the place and we were left to talk over a few of the details, not at first in an amicable atmosphere as George had been unaware of the rape.

George immediately sent the locket, with little Henry's hair safely rolled in it, to the forensic science laboratory to check whether Graham Smith's DNA could be established as the rapist. We all knew by now it would be, but you have to wait for official confirmation. We were still anxious to receive answers to the DNA on the Webley revolver.

Irvine returned home still as anxious as we were, but in his mind we were 80% home and dry, although George painted a less confident picture simply to ensure he would keep sending the titbits of information which would all help.

It was now the fifth day of the story, which had been serialised to run every day with each story detailing what to expect in the next edition and in Saturday's edition what to expect the following week.

I thought this was a little silly as it put a strain on everyone to get the story out, For example, in next week's editions we would be featuring the rape, so now we were both anxious to get the DNA results back and this was out of our control. It made everyone put pressure on everyone and the newsroom became an incredible hive of activity. We were already up fifty per cent on our readership and growing by the day and there were even calls being made in Parliament for an investigation, even though it had been many moons ago. However, in Saturday's edition George asked the following questions as an appetiser:

(a) Why did the police cover up the rape of Janet Gough?

(b) Who ordered the cover-up and what can be done?

(c) Was the Home Secretary involved?

(d) Which police force was involved?

(e) Who was the Chief Constable?

They were all tantalising questions designed to capture the imagination of the readers, which they did, but they also caught the interest of Whitehall.

The following Monday, it was if a bomb had been dropped as George was called into the Board Room where he was greeted by three members of the Board and a civil servant.

'George, good morning. Come on in sit down,' Sir John Plunkett-Ward our chairman said as George walked in.

'What's all this about then?' George asked. 'I'm sure you've not invited me up here for a social chat.'

'You know Jack and Walter?' (They were the Board members)

'Yes, of course. Good morning, gentlemen.' They nodded.

'This is John Fossdyke a Chief Secretary in the Home Office.'

'Yes, we met some months ago,' George replied. 'Yes we did. Good morning, Mr Stevenson.'

George nodded.

They sat round the table for a minute or so whilst Fossdyke got his papers together and then Sir John began:

'George, I'll come to the point straight away. Someone in Whitehall has decided that the story you are running–'

'Which one?' George asked, interrupting.

'Come on George, don't be facetious. You know which one – the Fred Wearing campaign. Well, it's got the spike and now it is not in the national interest or so Fossdyke here tells us and they have given us a D-Notice.'

'Forgive me Mr Fossdyke, I don't want to appear rude, but don't be so bloody daft. Come on, tell us which pathetic individual has dreamed this up? I'm sure it's not you. Or is it? Come on, tell us.'

'I know you will not like this, but I am here to tell you must not publish any further exposé on this subject and the story must be dropped indefinitely,' Fossdyke replied.

'Why? George snapped.

'It is in the national interest. That is all I am going to say on the matter.'

'Well, you can tell your boss that there is no chance and when I find out and I will, who it is, I will run their name into the story as well as yours. This is a continuation of the cover-up by the Home Office.'

'George, you mustn't act this way, please,' Sir Peter interjected. 'We have got the paper to think of and you must adhere to the rules.'

'And the consequences will be dire if you don't,' Fossdyke added.

'How dare you talk you me like that,' George said angrily. 'We are talking about a cover-up of a *murder*,' he said, almost shouting, 'and a rape and a robbery by a man whose father was rich and powerful at the time and bought off generals, politicians, policemen, the judiciary, you name it. We already have a direct witness as to the corruption aspects, who has made a statement and you want me to stop. What about freedom of the press and articles that are in the public interest? Oh grow up, Fossdyke,' George snapped.

There was silence in the room for a few moments, but George hadn't finished.

'That being the case, you can have my resignation at nine o'clock tomorrow morning,' George said, looking directly at the Board members.

'But let me warn you, Mr Fossdyke, *Berliner Zeitung* and

Der Spiegel are running the story as we have cooperated with them.

'How did that happen?' Fossdyke demanded.

'Fred Wearing saved the life of a German soldier shortly before he was murdered and the soldier concerned has taken his story to the German press, and as I won't be working for this paper tomorrow, I will see they get the full story.'

'You could go to prison for this,' Sir John said.

'Don't be silly, Sir John, they wouldn't dare. Think about it. We now have proof that Whitehall covered up a murder, possibly two and now we have cast iron proof that a Chief Constable covered up a rape by the same man. Won't the Germans have a field day?

'Sir John, I am wasting my time sitting here. I will pack my things and be out by 9 a.m. tomorrow morning.' George stood to leave. 'Gentlemen, Mr Fossdyke here has stirred up a hornets' nest and should have had more sense. He and his colleagues are perverting the course of justice and as a crime was committed which is not affected by any statute of limitations, I will personally see that his crime is recorded. I will also see that Mr Fossdyke's name features as one those helping to prevent the story appearing.

'I must go as I have to stop the publication. I will have to stop the presses to prevent the paper being in trouble. Good morning, gentlemen.'

George stormed out, leaving everyone open-mouthed and returned to his office where I was dutifully waiting.

'Get everybody together now,' he roared.

There were over a hundred employees in the main office when George began to relate what had happened:

'Colleagues, the Fred Wearing story has been given the spike. As of now we are not allowed to publish anything further on the matter. As of nine o'clock tomorrow morning, I shall cease to be the editor as I have resigned.'

There were huge feelings of discontent and mumblings of a walk out, shouts of disgraceful and more explicit words of disagreement as George continued: 'Now listen. We don't have to do anything. Let the British public do it for us. The front page of tomorrow's paper will be blank, except for the headline: Government blocks any further mention of Fred Wearing, our hero.

'Then we ask the questions again. It worked last time and it will be more effective now:

'Is this another cover-up by a Home Secretary?

'Why can a person murder, rape and rob with impunity just because he is the son of a member of the House of Lords?

'Why have the police covered up these crimes?

'Have they protected other people?

'Then at the bottom of the page: The British people deserve better. The *Mail* cannot protest or publish the story any more, but *you* can. People of Britain, rise up and protest. Contact your MP. Contact your Council and protest.

'On the back page, the words: George Stevenson, the Editor is forced to resign. Thank you all for your support.'

It was the first time a newspaper had a front page almost blank and yet sold out, but what an effect. It had stirred a sleeping giant. Two million copies were sold before lunch and another half million straight after. It had worked and within an hour of production, there were protests outside Parliament. By twelve o'clock there were that many protesting that they had to order the pedestrian barriers be erected as everything was grinding to a halt.

By 5 p.m. Parliament Square was blocked and so was half of Westminster. George had left the office, clearing his desk but I had hidden his stuff, knowing that this situation would be short-lived. The TV stations were interviewing him and he spoke nothing but the truth that someone in Whitehall was still trying to protect the reputation of a murderer and rapist, and the other papers, God bless 'em, joined in the protest saying how disgraceful things were as the very fibres of our democracy were threatened and why should anyone be protected from the law. Charles 1st was executed because the country didn't agree with him so who are we protecting?

Chapter 22
Last Minute Glitch

The action of the Home Office was just what the doctor ordered. On Monday morning, I put George's stuff back in his office and the D-Notice was lifted, with the *Mail* promising the continuation of the story at the weekend.

This really good result caused every section of the media to call for a public enquiry, as to whom they were still protecting and why, after all these years, did they need to protect anyone or anything.

George was a bit harsh towards the Chief Secretary, Fossdyke from the Home Office, as he was portrayed as a threatening bully, trying to stop free speech. He was then admonished in the Commons and there were calls for his resignation. In fairness, he had to take some of the blame for all the uprising of indignation; his attitude was very naïve and stupid.

There is an argument for not tangling with the press on matters of fairness and justice.

It was a wonderful moment indeed. The British have always been the most tolerant of people and it really takes a lot to make them open their eyes and take notice. Not since the Second World War or even the Falklands War have I seen such a spirit of togetherness to right a wrong.

As a result of all the publicity we had generated, things were going really well, when out of the blue we had the first fly in the ointment in the form of Benjamin Gremore, the son of Jonathan, who had long since passed away. He was also the grandson of Lord Winston Heath.

Our first contact with Benjamin Gremore was via Millbrook & Heath Solicitors who (a) objected to the fact that they hadn't been notified about the possible exhumation, (b) objected to the use of an illegal and unapproved source to obtain the DNA of a relative of his family and (c) made clear that these exposés were damaging the reputation of members of his family, namely Jonathan and Benjamin Gremore and their children.

They would be applying to the High Court for an injunction to prevent Fred Wearing's exhumation and any further publication of the story until the matter could be put before the courts.

'What a load of bloody crap,' George shouted angrily. 'Clive, come on in here.'

I walked into his office where he immediately handed me the letter from the solicitors.

'Can you believe this, Clive? How dare the bloody man do this! His grandfather was a bloody crook big time. His father's stepbrother was a murderer and a rapist and he wants us to stop the story because it's damaging his reputation. What about Fred's reputation! Who the bloody hell is he kidding. This really is a time waster, Clive. I'll arrange a cross table meeting with both sets of solicitors and hopefully that idiot will come too. And I want you to be there, to outline all the facts of the case. I don't want this to go to court. Not yet anyway.'

The meeting was arranged for the following morning and sure enough all parties were there, including Benjamin Gremore who quite frankly came across as a pompous and objectionable young man with a title.

George chaired the meeting and began by putting Benjamin in his place, telling him how his family got their money and how his grandfather became one of the most corrupt men in the British Empire.

Gremore's solicitors tried to stop George's passionate exposé, but he was on a roll. 'Look,' George said, 'we do not have the time to waste on trivia like this. This is our evidence. You can either hear it now or pay to hear it in court – because you will pay. This story is in the public interest and no court in the land will stop us publishing.

'Clive, tell him what he will face. And bear in mind, we not only had to persuade the Home Secretary of our case before the exhumation can take place, but also we had to show the scientific evidence and evidence from witnesses that were involved at the time.

'Clive, the floor's yours.'

I re-emphasised the points George had made and then detailed the positive evidence against his grandfather and then Smith. I also tried to soften the situation by saying what a wonderful man his father was and that there were several statements from people confirming it. For the first time, Benjamin Gremore was visibly shaken.

When I told him about the Freeworthys and their relationship with Winston Heath, he was finished.

'I had no idea about this,' he said with desperation in his voice. 'I thought it was newspaper sensationalism. I am so sorry to have caused you all this trouble and if there is any cost to bear please send me the account.'

George took pity on the lad. 'Look, Benjamin. Can I call you Benjamin?'

'Of course and it's Ben please.'

'Ben, everything you have heard is true and there is more, a lot more but you can come out of this smelling of roses. It's up to you.'

'How?' he asked, still sounding confused.

'Firstly you can give us a DNA sample so that we can confirm that your half uncle did fire the gun that killed Fred. We do have a lock of hair which will confirm it, but yours will make certain. This lock of hair will also confirm he raped a young lady and she had his child.

'Secondly, you could also be proactive in that you can make a statement to say that you want all matters brought to light and that no one should avoid justice.

'And finally, contribute something towards the inscription of Fred Wearing's name on the War Memorial or perhaps donate something to the poor. Whatever you do we will make sure you won't look bad.'

'I'll do that,' Ben replied.

I went out and collected the appropriate swab to take the sample which he duly gave and was very grateful to George for adopting the attitude of reasonableness. So that was that. I immediately sent the DNA sample from Gremore to the forensic science laboratory, which I was very pleased to say, came back as a positive match and proved that Graham Smith Jnr had raped Janet Guest. It also proved that the DNA found on the trigger and handle of the revolver was also that of Graham Smith.

All that was left with regard to the weapon was to check the DNA of a member of Seth Ambrose' family. I was pretty sure the DNA would match as Seth had been the only one who had touched it since the end of World War 1 – as far as I was aware. A sample was sent to the laboratory and it promptly came back as a match, confirming the second source.

All we had to do now was to exhume Fred's body and hope the bullet was still with him.

Our solicitors had now prepared the application, direct to a reluctant Home Secretary to exhume Fred's body and although he was loathe to agree to the preliminary negotiations, even with all the evidence that was put forward, which we thought made the case very strong, it was the indignation shown by the British public that had the desired effect. That, together with the letters written and submitted by our young lawyer, plus of course, the pressure put on by our editor, George Stevenson finally got the desired result and permission was granted. That was not before George had advised the Home Secretary that a terrible injustice would be reported in the *Mail* and that another Home Secretary was refusing the opportunity to right a terrible wrong.

Not really blackmail, just a little of the right pressure at the right time.

Of course, this exhumation attracted a great deal of publicity, not only with the local news but worldwide and I did my best to protect the family's privacy. But it was inevitable and they hounded poor old Irvine until he wished he hadn't started the thing, but I had warned him in the beginning that if the story was believed and I was sure it would be, then he would be subject to the full glare of publicity. However, I had no idea how much that may be. I had told him to refer everyone to me at the *Mail*, but of course the hardened reporters wouldn't let go.

Of course, they all wanted to know what had happened to Smith Jnr and that was left to me and the *Mail*.

I actually began a new story saying Graham Smith knew there would be a report about him the moment his father died and that, coupled with his stepfather's demise, he hotfooted it to South Africa. He had apparently embezzled a fortune from the factories which set him up for life.

We believe he had an African wife and would not come back to face any action and that he died in 1967 from venereal disease.

This seemed to come from me with an air of truth about it and it closed the book on the matter.

It was now incumbent on me to start the ball rolling to get the exhumation underway and thankfully, it was an old closed cemetery and no burials had taken place for years. Like all cemeteries that are no longer used it was becoming a little unkempt, but there were the odd one or two of the later ones still receiving attention.

Two weeks after the order for exhumation was granted, we notified the police that the exhumation would take place on a certain day and at a certain time. Fortunately, no one initially knew which cemetery was involved and by the time it became public knowledge the police had cordoned off the entire area.

Work began in the full glare of massive media interest, with the *Mail* in control, but before the exhumation took place, a standard tent was put round the grave to prevent prying eyes and the usual bright lighting put in situ.

It took very little effort to reach the coffin and it was obvious that Fred's Mum and Dad were proud of their son as Irvine had said because the coffin was of the finest quality. When you think of the near poverty they lived in, this must have been an enormous sacrifice for them. But they were proud of what he had achieved in his short life.

The ribbons which lowered the coffin to its final position were still visible although not strong enough to raise it again.

Four tapes were placed underneath the coffin and eight men gently, oh so gently, raised it to the surface where it was transported to the waiting police van.

The police were marvellous, not allowing any of the press or onlookers to enter the cemetery; they even used decoys when Fred's body was taken to the forensic lab to prevent the incident being overrun by the press.

I was invited to attend the forensic examination and walked into the morgue to watch. It was one of the most distressing moments of my life.

The coffin was placed on a table and you could see it was of the finest oak. Even the damp from those eighty years hadn't percolated through to the interior. The lid was gently unscrewed, raised and there he was, Fred

Wearing, this wonderfully brave man, his skeleton proudly wearing his uniform with his hat and his array of medals on his chest. I didn't see a skeleton, I saw Fred; I saw the smile that appears in his photographs; I saw him catching rabbits. I saw him silencing those machine guns, crawling round to save his friends and I shed a tear. Every time I think of him I shed another.

We all stood aghast just looking at him – the uniform beginning to fade, the dress ribbons hardly able to support the weight of the medals as they were deteriorating. Yet the hat was still in its correct position, still proud. I could sense everyone in that room was filled with the same emotions as me.

David Wilkins, chief of the forensic team brought us all back to earth quickly.

'It's very important we look for the bullet quickly to prevent any further deterioration.'

You could hear a pin drop as we all stepped back to let the chief move towards the coffin and, perhaps not for the first time, Fred had the last laugh.

The moment Wilkins leaned over the coffin we all heard what I can only describe as a gentle thud. The bullet had fallen out of Fred's head onto the floor of the coffin and remained in view.

Again we all stood in silence and we all knew what had happened. Fred had got his own back.

David Wilkins announced: 'It's here. He's put it where I can see it. There will be no need to disturb the body.'

It took a few seconds for the bullet to be gently picked up to prevent any possible marking and placed into a plastic bag, when it was immediately sent away for analysis.

It was a very sombre affair until one of the team whispered to me: 'I don't have to look at this. I can tell the bullet was fired from a similar calibre weapon to the one we already have. The examination will simply confirm what I already think.'

Wilkins ordered the coffin to be resealed, which was done as delicately as it was opened, following which it was placed in a room to be kept in storage for a few days as we understood that the Council, along with the family had plans for reburial in a different place.

Well, that broke the spell. I had not heard of this new development so I quickly went to find out.

In the meantime the bullet was taken to the forensic science laboratory for examination to be compared with those from the revolver and for the next two days, we were all on tenterhooks, waiting for any snippet of information to come.

We knew in our hearts there was always a possibility, remote though it was that Smith was telling the truth. That would leave us with his story to believe and a great deal of egg on our faces.

I left the morgue and raced over to see Irvine as I knew he would be the one who had been informed of any family arrangements and sure enough, I was right. I was glad that the timing of my visit left him free from press interference as they were all at the exhumation.

***

'Good morning Irvine, I hope I've caught you at an opportune time. I've just heard the family and the Council are planning to bury Fred somewhere else.'

'Yes, Clive and what's worse they are not interested in what we strived for because all we wanted was to get justice for Fred. These distant relatives know little of what happened and all they are interested in is getting some of the reflective glory. I heard that the son of Fred's nephew has been offered a tidy sum for his perspective on his great uncle's life. I understand that he will be contacting me to get some of the story. This demeans Fred's memory. If they felt so involved, why didn't they do something to help in the first place?

'They also want to separate him from his mother after he has been with her for the last eighty years, which is not on. By all means mark the spot with a special head stone which can tell the world what happened and by all means have something there to remember him, but don't disturb the family resting place and put Fred on his own, just for the temporary publicity because you know as well as I that he will be forgotten within a few years.'

'This is the world today, Irvine but I think we can do something about that. I'll have a word with my editor to see what we can do. But what is this I hear the Council want to do?'

'They're planning to put Fred in a grave next to the War Memorial as a special tribute and I also don't think that's fair to the others who were killed. All of them gave their lives for us so why single out Fred. We know he is a special case because of the circumstance we find him in but had he been killed and won the VC for example, his name would still be on the Memorial just the same as the others and that's what it should be. Some of these brave souls are buried far away in the lands where they fell.'

It was a far cry to what was said in the twenties and would be always to the Council's shame although all of those would be dead and gone now.

'One Councillor on the Wolverhampton Town Council suggested it would be a good idea to erect a statue at the entrance to West Park in the town as an apology for what they did to Fred's memory. We all thought this was a wonderful idea as it was the place where Smith was trapped in a tree where Fred tried half-heartedly to rescue him. It was also the place where my mother was raped by that animal and with Fred's statue there, it would help cleanse the place for me.'

I returned to London to update George on all matters. It's a date I will always remember – Wednesday 6th September at 4.00 p.m. The receptionist came running up the stairs excitedly, bursting into George's office.

'Well, what is it?' George demanded.

'I've got a Dr William Field of the Firearms Section of the forensic science laboratory on the phone. He wants to speak to Clive and you've switched your phone off,' she said nervously in front of the boss.

'I'll make an exception this time. Put him through,' he said, almost breaking into a smile.

She left quickly and we could hear her running down the stairs still excited, as she knew, as we all knew, this was the call we had been waiting for.

There was a click and the extension rang. George signalled for me to pick up the phone. 'Clive?' the voice on the other end asked.

'Yes,' I replied, my heart beating nineteen to the dozen.

'Bill Field. You can stop worrying. It's a positive match. It is 100% accurate. It *is* the bullet that killed Fred Wearing and it was fired from the revolver with the identification number 198342 and you already have the DNA results.' He paused for a moment to allow the words to sink in. Adopting the same formal tone, he continued:

'The bullet which fell from the neck of Fred Wearing and retrieved from the coffin base was fired from the Webley revolver issued to Second Lieutenant Smith. The casing from the bullet was still in the chamber and when forensically examined there was a positive match. It is therefore conclusive that Lieutenant Graham Smith murdered Private Fred Wearing. Now you can stop worrying.'

I didn't reply; I was speechless.

'Clive? Clive?'

'Yes. Sorry Bill, it's the excitement of it all. Thank you,

thank you very much,' I replied.

'It's a pleasure. We'll speak soon.' He put the phone down.

I felt a huge weight lifting from my shoulders, but just wanted to sit and let it all sink in. George stood up walked round to my side of the desk.

'Stand up,' he said in a commanding tone.

I stood up. He grabbed me round the shoulders and hugged me. 'Well done, Clive. A bloody good show!'

That was the picture complete. We had all the evidence and the statements from over thirty people who had seen the shooting or were close enough to know what had happened and we could now conclusively call Graham Smith Jnr the First World War murderer, something Irvine said he would always be known by. What a pity he didn't meet Ellis, the hangman, after a public trial, but he did at least see Frank, the foundry man's apprentice who got his own back for all of them.

I acquainted George with Irvine's latest worries and quite frankly he agreed with everything Irvine had said, George felt all these ancillary stories would denigrate what had been achieved and devalue the main crux of the campaign, that of obtaining justice and righting a wrong. He also agreed with me that we should let the public decide where Fred should be reinterred.

Whilst discussing matters with George, Irvine rang to advise me that the family had been persuaded by one of the *Mail*'s competitors to have a ceremony to place Fred's new gallantry award and his service medals in the coffin with him and that they wanted him to attend.

'I think it's a bit sick, Clive. What do you think?'

'I agree with you, Irvine, but look, I am tied up at the moment. I'll ring you back. OK?'

'OK,' Irvine replied.

George decided there and then that we should run the

campaign straight away whilst we were in the full glare of publicity. We both felt Irvine was right but in this day and age when a story is good, everyone wants a slice and when people have little and they are offered what they consider a lot, it's inevitable they will take it.

Chapter 23
The Last Piece of
the Jigsaw

It was a lovely story and all those involved had done their best and achieved what they set out to do. It was a pity that selfishness and some opportunistic greed had soured matters a little, but it didn't end there. The Prime Minister, influenced by the Home Secretary had persuaded the Queen to posthumously award Fred with a bar to his Military Medal and at the same time remove the award granted to Second Lieutenant Graham Smith on the grounds that he had murdered Private Fred Wearing who, through his conspicuous gallantry had saved the lives of many men. It was also acknowledged that Second Lieutenant Smith had falsely claimed he was involved.

This now opened up the door for the final arrangements to be made.

The *Mail* had already received many thousands of pounds from its readers who were all asking for a statue to be erected in his honour and felt that Wolverhampton Council should be the beneficiary of the money, but when George learned the Council had already approved a motion to place Fred in a special grave at the War Memorial, it worried him and he felt he would like to discuss the matter with the Council.

It was agreed that George would address the Council at the next meeting, a month from then. He immediately set up a team to get the public to decide where Fred should be reinterred and with it several very emotional articles supporting either case.

The response from the public was amazing, not only with the tear-off slip that was in the paper, but the thousands of calls made on the phone, where the public had to choose the various options by clicking on either one, two, or three. The fact that over half a million people voted twenty to one for Fred to be reinterred with his family was extraordinary.

Irvine and all those who knew Fred from Tremont Street voted one hundred per cent to place Fred's name on the War Memorial.

Armed with this, George attended the Wolverhampton Town Council meeting, having already agreed that Daniel Free, a very famous sculptor would be responsible for sculpting the statue. Irvine had loaned him several photographs, one showing that enigmatic smile that so annoyed Smith and I asked Daniel if that could be featured.

At the meeting, George made an impassioned plea to have Fred placed with his family, quoting the views of all those who voted for this. He also made a plea that with permission from his family, Fred's medals be placed on view at the Town Hall where it all started and that his history be placed on a scroll alongside his medals to remind Wolverhampton of his bravery and of the terrible injustice done to him. They wholeheartedly agreed with the proposal so it was now up to George to ask the family.

He convinced the family by telling them their names would be mentioned as giving permission for this to happen and that the record will remain in the Town Hall forever. Thankfully, they seemed satisfied with that.

Initially, there was to be a Service of Remembrance at the local church in Penn Fields, but this was considered too small, so the next venue was St Peter's Church in the centre of the town. After discussions with the police, that too was considered too risky because they were expecting many thousands to turn up; so believe it or not, it was held in a packed Molineux Stadium.

Draped in the Union Flag, Fred's coffin was carried by members of the 1st Battalion of the Mercian Regiment, which later merged with the South Staffs. It was a wonderful service, ending with a rounding three cheers from the capacity crowd. Fred was then taken to be re-united with his parents and with that, the cemetery returned to the quiet little place it had been, only this time the youngsters of the town had cleaned up the graves and the grounds for the occasion. A plaque was erected by his grave which explained the history of Fred's demise.

Digressing for a moment, the statue was superb. It was erected at the front of the park and Daniel Free, the sculptor had created a wonderful image with Fred in his uniform. What was most important for those who had been close to him was that the sculptor had captured that smile. All those who knew of Fred and the family could look up at him and imagine he was there with them.

Chapter 24
Epilogue

'You'll get the Pulitzer Prize for this, Clive,' George called out when I returned to the office, where all the staff were waiting in the main office to congratulate me on the story and toast our success.

'Well done, Clive!' I was handed a glass of bubbly and invited to respond which I did by thanking all of them for their help and giving special thanks to Irvine Rawson for leading us into the story. I ended by saying it wasn't finished yet; we needed to expose those responsible for the corruption.

But it was the headline the following day which gave me the most pleasure and what a headline it was in Saturday's *Mail* of 7th September: 'Justice at Last for a British Hero', under which was the story of all the families' and their friends' quest for justice.

After an investigation like this one, the *Mail* could not let things pass without naming or shaming. Just how the Home Secretary would handle the evidence compiled and instigate a review into the corruption remained to be seen.

After talking to so many people and listening to all their stories, I was convinced that not since the entire Irish nation north or south or the families of the Liverpool football fans who died in the Hillsborough disaster have so many people fought so hard for the justice they believe they were entitled to; and even after several generations have passed, many still fought as they believed right was still on their side.

The Queen approved that Fred Wearing would posthumously receive a bar to his Military Medal and at last his name was added to those who lost their lives on the battlefield. Justice was done and seen to be done. I immediately contacted Irvine inviting him to phone me the following day because I felt this was somewhat of an injustice.

Fred was awarded the Military Medal; it was the same award for Smith, only being a commissioned officer, he was awarded the Military Cross. However, everyone I have spoken to on this point expressed their dissatisfaction in giving a higher award to a man where there was doubt, particularly in these circumstances. Fred deserved more. There was no doubt with Fred. Even a German soldier verified Fred's action and of course there were several witnesses on the British side able to confirm they saw the various parts of his lone action. When you read or hear the citations for those men and women who were awarded the Victoria Cross and their wonderful exploits, there really is no difference between theirs and Fred's. It is a pity but at least the statute recognition is now there as to what he achieved.

***

The last part of the story had to be the naming and shaming of all those who had used and abused the law for their own ends; those who had forgotten the meaning of the words fairness and justice and who had destroyed the lives of many families because of their greed and corruption.

It was now our time to expose the corruption of those wealthy individuals who perverted the course of justice and, due to lapses in time will never face the consequences of their actions. We can however change the history books but it will be for all future generations to judge what they were really like:

Lord Winston Heath, a perverted man, the mastermind with all the money.

General Lord Malcolm Weatherall, the evil and crooked General.

Chief Constable, Sir Tim Tenant who covered up the crimes.

Brigadier Reed, unlike Captain Harmsworth, was too scared to tell the truth.

Major Fortesque, who could have done better to ensure the truth was told.

And finally, the courage of all those, who had for years continued with their campaign to get justice for the families of those involved:

Irvine, with his comfy chairs, his lovely cups of tea and scones, of course.

Bill Ambrose whose family suffered from Seth's agony for his friend.

Mrs Freeworthy, persuaded by her grandson, a direct descendant of General Malcolm Weatherall to tell the truth about her father.

Ben Gremore, who stood up to be counted when it mattered.

George Stevenson, the *Mail*'s editor who put his job on the line to ensure the truth would be told.

The list is endless...

Then of course there's me. Well, I'm just the reporter, no real responsibility but it was truly a pleasure to meet these people and even more so when I was able to get the truth published and let them rest from their torment.

Finally, it wasn't quite finished...

The *Mail* started its campaign to get the award removed from Graham Smith Jnr which was soon achieved and given to Fred, but it begged the question: Where is this monster now? Of course I knew the answer, but I was left debating whether or not to expose the foundry man's apprentice, or let sleeping dogs lie, thus leaving families and friends to enjoy their moment of reflected glory and show the world what a wonderfully brave man Fred Wearing was and that there were many people who survived as a result of him. I chose to let the matter rest.

At the end of it all, George decided we would put on a rather fancy buffet in the *Mail's* offices to celebrate the success of the story and the subsequent campaign, sending invitations to several of those involved.

Even Ben Gremore turned up, along with Hans Leberfeld and his daughter, plus of course, all the locals who had played their part.

It was a wonderful affair with very many happy faces and the realisation that at last justice had been served.

George gave a speech congratulating Irvine on his approach and determination and for the help he gave to the story and when finished, we asked Irvine to respond.

We were all astonished to discover how eloquent he was, how humorous and how sincere, only breaking off to remind me of my promise to pay him two hundred pounds for his story. George immediately wrote him a *Mail* cheque for that sum which I believe is still framed and standing above his kitchen range in Tremont Street.

Irvine continued his story, thanking all at the *Mail* for restoring old friendships and making new ones and then at the end he proposed a toast:

'To my uncle Frank – the foundry man's apprentice.'

We could all see the quizzical looks around the room. What's this about? Who's he? What's he got to do with it?

Everyone raised their glasses and toasted: 'To Uncle Frank.'

Irvine raised his glass and winked at me. I couldn't help but smile.

Dear Reader,

This story was related to me as true, but of course a hundred years have passed. Memories become stretched as does the imagination and stories become exaggerated. I have changed the names just to protect the families who may have been involved and have put my two penn'orth in, hopefully to make it flow better. You however must decide whether or not you believe it. If you get the time let me know. My address is on the back cover and thank you for supporting this impoverished writer.